LIST OF SUSPECTS

"So, what do we know so far?" Gin asked.

I ticked off possibilities on my fingers. "Shelly was close to him. Harini seemed nervous yesterday when I brought up his death and said he was Shelly's friend, not hers. According to Tulia, that Lawrence guy is probably a relative. Peter Zelensky might have been Enzo's investment adviser. Peter didn't think at all highly of him, at any rate. But would any of them murder Enzo? I have no idea."

"Sounds like we have our work cut out for us."

"Yes, unless today is when the able state police detective arrests the killer."

"If Lincoln and team are successful, the Cozy Capers could discuss the book of the week instead of homicide . . ."

Books by Maddie Day

Country Store Mysteries
FLIPPED FOR MURDER
GRILLED FOR MURDER
WHEN THE GRITS HIT THE FAN
BISCUITS AND SLASHED BROWNS
DEATH OVER EASY
STRANGLED EGGS AND HAM
NACHO AVERAGE MURDER
CANDY SLAIN MURDER
NO GRATER CRIME
BATTER OFF DEAD
FOUR LEAF CLEAVER
DEEP FRIED DEATH
SCONE COLD DEAD
CHRISTMAS COCOA MURDER
(with Carlene O'Connor and Alex Erickson)
CHRISTMAS SCARF MURDER
(with Carlene O'Connor and Peggy Ehrhart)

Cozy Capers Book Group Mysteries
MURDER ON CAPE COD
MURDER AT THE TAFFY SHOP
MURDER AT THE LOBSTAH SHACK
MURDER IN A CAPE COTTAGE
MURDER AT A CAPE BOOKSTORE
MURDER AT THE RUSTY ANCHOR
MURDER AT CAPE COSTUMERS

Local Foods Mysteries
A TINE TO LIVE, A TINE TO DIE
'TIL DIRT DO US PART
FARMED AND DANGEROUS
MURDER MOST FOWL
MULCH ADO ABOUT MURDER

Cece Barton Mysteries
MURDER UNCORKED
DEADLY CRUSH
CHRISTMAS MITTENS MURDER
(with Lee Hollis and Lynn Cahoon)

Published by Kensington Publishing Corp.

MURDER AT CAPE COSTUMERS

A Cozy Capers Book Group Mystery

Maddie Day

Kensington Publishing Corp.
kensingtonbooks.com

KENSINGTON BOOKS are published by

Kensington Publishing Corp.
900 Third Avenue
New York, NY 10022

All Kensington titles, imprints, and distributed lines are available at special quantity discounts for bulk purchases for sales promotion, premiums, fund-raising, educational, or institutional use. Special book excerpts or customized printings can also be created to fit specific needs. For details, write or phone the office of the Kensington Sales Manager: Attn.: Sales Department. Kensington Publishing Corp., 900 Third Avenue, New York, NY 10022. Phone: 1-800-221-2647.

KENSINGTON and the KENSINGTON COZIES teapot logo Reg US Pat. & TM Off.

First Printing: September 2025
ISBN: 978-1-4967-4059-5

ISBN: 978-1-4967-4060-1 (ebook)

10 9 8 7 6 5 4 3 2

Printed in the United States of America

The authorized representative in the EU for product safety and compliance is eucomply OU, Parnu mnt 139b-14, Apt 123
Tallinn, Berlin 11317, hello@eucompliancepartner.com

For everyone who feels threatened. For those standing up at great risk for justice. For democracy, may it survive and thrive again.

ACKNOWLEDGMENTS

I was inspired to write this particular story after I read a short squib in the *Boston Globe* in March of 2024 about two women in Ohio who attempted to pull off a kind of scam having to do with a drive-through window at a bank and someone else's bank account. I won't spoil the book for you by providing any more details, but you can look it up yourself and see how I changed the facts (and the names) for my own (fictional) nefarious purposes.

Many thanks to Brian Stokes, interim director of the Falmouth Public Library, for giving me tips about the library program at the Barnstable County Correctional Facility and answering all my questions. I first heard about the library in a story researched and reported by Simón Rios of WBUR, a Boston-area NPR station. He was kind enough to answer a few questions, too, and I knew I wanted to include this access to books in one of my Cozy Capers mysteries. The inmates now have a complete set of the first six Cozy Capers Book Group Mysteries in their library. I also read the memoir *Running the Books: The Adventures of an Accidental Prison Librarian* by Avi Steinberg (2011), which gave me even more ideas.

Thanks also to an officer at the Falmouth Police Department who patiently answered my questions about filing a missing person report. I regret I didn't record his name. Sergeant James Cummings of the same department informed me about body identification and where it would take place; my apologies for slightly fudging the procedure.

Thank you to Jackie Brisbois, who introduced me to the pickleball community in my town. Paddle and ball sports are not for me, but I was happy to watch as well as to pick her brain later about tensions on and off the court. Thanks, too, to my good friend Lyndsie Reynolds, who generously shared her recipe for the yummy Crabbies appetizer, and to Kathie Grant Brush, who contributed a colorful phrase for Reba from her own grandmother.

I finished this book while on a writing retreat in the area of Cape Cod where fictional Westham is set. While occupying the Quaker cottage I rent during the off season, I met several West Falmouth Friends who had worked hard in the cottage garden all summer to grow food for a local food pantry. I knew I needed to include mention of their worthy project in this book.

I'm ever grateful to Jennifer McKee for assisting with many non-writing aspects of my business, even on the edges of Florida hurricanes. You rock, Jen. Once again, Amy Glaser gave a close look to this manuscript and sent along many insightful comments, which improved the story considerably. Bless you, Amy.

No book of mine can go out without thanking my current and former Wicked Authors blogmates—Jessie Crockett, Sherry Harris, Julie Hennrikus, Liz Mugavero, and Barbara Ross (and all their pseudonyms)—for their ongoing support and friendship. Two have left the blog, but I hope you come visit the rest of us over at wickedauthors.com. Please also check out my posts on the second and fourth Fridays and the eleven other talented author-cooks at Mystery Lovers' Kitchen, where you can find an original recipe (and regular giveaways) every day of the week.

Note to readers: The ideas and words in this novel were generated entirely by the author without contribution from an AI application. No one has permission to use this book to generate AI content. I wish I didn't have to include that statement, but you should know where your fiction comes from.

I'm grateful to John Scognamiglio and Larissa Ackerman and everyone at Kensington Publishing who makes the process of getting my books into print seem nearly seamless. Seven books into this series, I'm as happy with them as I always have been. I also owe thanks to my former agent, John Talbot.

To my family, I love you. And to enthusiastic librarians, book bloggers, and readers, I wouldn't be on this path without you.

MURDER AT CAPE COSTUMERS

CHAPTER 1

The streets of Westham, Massachusetts, were filled with pirates and princesses, devils and angels, skeletons and superheroes on this Friday afternoon in late October, but our coastal Cape Cod town wasn't the site of a movie filming. The costumed residents were all in various sizes of miniature and were making their way along Main Street in our annual merchants' trick-or-treat event.

Shops and restaurants were decorated to the hilt for Halloween, with spiders and bats and jack-o'-lanterns everywhere you looked. Candy was at the ready in baskets and bowls to slip into kids' bags or hollow plastic pumpkins. Actual Halloween wasn't until Monday, but this was a special afternoon event downtown. We'd had a steady stream of kiddos coming into Mac's Bikes for candy since an hour ago when the event began at two o'clock.

A three-foot-something Wonder Woman skipped into my retail, repair, and rental shop.

"Titi Mac, look at me!" my niece Cokey exclaimed as she twirled in a circle with all the happy energy of a six year old, her red cape flying out from her back. Red tights and yellow sneakers replaced the knee-high boots of the original superhero.

"You look powerful." I came around from behind the counter at my shop and knelt for a hug.

"I am."

My grandmother Reba, a rather miniature person herself, followed Cokey in. On her short-cropped white Afro she wore a pointed wizard's hat studded with stars and moons. A midnight-blue cape to match nearly swept the floor. I hugged her too.

"Are you getting some good loot, Cokester?" I asked my niece.

"Yes." She held out her bucket and began detailing all the candies.

"Pick one from our bowl, okay?" I picked up the big bowl on the counter, now only half full, and held it down for her.

"Thank you." She rifled through until she found a candy bar she liked. "I saw a scary skeleton in the window."

"What window?" I tilted my head.

"In that new shop, Cape Costumers," Reba said.

"It was moving, Titi Mac." A curly blond lock fell over Cokey's yellow satin headband.

I smoothed the hair away from the red star on her forehead. "Was it a puppet or an animation?"

"It was as big as a person." Her eyes were wide. "What's a amination?"

"It's like in the cartoons or the movies, like Moana or SpongeBob SquarePants." I mentioned two of her favorite animated characters. "Were you frightened of the skeleton?"

"A little bit." She nodded slowly, 100 percent serious. "But Bizabo held my hand. We stayed outside, and it was inside the store."

"We decided against picking up candy at that location," Reba murmured.

My mechanic, Orlean, appeared in the doorway of the repair room. "Cokey? I have something for you."

The girl skipped back there. Orlean, usually a woman of few words, had a special soft spot for Cokey.

"Why would they display something scary on a day meant for children?" I asked my grandma.

"I have no idea. It was, you know, a regular costume, white on black, not just the bones of a skeleton, plus a head mask. I also thought it looked like a real person was wearing it, but maybe the getup was rigged to move around."

"Have you met the owners?"

"Not as yet, no," Reba said. "I've heard that Harini Whitt had a long career as a ballerina."

"I didn't know that. Gin Malloy said Harini asked if she can join our book club. I haven't met her or Shelly Hitchcock yet."

Cokey twirled her way back to us, her star-spangled blue skirt flaring out around her.

"Let's go, Bizabo. There's lots more stores, and Tio Tim said he was saving a special treat for me."

Tio Tim, a devoted uncle who adored Cokey, was also my handsome and brilliant husband as well as owner and chief baker at Greta's Grains, the bakery down the street.

Reba smiled as Cokey tugged at her hand. "I guess we're off."

"Happy Halloween." I watched the wizard and the superhero trundle down the sidewalk hand in hand.

Cokey wasn't a fearful child. She'd always been curious and confident. For something in a costume shop window to scare her took a lot. I would take a stroll down there after we closed at five today and have a look at this skeleton myself.

Harini and Shelly, apparently friends and business partners, had opened Cape Costumers only a month earlier in what had been an empty storefront. I wasn't the only Main Street shopkeeper to hope it was a permanent business and not merely a pop-up for the spookiest holiday of the year.

CHAPTER 2

By the time I arrived at Cape Costumers at five thirty, the sun was about to set and a chilly wind whipped in from the bay. The change from daylight saving time to standard wouldn't happen for another eight days, but the evenings already came early, and the nights were dark.

Store windows along Main Street were lit, as were the antique-style lights on lampposts. Tim's bakery was dark, as always at the end of the afternoon, because it opened early every day. The Rusty Anchor Pub looked so warm and welcoming I was tempted to stop in. Tim and I had a date night planned, though, and I'd promised to be home by six.

At the corner I crossed to the other side of the main drag. The costume shop was beyond the library nearly to Salty Taffy's, my friend Gin's candy store.

When I got to Cape Costumers, I skirted a real black

cat staring at me from atop a hay bale on the sidewalk. Cats and most dogs didn't play nicely with my allergies, which was why I was the human for an African gray parrot named Belle.

One front window of the shop was devoid of a life-size skeleton, bones or otherwise. Bats and spiderwebbing and pumpkins, sure, along with a suit of armor and a Darth Vader getup. In the window on the other side of the entrance, though, an all-bones skeleton slumped in an antique armchair, with a dog skeleton waiting eagerly in eternity for its treat. The skeletons were flanked by a ghoulish, person-sized lobster, its mouth agape as if *The Scream* painting had come to live in a crustacean. Wearing the uniform of a police chief, a white-faced, featureless mannequin with no hands stood at attention on the opposite side.

I shuddered but pulled open the door. While I was here, I might as well introduce myself.

"Welcome to Cape Costumers," a woman said. She came around from behind a counter at the side of the store.

"I'm Mac Almeida." I extended my hand. "Owner of Mac's Bikes down the street. Welcome to Westham."

"Shelly Hitchcock, co-owner here. Good to meet you, Mac." She shook my hand. Hers was bony and cool, with heavy silver rings on both hands. She looked to be in her sixties, with reddish-brown hair in a short chic-shaggy cut. She stood a couple of inches shorter than my five foot seven. A black-and-white silk scarf was artfully loose around her neck, and she wore a black-and-silver long-sleeved dress on her lean frame.

"You had good timing, opening close to Halloween," I said. "The nearest party store is quite a drive away in Hyannis." I glanced around the space. Racks held costumes ranging from a medieval maiden to Princess Leia to a classic cowboy to a Ghanaian king. I didn't see a single sexy nurse outfit or cheap polyester costume made overseas.

"Halloween's a big time for a costume shop, even a high end one like ours. We hope to do business throughout the year, of course, and we can fill custom orders. We also have a dance section for all ages." She gestured to the far wall.

"That's smart. What brought you to Westham in particular?"

"Who doesn't love Cape Cod?" Her smile was tight.

"For sure."

Shelly cleared her throat. "And I have a friend with ties to the area."

"Your business partner? Harini, right? I haven't met her, but she asked to join a book club I'm part of."

"That's her name, but no. Someone else." This time her cheeks pinked up.

"Well, we're glad to have you among the merchants here. Our Chamber of Commerce is pretty active. I hope I'll see you at a meeting soon."

"Thank you. I've already been approached by the director. Are you from Westham?"

I laughed. "I sure am. My whole family is here. My grandma's a fixture around town. My dad's a minister, my mom is a popular astrologer—"

"Astra MacKenzie?"

"The same."

"She's wonderful. I've already had a consultation with her."

"That's great." I kept myself from rolling my eyes. I adored my mother, but I considered astrology a sham. At least it was a harmless one. "Well, I'll let you get back to whatever."

"Are you all set for the holiday?"

"Yep." By that I meant I had several big bags of mini candy bars hidden away at home. I didn't do costumes. Ever.

"If you need a last-minute accessory, you know where to find me."

"You bet. Speaking of costumes, my niece said she saw a skeleton moving in your window earlier this afternoon. She thought it was a real person, but I didn't see a skeleton there when I came in."

"She wasn't mistaken. A friend of mine was trying on that costume and started fooling around, playing at being a mannequin."

"I see. Thanks." I turned to go, then turned back. "Why costumes, anyway? I mean, it's an unusual kind of business to open."

"I was a costumer on Broadway for many years." She lifted her chin in pride. "My costumes were highly prized and contributed to more than one Tony Award for productions. It's hard to detach from that kind of career."

"That makes sense," I said. "So you moved here from New York?"

"I did. I'm a real city girl, and it's the first time I've lived somewhere so quiet."

"I know what you mean, but you'll get used to it." I smiled. "I went from owning a condo and working in busy downtown Boston to two years in a village in Thailand. The quiet there spoiled me, and after my Peace Corps stint was up, I came back here instead of resuming the urban lifestyle."

I said goodbye and made my way out. Shelly had blushed when she mentioned the friend with ties to here. I would have asked the friend's name, but I'd already been nearly grilling the newcomer. I was pretty sure Shelly had a romantic situation with the *friend*.

Cokey might not be reassured that her skeleton was merely a real person in a costume. Something must have been way off for her to be so freaked out about what she'd seen.

CHAPTER 3

A slender man walking with a cane browsed the display bikes in my shop the next afternoon. His dark hair, which fell over his collar, had a fair bit of silver highlighting it. When I approached, he turned slowly and with care. I didn't think I'd ever seen him before.

"Can I help you, sir?" I asked.

"Thank you, miss." He flashed a smile full of perfect white teeth. His skin was lined, but his brown eyes were warm and not faded, and his features went together in a way that spelled handsome and possibly leading man. "I'm afraid with the advancing years my balance has become precarious. I'd still like to keep moving, however, and my friend Reba said I might find a three-wheeled bicycle here." His voice was still strong and smooth.

"Reba is my grandmother." My eyebrows rose.

"So she mentioned."

"I'm Mac. Mac Almeida, and of course I can help you with an adult tricycle." Sofia Burtseva, one of my weekend employees, had called in sick this morning. I'd made my way over to the shop to replace the former waitress who had become a cycling enthusiast.

"Enzo Lawrence at your service, Mac."

"I'm so pleased to meet you, Enzo. Are you visiting Westham?"

"No, I moved here several years ago," he said.

I waited for more, but he stayed silent. Sometimes it seemed like I knew everybody in town, but I didn't, and it wasn't my place to pry about where he'd come from and where he now lived. I could always ask Abo Reba.

"Well, our Shining Sea Trail is perfect for cycling on," I said.

"Is the path very hilly?" he asked. "I'm afraid my heart is going the way of my balance, and my doctor has ordered me not to overly stress it."

"The trail is a former rail line, so it doesn't have many hills. Reba takes her three-wheeler on it, and my mother rides one too."

"If your dynamite grandmother can ride the trail, I expect I can, as well. Sell me a transport, my dear." Enzo beamed.

"I'd be happy to. We have one back here in green, or I can order a model in another color."

"Green would be splendid." He ran a hand down the front of his Pendleton shirt, which was plaid in muted shades of green. "I am fond of the color."

"Would you like to try riding the trike in the parking lot before you commit to buying it?" I asked.

"I don't think so. I have somewhere I need to get to after I leave here. But I suppose I should get kitted out with a helmet, a reflective jacket, lights, and all whatnot. You'll put together the whole package for me, yes?"

"We can certainly do that." I pushed a slip toward him. "Please jot down your phone number and address for our records."

After we talked about his size, I assembled a full riding ensemble, and he didn't blink at the price of anything. After I rang up his purchases, he handed me five hundred-dollar bills.

"I know it makes me seem old-fashioned, but I prefer to deal in cash. That way, if I fall down dead one of these days, my estate won't have credit card bills pending. And I don't trust those app thingies."

"It's no problem. I still have a cash drawer." I gave him his six dollars of change and thanked him.

"I've been enjoying your Halloween decor in here, Mac." He gestured around the shop.

"Thanks." With Cokey's help, I'd decorated with twisted orange and black streamers. Ceramic jack-o'-lanterns were scattered about, and bats were suspended from several of the wall racks. A small plastic skeleton wearing an orange bike helmet sat on a child-sized tricycle.

"What costume will you be wearing Monday?" Enzo asked.

"I don't wear costumes."

His jaw dropped. "Not for any occasion?"

"Nope. I'm never in a performance, and it's not my thing to dress like a character or whatever."

"I have worn splendid costumes in the past." He got a dreamy look in his eyes, gazing into the distance.

"Are you an actor?" Maybe my thought about him being a leading man had been correct.

"I did have my modest successes on and off Broadway."

"Isn't there a Cape Cod repertory theater?" I enjoyed the symphony, but I'd never been to a Broadway musical. Going to plays in the summer alongside all the zillions of Cape tourists didn't appeal to me.

"Indeed there is, the Cape Playhouse," he said. "In fact, I appeared in several performances there over the summer. Cape Cod Theatre Company is good too."

"What are you going as for Halloween?"

He pointed at the skeleton on the trike. "A much larger version of that."

A rosy-cheeked group of women in biking togs pushed through the door.

"I'll let you get back to work," he said.

"We'll give your three-wheeler a quick going-over, and I'll call or text you when it's ready."

"Perfect. If you should change your mind about a costume, there's a fabulous shop down the street. I happen to be friends with the owner, and she's a professional."

"Got it. Thank you for your business, Enzo."

He slipped past the women and headed out.

So, he was friends with Shelly and was going to be a skeleton on Halloween. He must have been who Cokey had seen in the window. It was interesting that Reba knew Enzo, but I didn't find it surprising. She was one of those people who had never met a stranger.

I headed over to put a Sold tag on the green tricycle. "Let me know how I can help you all," I said to the women, who were browsing the retail shelves holding shirts, shorts, and socks.

By four thirty the shop was empty. Edwin Germain, my weekend mechanic, had gone home. We didn't have any rentals due in today that hadn't already been returned. I brought in the Open flag from outdoors and flipped the sign to read Closed.

Tim had driven north to Logan Airport in Boston to pick up his sister Jamie and her two youngest children, who were traveling here from Seattle for a visit. Her plane should be landing about now. Tim wouldn't arrive with them for a few more hours, depending on traffic.

At least this time Jamie hadn't canceled her trip at the last minute. She and the kids, including the two older ones, had bailed on our wedding last December, and the change had crushed Tim. She was his only sibling and he adored the children.

The older ones lived with their father. Jamie had given birth in August to a little boy, Luca. Her younger daughter Daniella, whom everyone called Ella, was now three and a half. She had yet a different father from Luca and from Jamie's first two.

Jamie suffered from addiction and episodes of mental instability. It broke Tim's heart to live so far from her, although he had dropped everything to fly West and take care of the kids more than once during his sister's crises.

We'd borrowed a portacrib for the baby from one of Pa's parishioners, and I'd pretty well childproofed the house in case Ella was a rambunctious little girl, but I wanted to do a last sweep through to elevate breakables.

The impending visit, which meant so much to Tim, was making me anxious. I tried to practice slow breathing to tamp down my nerves. I'd always been borderline obsessed with things being tidy and organized, and I knew young kids in the house were about to wreak havoc with all that. Still, they would only be here for a week. Ella was bound to love Halloween, and Jamie would take them home next weekend.

I could do this.

CHAPTER 4

Sure enough, semichaos ensued in the house. By nine the next morning, two of the West Coast crew were out of bed. Tim was mixing up batter for blueberry pancakes. Ella, wearing an adult-sized apron over her rockets-and-stars pjs, stood on the step stool next to him. One end of the counter was covered with baby bottles and a can of formula. The infant car seat sat on the floor in the corner, and Jamie had left a cloth bag of snacks on the table.

She had gotten up an hour earlier, fed Luca a bottle, and handed him off to Uncle Tim before going back to bed. Last night they arrived home after eight. After we'd all had a bite to eat, getting them settled and the kids to sleep had taken so long I didn't have much of a chance to get to know my sister-in-law. I hoped I would today.

After Tim had finished burping the little guy, he

sang him to sleep and asked me if I could handle him. I took another sip of my coffee and sat with the baby at the table.

I gazed down at Luca's tiny round cheeks as he slept. His pale hair was a silky tuft on top of his head, his mouth a wee rosebud, his nose a little button. He had all his body parts intact and had made it out of the womb without issue. Importantly, there hadn't been any drugs in his blood. Tim, knowing Jamie, had worried about that.

Luca's life was at the beginning. He hadn't been hurt or lied to. He had people who fed him and loved him and kept his world safe. May it stay that way for a long, long time.

"Auntie Mac, look at me." Ella brandished her wooden spoon. "I'm cooking."

"That's great, sweetie." I smiled at her as Tim wiped up the batter the girl had sprayed around with her gesture. "I'm hungry for pancakes."

Luca stirred at my voice. I stroked his head, and he settled again. Belle, my parrot, stirred too. She'd been on her perch, snoozing. Now she jumped down and waddled over to Ella's stool.

"I'm hungry," Belle said in an exact imitation of my voice. "Snacks, Mac?"

Ella giggled. "Can I give her a blueberry, Uncle Tim?"

"Sure, honey," he said. "Here, let's put a few in a bowl. You can set it on the floor for her."

"Sure, honey," Belle said in Tim's voice. She gave one of the wolf whistles she always did at the sight of him.

"Belle loves frozen fruit," I added.

Ella climbed down and took the small bowl from Tim. She squatted and set it on the floor. "Here's your snack, Belle." Her speech was clear and she didn't lisp like Cokey did. She also seemed fearless around Belle and her enormous beak. "Can I pet her, Auntie Mac?"

"After she's done eating, you can. Only on her head, okay? And touch her softly."

Ella nodded, her loose black curls bobbing around her shoulders. "I know how to be gentle. Mommy showed me with Luca." Her big brown eyes were serious. With her skin that looked tanned even in winter and her dark hair and eyes, she clearly had a different father than Luca. Tim, Jamie, and their parents were all as blond and blue-eyed as they came.

I knew about mixing up the gene pool. My father, with a Cape Verdean father and Reba, his American Black mother, was a blend of African and Portuguese. My mom, with her British Isles heritage, was green-eyed, pale-skinned, and light-haired. I was a scrambled-up mix of all of them, with green eyes but skin and hair like Ella's, except I wore mine two inches long in a style that I didn't have to fuss with.

Ever since our marriage last December, Tim and I had been hoping we'd get a baby underway and have our own experiment in diversifying the gene pool. So far, nothing had happened. I wasn't eager to experience the mess of pregnancy and birth, but I loved children and family as much as he did.

Half an hour later Tim had helped Ella set the table and bring over butter and syrup. He served up three plates of luscious puffy pancakes studded with dark berries.

"These look wonderful," I said. "Thank you both."

"I can take the baby," Tim offered.

"Eat your breakfast and then we can swap," I said. "If I eat one-handed, more will get on the baby than on me."

"And he's too little for pancakes," Ella declared. "All he gets is milk from a bottle. Not like me."

"Do you want a glass of milk?" Tim asked her.

"No, thank you. I'm lactose intolerant." She pronounced each syllable carefully.

Tim raised his eyebrows and smiled at me in one of those grown-up communications between parents or caregivers I'd only observed until now.

"How about orange juice, then?" I asked. "I bet Uncle Tim will pour you a glass."

"Yes, please."

The kid knew big words and was polite. Jamie was doing more than one thing right as a mom. Ella thanked Tim when he brought her juice.

"Are you excited about Halloween, kiddo?" he asked.

"Yes. But I don't know when it is."

"It's tomorrow," I said.

Her mouth wobbled. "We didn't bring my costume. I was going to be an astronaut."

The poor thing. "I saw that you have space stuff on your jammies," I said. "I bet your cousin Cokey has a costume you can wear. She's six now, but something she wore last year or the year before would probably fit you."

"Did she go as an astronaut?" Ella perked up.

"No, but I'm sure she has a couple of great costumes," I said. If she didn't, we could outfit Ella at the new costume shop. "You'll meet her at dinner tonight."

"Does Cokey have a little brother too?"

"Not yet. She's going to have a baby sister or brother, but it's still in its mommy's tummy."

"Like Luca was." Ella forked in a bite of pancake.

"Exactly," Tim said.

My brother Derrick and his new wife, Neli, had had no trouble at all conceiving in the summer, and she was due in January. They were mixing up the gene pool too. Neli was Black and Derrick's father had been Mom's first husband and white, although Pa had raised my half brother as his own. Derrick looked a lot like a male version of our mother. I couldn't wait to meet their baby.

Jamie appeared in the doorway with bed hair and bleary eyes. A hip-length sleep shirt hung off her too-thin frame, and bare feet peeked out from pajama pants with rockets and stars on them.

"Mommy!" Ella said. "We made pancakes. There's more for you."

Belle waddled over to the car seat muttering in Ella's voice, "We made pancakes. Mommy, we made pancakes."

"That's the bird?" Jamie sounded horrified.

Belle had been asleep in her covered cage last night when they'd finally arrived. Jamie must not have noticed her when she'd gotten up earlier.

"Get it away from the baby carrier!" She took a step toward Belle.

Tim rose. "It's okay, sis. Belle won't hurt the seat." He moved between his sister and the parrot.

"Belle's nice, Mommy," Ella said. "I fed her blueberries."

"I hope you scrubbed your hands after that." Jamie sank onto a chair and rubbed her face.

Ella looked worried. Luca's eyes drifted open. Tim set a steaming mug of black coffee in front of Jamie.

"Do you take anything in it?" His voice was even more gentle than usual.

She shook her head without speaking.

The week would be a long one if Jamie was going to be freaked out about Belle.

CHAPTER 5

The day ended as planned, with family dinner at my parents' home in the parsonage. Earlier, Tim had taken Jamie and the kids on a driving tour of this part of the Cape. Since it would have been tight fitting me in between the borrowed car seats for the baby and Ella, I'd stayed back. I took myself for a long solo walk and caught up on my book group reading at home.

Last year I'd shifted to not working on weekends. That was what employees were for. Yesterday had been an exception, with me subbing in for Sofia. I wanted to have tomorrow free, too, because I hoped to get to know Jamie better. Maybe she and I could get out for a walk together, or I could treat her to a manicure later in the week. Tim was taking the whole week off to be with his sister and the little ones. He wouldn't mind watching the kids while Jamie and I had some girl time.

If she wanted to, that is. So far she hadn't seemed to

warm to me at all. It might be that she was generally unhappy. She was tender with her children, but I hadn't seen her smile at me once. I'd be willing to bet that a week hanging out with her sweet, generous, supportive big brother and having help with her children might ease her mood at least for the short term.

Now we were immersed in the bustle of my family. Neli had made a big West African stew for everyone and stood stirring the pot with an apron over her growing baby bump. Abo Reba was holding court in the living room and held Luca on her lap. Cokey had already taken Ella under her wing. Derrick and Tim chatted about something. I headed into the kitchen, where Mom cut vegetables for the salad and Pa slid a fragrant loaf of fresh bread out of the oven.

In a family text thread last week, everyone had agreed not to have wine or beer tonight, so as not to tempt Jamie. She'd told Tim she'd been clean and sober for a year, and nobody wanted that to change, at least not on our watch. I sipped seltzer as I leaned against the kitchen counter absorbing the yummy smells and letting the buzz of multiple conversations wash over me.

After being introduced to everyone, Jamie stood in the doorway between the kitchen and the living room. She picked at her cuticle with her other hand. Her left knee jiggled in black leggings. She wore a long black sweater that made her look paler than usual, but her flax-colored hair was neatly tied back and she'd applied light makeup and lip gloss before we left the house.

Pa gave her his warmest, most welcoming smile. "Can I get you an iced tea or some cider, Jamie?" He spoke softly in that deep, reassuring voice that inspired both confidence and confidences. Being a minister was the perfect job for him.

She looked startled. After a moment, she said, "Thank you, yes. Cider sounds good."

He came back with a glass of the classic fall drink. "This family can be a bit overwhelming, but we're so happy you're all here with us."

"My brother's been bugging me to come East. I figured this was as good a time as any. I'm between jobs right now, and . . ." Her voice trailed off.

"We're glad to have you." He leaned closer and murmured something I couldn't hear.

I expected he offered to speak with her in private at his church office if she should want that. Jamie stared at him, then nodded.

"Look, Mommy! Cousin Cokey lended me a costume." Ella burst into the kitchen with a grinning Cokey behind her. "Can you guess what I am?" Ella wore a miniature white lab coat and big black-rimmed plastic glasses, and she carried a clipboard. The lab coat included a pocket protector and two pens in the breast pocket.

Jamie smiled at her daughter, one of the first smiles I'd seen from her. "Um, an astronaut?"

"No, silly." Ella looked at me. "Auntie Mac, can you guess?"

From behind Ella, Cokey put her finger on her lips and shook her head. She knew I'd remember the costume from two years ago. I was glad Derrick had kept the getup. When I phoned him this afternoon, he said of course they had a costume for Ella.

I cocked my head and studied her for a moment. "I think you're a doctor."

"No!"

Neli came over and squatted in front of Ella. "Let's see. Lab coat. Clipboard. Glasses. I'd say you're a scientist, or maybe an astrophysicist."

"Yes!" Cokey clapped her hands.

"Because astronauts are usually also scientists," Ella explained. "What are you going to be for Halloween, Auntie Neli?"

Neli pushed up to standing with a little grunt. "I think I'll go as a pumpkin."

My mom laughed. "An orange T-shirt and a green beret and you'll be all set."

The children seemed to relax Jamie. She leaned against the doorjamb sipping her glass of apple cider.

"Do you like to dig in the dirt, Ella?" Pa asked her. "Cokey does."

"Do I, Mommy?" Ella scrunched up her little nose.

"When you get a chance, yes." Jamie glanced at the rest of us. "We live in an apartment, so we don't have a garden."

"Well," my father continued, "I'm thinking of planting a church garden out in front. Several of our Quaker neighbors down the road have had a big garden behind their meetinghouse since last spring. Everything they grow goes to the Free Food Market in the basement of our church, and the Friends are also teaching others how to grow food at home. Isn't that splendid?"

"Can we help you in the garden, Abo Joe?" Cokey asked.

"Of course."

The rest of the evening went smoothly. Cokey and Ella had become instant friends, giggling and chattering away. Luca just seemed to take it all in.

I still hadn't figured out what to do with Belle when Jamie was around. The only solution seemed to be to bring the bird and her roost and cage upstairs. Tim and I had given our bedroom and bathroom off the living room to Jamie and the kids. She needed to feed Luca in the night, and that way she wouldn't have to negotiate stairs when it was time to fix a bottle.

As I reminded myself, it was only for a week.

CHAPTER 6

The next day was an odd one. Tim and I were both home, but Jamie turned down our suggestions of things we all could do, outings we could go on together. She claimed she had a headache and retreated to her room, leaving us with the kids. Tim and Ella made hearty pumpkin muffins while I hung out with Luca.

That part Tim and I didn't mind. Between us we could handle a baby and a bright little girl, but he murmured his concern about Jamie to me. I had borrowed a few simple board games and puzzles for Ella from Derrick, and I'd also laid in a supply of crayons. She kicked around a child-sized soccer ball in the yard with her uncle while I watched Luca sleep.

Tim had found a mini-basketball hoop at Goodwill and picked up a small basketball at the toy store. Ella loved learning how to shoot baskets on the driveway. Having a yard was new for our niece. The weather was mild and sunny and perfect for playing outdoors, and Cokey would love using the hoop and ball after Ella went home.

Jamie also refused our offer to go out for lunch. Tim popped Luca into the soft front carrier my parents had loaned us and we walked downtown to the Miss Westham Diner. It had been a favorite of mine growing up and still was today. The outside of the diner was a classic silver rail car, and inside it was as retro as they come. The decor was black and white, with a checkerboard linoleum floor and Naugahyde paired with chrome for seating.

Ella, sitting on a booster seat, enjoyed her fish sticks and fries. Too bad she couldn't order the traditional thick, creamy milkshake because of her lactose intolerance.

"She's a tidy eater for a kid," I murmured to Tim, watching her wipe her hands on her napkin and delicately dip each fry in the little paper cup of ketchup.

I savored a bowl of the diner's fish chowder, the best around, and Tim downed a double cheddar cheeseburger with mushrooms. He and I split an order of onion rings, and we shared two brownies among the three of us. Ella would get plenty of sweets later in the day. Luca stayed asleep in the carrier the entire time, with a napkin draped over his head while Tim ate to keep food out of the baby's hair.

"Uncle Tim, do you think I'll get a lot of candy at trick-or-treating tonight?" Ella asked.

"I bet you will." He smiled at her. "Everybody loves a scientist."

Luca let out a little wail.

"I think that means it's time to get moving," Tim said.

"I'll pay and meet you outside." I slid out of the booth.

"Uncle Tim, I have to go pee-pee." Ella looked panicked.

"Then let's go." He took her hand and headed to the unisex bathroom, baby and all.

On our walk home, we slowed as we passed Cape Costumers. Ella pulled on my hand.

"Auntie Mac, look at the devil." She pointed at the window.

Sure enough, a devil leered out at us, but this one was a cardboard cutout, not a real person in a costume. A mermaid outfit hung next to it, with shiny gold scales decorating the aqua tail, and a SpongeBob SquarePants getup flashed a buck-toothed grin from where it perched on a big seashell. Shelly must like to change up her window displays.

The door stood wide open. Inside near the entrance was a bowl of candy corn packets on a table.

"Can we go in and get candy?" Ella asked. "Plus, I want to see all the costumes."

I glanced at Tim.

He patted Luca's back. "This little guy's getting restless, and I think it's time for a diaper change and a bottle. I'll meet you two back at home, okay?"

"Deal." Ella gave him a thumbs-up.

Tim and I exchanged another amused look at the paired word and gesture, which made the little girl sound older than her years.

"See you back there." I laid my hand on her shoulder. "Let's see what's inside."

The bowl had a Help Yourself card in front of it.

"Do you like candy corn?" I asked Ella.

"I've never had it. I like corn on the cob. Does it taste like that?"

I laughed. "Not a bit. Put a packet in your jacket pocket, and I'll show you the right way to eat it when we get home."

"Happy Halloween." A slender woman approached us from the back of the store. Her gait was fluid, and she held herself with a straight back and perfect posture, as if she were a dancer on stage. Her salt-and-pepper hair was pulled back into a tidy bun, which added to the ballerina look. This must be Harini Whitt.

"Happy Halloween," Ella piped up.

"We still have a number of costumes in small sizes," the woman said.

"But I already have one," Ella said.

"Do you? What are you going to be, dear?" She put her hands on her bent knees and gazed into Ella's face.

"A scientist."

"Very good." She straightened. "Let me know if there's anything I can help you with, ma'am."

"Thanks. Welcome to Main Street, by the way." I extended my hand and introduced myself. "I met Shelly last week."

"Thank you. I'm Harini Whitt." She shook my hand. "Your name sounds familiar. Might you be part of the mystery book group?"

"I am. I understand you're going to join us."

"I'd like to check it out, at least. I prefer my mysteries on the gentler side."

"That's all we read." I smiled. "And we've had a few regulars grow too busy in recent months to come to our meetings, so we're happy to have you." My brother had been a founding member, but he'd dropped out, and now Zane King had, too, at least for a while, having become the proud father of twins.

"Auntie Mac, look!" Ella grabbed my hand. "It's a grown-up astronaut costume. That's what they wear under their space suits."

I smiled at Harini and let myself be pulled away to check out the adult-size NASA flight suit.

CHAPTER 7

When Tim offered to take our mini-scientist out trick-or-treating, Jamie said she would stay home with the baby and hand out candy.

I was off to a party at Gin's. It ostensibly was going to double as a book group meeting to discuss this week's cozy mystery. *Nine Lives and Alibis* by Cate Conte was a Halloween-themed story, but we might socialize instead. I'd forgotten to ask Harini this afternoon if she was joining us. If they kept the store open until late tonight, she might not be able to.

I slung my EpiPen bag across my chest. I was deathly allergic to insect stings and never left the house without my injectable epinephrine. The bag also held a couple of Benadryl pills as backup.

"Auntie Mac, aren't you going to wear a costume?" Ella asked at nearly five o'clock.

"No, honey. I don't like dressing up. But you look

great." My sole nod to the holiday was an orange silk scarf and a black shirt.

"She's the picture of a scientist doing important work." Tim held Luca on his shoulder, gently patting his back.

Luckily, the night wasn't too cold, and a thick sweater was all Ella needed for warmth under her lab coat. After I made sure our porch light was on, I emptied a bag of bite-size candy bars into a wide bowl.

"You'll be all right, Jamie?" I asked. "There's plenty of food in the fridge for dinner and two more bags of candy on the counter in there." I had put Belle to bed early so she wouldn't bother my sister-in-law. It was too bad I hadn't gotten any time with Jamie today, but the week was young.

"I'll be fine." She knelt and kissed Ella. "Bring back some goodies for Mommy, okay?"

"You can have all the ones with coconut in them."

"Deal." Jamie straightened and took Luca from Tim.

The three of us set out. Ella headed up the well-lit front walk of the house next door.

"Have fun." I bussed Tim's cheek. "I won't be too late."

"You too." He kept his gaze on his niece.

As I walked on, her tiny voice proclaimed, "Trick-or-treat!" Tim was in his element with little kids in the house. He seemed to know exactly what to do with both Ella and her little brother.

I was looking forward to experiencing Tim as a father to our own child or children, even though I still wasn't pregnant. I was thirty-eight, and we'd been trying for ten months. My doctor had said we needed to give it a good year before we could consult a specialist.

Adopting a newborn was a possibility, although I'd heard it could take a super long time to match with a pregnant mom through an agency.

There were alternatives. Some people fostered an older child through their state's social services department and then adopted them, while others went outside the system entirely. Zane and his husband had made a private arrangement with a friend of theirs who had agreed to donor insemination. After all parties signed a legal agreement and the biological mom gave birth to healthy twins, Stephen and Zane were now happy and harried parents of two one-month olds.

This neighborhood wasn't wanting for children. The paved sidewalks of our street were full of superheroes, devils, lions, and princesses, plus the odd ghost or train conductor. I didn't see a single other scientist or astronaut of any size. Ella was a unique trick-or-treater tonight.

I continued toward Gin's place downtown. Cape Costumers was closed and dark inside, with nothing but strategic spooky lights illuminating the display windows. Two doors down was the First Citizens' Credit Union. Five thirty was after hours, but the drive-through window stayed open until seven o'clock several days a week. A red sedan pulled into the drive-through lane on the side of the building.

I stared. The driver seemed to be dressed as a clone of Morticia Addams. Red lips pierced an ashen face and a black half mask covered her eyes. Long straight black hair hung down over the deep vee of her black dress, and clawlike red nails gripped the steering wheel. The front-seat passenger was a skeleton with a black hood painted like a skull covering the entire head. The mouth was pulled back in a classic skull creepy grin. If this was the skeleton Cokey had seen—with Enzo Lawrence in costume, perhaps—I understood why she'd found it scary. Someone in a jester's hat and harlequin tunic sat in the back seat, also wearing a half mask.

I shrugged. These folks were out for a night of partying and needed an influx of cash. Or maybe they'd gotten a big check in the mail and weren't up to speed on how to deposit using an app on their phone. I headed on to Gin's for a night of fun with my bookish buddies.

CHAPTER 8

Gin and I set out on our usual weekday walk at seven the next morning.

"That was fun last night," I said after we'd hit our stride on the former rail trail. "Thanks for having us."

"I don't think anybody minded not talking about the book, do you?"

"Not a bit. And since Harini couldn't be there, we can save book talk for next time." The five of us—Gin and me, plus Norland Gifford, Tulia Peters, and Flo Wolanski—played silly party games, ate pizza and sipped the drinks of our choice, and caught up with one another.

"Did you hear the news this morning?" she asked.

"No. What happened?"

"A man was found dead, and they seem to think there was something suspicious about it."

Not again. "In Westham?" I asked.

"Yes. On the deck of his condo. You know the development out on Short Sand Road next to that theater place?"

"Bay State Light Opera?"

"That's the one," Gin said. "It's the facility they renovated a couple of years ago."

A stately mansion with a wraparound veranda was on the property, but the summer theater organization had built a new performance and teaching space next to it. They rented it out for events like weddings and fundraisers when performances weren't on the schedule, and it had proved to be a popular venue.

"Did the news say who found him?" I asked.

"A neighbor, apparently." Gin slowed and stared at me. "But the weird part is that he was wearing a skeleton costume."

I came to a complete stop. "What was the man's name?"

"Being withheld pending notification yada, yada, yada."

"Of next of kin. Of course. Gin, this might be a complete coincidence, but a person in a skeleton costume was moving around in the window of Cape Costumers Friday. The sight of it scared Cokey when Reba was taking her around for the merchants' trick-or-treating thing. One of the shop's owners, Shelly Hitchcock, said it was only a friend of hers fooling around."

"And you think that he was the dead skeleton on the deck."

"It's possible. Another strange thing might be related."

"What's that?" she asked.

"On my way to your place last night, I saw a car pull into the bank drive-through window. All three people were in costume, including masks, and the passenger in the front seat was a skeleton. Full head mask and everything."

"You should tell the police."

"I will. Or Lincoln, or both."

Lincoln Haskins was the state police homicide detective I'd gotten to know over the last couple of years. After his earlier stern warnings to stay out of his homicide investigations, we'd eventually arrived at a good place. He'd come to accept that the Cozy Capers and I were going to investigate murders when one of us had something at stake in solving it. But we'd learned to be safer in our digging, and Lincoln appreciated information I passed along to him.

"If it was the same guy, it's at least a data point," I added.

"Right. And it could help narrow the window for his time of death." Gin laughed. "Listen to me. I'm starting to sound like a cop in one of the mysteries we read."

"We've learned a lot, you have to admit."

"Kind of hard not to."

"Let's get walking again," I said. "Tim's got both the baby and Ella right now. He wanted to let Jamie sleep in, but I don't want to be out too long."

We resumed our fast stride, swinging our arms. Frost-reddened poison ivy lined the edge of the paved trail, and a twisty vine hanging from a bare tree looked just as lethal. Dry leaves hung on to a few of the branches of any tree not an evergreen. These leaves were brown and dead, not the glorious colors of the typical and famed New England fall. The Cape didn't have many maple trees, anyway. Tourists had to go farther north for real leaf-peeping.

I'd once read an Annie Proulx essay about autumn. She wrote with eloquence about the senescence of late summer and fall, about everything dying and for a reason. The skeleton on the deck might have died for a reason, but it couldn't be a good one. If it was a homicide, it wasn't in the natural order of things, unlike these sap-starved leaves.

When we emerged from the wooded area onto a boardwalk over the marsh, a brisk wind hit me in the face. I could taste the salt in the air. Colder temperatures would keep company with ever-shortening days for two more months, a prospect I found depressing. Maybe I'd get around to ordering one of those SAD lights to keep my seasonal affective disorder at bay. My short-day blues seemed to grow worse every year.

"Are you working today?" she asked.

"I am. Tim has plans with Jamie and the little ones."

"Have you gotten to know her at all? I know you were hoping to."

"Not really," I said. "She's been keeping me at arm's length. I plan to ask her to go out for a manicure with me one day this week, or for a bite to eat."

"But not at the pub, right?"

"No way."

I'd told Gin about Jamie's struggles with addiction. The Rusty Anchor would not be our destination for a sister-in-law supper.

"By the way, I can't serve at the Free Dinner tomorrow," I said. "I let the organizer know." Gin and Norland

and I had been volunteering as servers at the weekly free dinner Pa's church offered. All were welcome, no questions asked, and it was a popular meal for those whose income and bills didn't quite match up.

"You do have a few things on your plate this week." She smiled.

"You could say that again."

CHAPTER 9

By ten o'clock Mac's Bikes was open and busy for a not particularly warm first day of November, which surprised me. A group of twentysomethings in Day of the Dead attire wanted to rent bikes so they could tour area cemeteries. A bit of morning drinking might have already gone on, but they all signed the required waivers about responsible riding and being liable for damage. A couple in matching jackets brought in their preschool-age grandson to buy him his first two-wheeler for his birthday. A regular customer who was a serious cyclist dropped off her Cannondale for a tune-up.

A group text thread with the members of the Cozy Capers group was also busy. Everybody wanted to talk about the murder. Speculation in the group was high about the man's identity, but his name and details of the death still hadn't been released by the authorities.

All I could do was glance at the messages on brief breaks between helping shoppers and renters.

Orlean was working away in the repair shop, and I was in charge of everything else, meaning retail and rentals. My most recent part-time employee had left last month for a full-time job in Providence, Rhode Island, which I thought would be fine. Fall and winter were usually my quiet seasons, but not today.

My grandmother bustled in at about eleven thirty, wearing her customary hot pink track suit and rainbow-colored Rasta beret. For the moment, the store was empty of customers. I had taken a quick facilities break and now perched on the stool behind the counter, perusing my texts. I looked up and smiled at Reba, inhaling her scent of coconut tinged with chlorine from her daily swimming habit.

"MacKenzie, darling, I just heard the news."

My abo was pretty much the only person who called me by my full first name.

"Good morning, Abo Ree. Do you mean the man who was found dead?"

"Of course." She set her fists on her tiny hips. "What else?"

"It could be any other news. I don't know, the election? Maybe Cokey lost another tooth, or there's flooding in Madagascar."

"Don't be obtuse, now. Of course I mean the murder. Is your group already on the case?" Her brown eyes were bright, as bright as the slightly rheumy eyes of a person over eighty can be.

"They're trying to be, but nobody has any information, including whether it was actually murder."

"See? That's the reason I'm here. I'm afraid it was my friend Enzo Lawrence."

The man in the skeleton suit. As I'd suspected.

"I'm so sorry, Abo Ree. Were you two close?"

"No, not in so many words," she said. "He was more of an acquaintance. We had mutual friends, which is how I found out."

"He came into the shop and told me you recommended that he get an adult tricycle here."

"Well, of course I did. Where else should he buy one?"

I smiled at my biggest supporter. "Unfortunately, we completed the sale and it was waiting for Orlean to make sure it was ready for him to ride. I guess I should cancel out the purchase."

"Good idea."

"Hey, Reba." Orlean appeared in the doorway to the repair area. "Couldn't help but overhear the talk. That mean you want to cancel the trike check over, Mac?"

"I'm afraid so," I said. "I doubt whoever his relatives are would want the expense to his estate."

"Got it." She turned away. Orlean always spoke tersely, but she got the job done, and that was all I needed.

"Did you see the announcement of his name on the local news?" I asked my grandma. "I've been so busy all morning, I haven't had a chance to look at anything but receipts and rental forms."

"No." She shook her head. "My girlfriend called. Her great-niece works for the Barnstable police, and they got word. Naturally, she called Bea, who phoned me."

"Naturally." I studied her. "Do you have any idea who might have wanted Enzo dead and out of the way?"

She tapped her temple. "Not yet, but I'm putting my little gray cells to work."

As she spoke, Norland Gifford pushed through the door. Westham's retired police chief was a member of the Cozy Capers and a friend. He also maintained close ties with the WPD.

Reba brightened. "There's someone who might know."

"My thoughts, exactly," I said. "Good morning, Norland."

"Morning, ladies." He didn't return our smiles. "Did I hear something about little gray cells?"

"You sure did. I suppose you're here to talk about Enzo Lawrence's homicide with my granddaughter," Reba said.

He gave a slow nod. "I suppose I am, and I'm not surprised you've already heard."

"She has a friend with a relative in the Barnstable police," I murmured. "You know how it is."

"I do."

"Well, I have a mani-pedi scheduled, hon." Reba's words rushed out as if she didn't want Norland grilling her on who the contact was. "I'll be getting along, but, Mac, I wanted to ask if you'll come to the cemetery with me tonight, as we always do."

"For Abo Alcindo?" I asked. "Of course I will." Although our annual pilgrimage had slipped my mind this year, she'd been bringing me with her to my grandfather's grave on the Day of the Dead since his death over a decade ago, at least when I was living in the state and not off on my travels. And before that, I'd gone with both my abos to leave flowers and pour a little grogu on the grave of Alcindo's late brother. They would each sip a small glass of the clear sugarcane liquor, which I joined them in after I'd graduated from high school. "I'll close up at four thirty today."

"I'll come by about then. Toodle-oo, Norland." With that, she was gone.

"Good heavens, a fly couldn't land on that woman," Norland said.

"Not a one. So, you looked pretty serious when you came in. What do you know?"

"As you're aware, I'm still in close contact with several former contacts on the force. The victim's name was the main piece. Sounds like Reba knew him."

"She said they were acquaintances, but you know my grandma. Everybody in the universe is her friend, and she's drawn like a magnet to anyone new or interesting in town."

He smiled for the first time. "True words, although I must point out that the death hasn't yet been definitively identified as a homicide."

"I didn't think so. I might have something to share about Enzo." I explained that I'd seen a person dressed as a skeleton in the passenger seat of the red sedan going through the bank's lane. "I told Gin, but I haven't had a free minute to let the group know."

"Have you told Haskins or Detective Johnson?" Norland frowned.

"Neither. We've been busy here until ten minutes ago, and I'm the only one out front these days."

"You heard that the dead man wore the same kind of costume."

"Yes, Gin told me about it on our walk. Do you know who reported Enzo dead?"

"Not yet. As you know, they might become a person of interest, depending on who it was."

"Right. There's another piece." I relayed the experience Cokey had had seeing the window of Cape Costumers. "She was totally freaked out about the skeleton she saw. If it was also Enzo, I know he and Shelly Hitchcock were friends, and possibly more, by the way Shelly blushed when she mentioned him."

"And who is this Shelly person?" he asked.

"One of the new owners of Cape Costumers."

"I see. Share what you know to the group, okay? I have to run. I have an OFL today."

"What's that?"

"Old Farts' Lunch." He smiled. "We're a few geezer men talking every month about nothing. But it's fun, and it's company."

"I love it. Where do you meet?"

"The Rusty Anchor, of course. Even old farts like a glass of beer with lunch."

"Have a great time."

"Thanks. I always do." He zipped up his jacket, snugged his navy Greek captain's hat onto his head, and made his way out, holding the door for another set of customers coming in.

So much for having time to text the group, or Lincoln, for that matter.

CHAPTER 10

My shop fell quiet by one o'clock. I perched on a stool at the counter to eat my sandwich and took the time to text Lincoln the few things I knew. It wasn't much, but if I could help, I would.

He wrote back within the minute.

Got a little free time?

I replied that I did, and five minutes later he ambled through the door.

"Don't take this the wrong way," I said. "But I'm glad I haven't seen you since July."

He gave a low laugh. "Same. The more months that go by without a homicide, the better." He was a big guy, six foot three, but he'd been working on his fitness on his doctor's recommendation. Now he sported a slimmer profile than he had a year and a half ago.

"And, yet, here you are," I said.

"Alas, yes."

"Does that mean the death is for sure a murder?"

"We now believe so, yes," he said.

I tilted my head. "You got new glasses." He'd always worn heavy black frames. Now his eyeglasses were rimmed with a thinner tortoiseshell.

"I did." He blushed, something I'd never seen him do before.

"I like them." I smiled, wondering if a romantic interest might have something to do with his new look. In his midforties, he'd been divorced and single since I first met him. "They suit you."

"Thank you." He cleared his throat. "You said you had something to share."

"Maybe. You might want to talk with Shelly Hitchcock about the victim. She's the new co-owner of Cape Costumers." I explained for the third time today about the skeleton in the window. "And then I saw one in the passenger seat of a red sedan driving through the bank last evening at about six. I don't know if either was Enzo, but he was in costume when he was found dead, wasn't he?"

"He was. Which bank?"

"The credit union on Main Street."

"So noted." Lincoln asked, "And you know the victim's name how?"

"From Reba. Yeah, don't ask. She has her ways. But now it's my turn to ask a couple of questions, if that's okay."

"You can try me."

"Gin said a neighbor reported Enzo dead. Who was it?" I asked. "And do you have any idea what killed him? Oh. I have three questions. I guess the most important is who wanted the dude gone bad enough to end his life?"

"If I knew the answer to the last one, Mac, I'd be booking a killer into a jail cell right now, not sitting here picking your brain."

"All right. But what about the first two?"

"The neighbor was simply a neighbor, as far as we can tell. She reported seeing something on the deck next door early this morning, and she went over to check. We're canvassing the area now to find anyone who might have seen unusual goings-on or anything suspicious last night."

"Why do you think it was homicide? Was Enzo shot? Knifed to death?"

"Nothing like that, but the medical examiner didn't like the look of his skin, and the body was in rigor mortis in an odd position."

A man came through the door, followed by three women. I greeted them, then turned to Lincoln.

"Thanks for the info," I said. "I have to get back to work."

"Thank you for sharing what you know."

"You're always welcome to it. Good luck with everything."

He slid past the customers and out the door. I had so many questions and no time to think about them.

The women were browsing the retail shelves, but the man approached. Looking a hair under six feet, he had the trim figure and erect bearing of an ex-military person, or maybe a current one, and the short hair to match.

"Welcome to Mac's Bikes," I said. "I'm Mac. How can I help you?"

"I'm visiting town for a bit and didn't bring my bicycle. What's the highest-end model you rent?"

"I'm afraid all the rentals are the same except for size, and they're sturdy rather than high-end. Plus, we have a couple of tandems."

"Hmm." His lip curled. "I'm not accustomed to anything but the best."

I kept silent. Unless he wanted to buy one of the Bianchis I had in stock, he was out of luck.

"Very well," he said. "I'll rent, and for a week, please."

I handed him the rental application and a pen. "Will you want a helmet too?"

"No."

"Fill out the top section, initial the box to decline a helmet, and sign at the bottom, please." We required children under eighteen to either bring or rent a helmet, but I couldn't do anything about adults who wanted to risk the safety of their brains. Even then, I'd seen teens ride away with the helmet unbuckled. If their parents didn't enforce safety, I couldn't either.

He took the pen in his left hand and filled in the blanks in an over-the-top writing style. He slid the paper back to me. "I understand there was a murder in town yesterday. Am I going to be all right riding the public trails?"

"I did hear about a person being found dead and maybe not of natural causes." I didn't think it had hit the news by now. "But I believe the police are on the case, and Westham is a safe town. I'm sure you'll be fine."

"Good."

I told the women I'd be right with them and asked the man to follow me to the rental bikes area out back. I really needed to hire another employee.

After I'd fixed up the guy with a bike, I asked, "What brings you to the Cape at this time of year?" It was well after the Cape's tourist season.

He didn't meet my gaze. "I have family business to attend to."

"Have a good ride. Let us know if you encounter any problems with the bike."

Once things had quieted down again, I went to file his paperwork. *Huh.* His name was Herbert Lawrence, and he listed his address as Bedford, a town northwest of Boston that hosted Hanscom Air Force Base. I took a second look. He'd omitted a street address. Well, I had his cell phone—if it was correct. I could find him if he didn't return the bike, which I thought was un-likely, given the way he'd turned up his nose at it.

Could his family business be with Enzo Lawrence, now deceased? Probably not. Lawrence was a common surname. Even if Herbert was a son or nephew, it was too early for him to have heard of the homicide.

CHAPTER 11

Unlike their Portuguese colonizers, Cape Verdeans didn't fuss much with All Souls' Day. But my grandfather had spent time in Mexico. There the Day of the Dead is a big deal, with graveside family picnics and music, costumes and parades. It's a holiday with somber origins that sometimes turns into a cemetery dance party.

The annual ritual of tidying up graves and remembering those who had gone on before had been important to Alcindo. I loved having that connection with him and with Reba, and I dreaded the day when I would also be toasting her departed soul. I hoped that time was a long way in the future, and perhaps by then I'd have a little Reba great-grandchild to bring along and continue the tradition with.

At five twenty the shadows were deep and long next to my grandfather's grave at Seaview Cemetery. Aptly named, it was one of the oldest burying grounds in Westham and, situated on a hilltop, provided a glimpse of the sea.

My grandma interrupted my thoughts by handing me a small glass of bagaço, the Portuguese aguardente made from the lees of wine. It was hard to find grogu around here, and in recent years Reba had substituted the Portuguese version.

"To my beloved Alcindo." She raised her glass.

"To Abo Alcindo." I sipped.

She took a small drink at the same time, then poured the rest of her glass onto the grave. I held out the open bottle. When she nodded, I refilled the glass.

We clinked our drinks again.

"I wish your father would join us here one year," Reba said after taking a sip.

"Pa never does. Do you know why?"

"Joseph has said he wants to hold the memory of his father close in other ways, not with a reminder of his death." She gave a little shrug. "That's his choice. Shall we sit for a moment and reminisce? My bones are tired today."

"Of course." I followed her to the stone bench a few yards away. My grandma almost never complained of ailments, and this had me worried.

Instead of reminiscing, she asked about the present. "How are things with Jamie and the children?"

"Good question. She is great with them and is responsible, making sure little Luca is fed and clean, and she's sweet and fun with Ella. But something's going on with her."

"Is she staying sober?" Reba asked.

"She says she is, and I haven't detected any smell of alcohol or strange behavior. The thing is, she's so thin, and she seems withdrawn. Tonight I want to make a date for the two of us to do something fun, see if I can get her to open up."

"That's a good idea, sweetheart. Those babies are darlings, for sure. Well, little Luca is at the lump stage, as my sister used to say, but he's a cutie, and we'll see his personality emerge by and by."

"A lump." I laughed. "I know what you mean. He drinks and sleeps and poops but isn't smiling or doing much otherwise yet."

"So, what news about the murder? Did Lincoln have anything juicy to share?"

"Way to pivot, Abo Ree."

"I'm much too old not to ask the things I'm curious about."

"I get it. Well, Lincoln didn't have a lot," I began. "The police don't seem to know the cause of death, and the person who reported Enzo lying on his deck was only a neighbor."

"I wonder if he'll be buried here." She waved her hand, taking in the scope of the burying yard. "I don't suppose Lincoln knew about Enzo's family."

"We didn't talk about the next of kin." I took another small sip of the clear liquor, which warmed all the way down. "A man came into the shop after Lincoln left. He rented a bike and left. It all seemed normal except for him wanting a higher-end style than I stock for rentals. But after he left, I checked the rental agreement. Abo Ree, his name is Herbert Lawrence, and he said he was on the Cape for family business."

"The last names match, but it's not an uncommon one."

"I know. It might be total coincidence."

We sat sipping until our glasses were empty. My grandma held up hers.

"Promise me you'll keep coming on *Día di Dufuntu* after I'm in the ground?"

I wrapped my arm around her shoulders and pulled her close. "I promise, but you have to promise to take care of yourself on top of the ground."

"No worries, MacKenzie. I have no intention of going anywhere." Her laugh was an infectious tinkling sound.

A man walked toward us along the grassy path next to my grandfather's grave. Hands in his pockets, the man gazed down. He appeared lost in his thoughts.

"Peter," Reba called out. "Visiting your beloveds?"

He looked up, startled. "Hello, Reba. Yes, I am. It's a tradition."

"That's why we're here, too. MacKenzie, this is Peter Zelensky. Peter, meet my granddaughter, MacKenzie Almeida."

I extended my hand. "I'm Mac."

He gave my hand a quick shake. "Good to meet you, Mac. You have the bike shop."

"I do."

"My daughter is back living at home until she figures out what to do with her entirely useless degree in history, and she wants to ride her mom's old bike. I'll bring it in one of these days."

"We can make it rideable, as long as it's not too rusted," I said.

His eyes drooped and his mouth turned down. He gave a longing glance behind him. "My wife last rode it five years ago, not long before she died."

"I'm so sorry," I murmured.

"It's okay." He patted my grandfather's gravestone. "Alcindo was a good man. You ladies take care, now."

"You too, Peter." Reba watched him until he was out of earshot. "Poor fellow. He and his wife were so in love even after twenty years, but cancer doesn't care about the heart."

"It sure doesn't. How do you know him?"

"He's been the investment adviser for pretty much everybody around here. Those with funds to invest, anyway."

"I don't think I've seen him before," I said.

"After his wife went on ahead, he moved up to North Falmouth. Couldn't bear staying in the house, according to what I heard."

"That would have been before I moved back to Westham, which explains why I didn't recognize him."

"Yes," she agreed. "Before we go, I have a piece of nonmurderous gossip for you."

"Ooh, do tell."

"Did you know Lincoln has been stepping out with a lady?"

"I wondered," I said. "He's looking kind of spruced up lately, and he has new glasses. Who's the woman?"

"It's his ex-wife."

I gaped. "No way"

"Indeed. Delia Haskins."

"I met her last summer at the Rusty Anchor, and I remember wondering about the name. So, they've gotten over whatever reason they got divorced and realized they missed each other?"

"Those two suffered a tragedy no parent should ever go through," Reba said.

My heart sank. "They lost a son or a daughter."

"Yes, their little girl and their only child. Their daughter passed from leukemia at age three. People grieve in different ways, and certain couples can't find a way to reconcile their sorrow and their love for each other."

"But now they have," I said. "That's awesome."

"I hope it sticks." She stood and handed me her glass. "Let's go. I don't like being in a graveyard after dark."

A shiver ran through me. I didn't believe in ghosts, but I agreed with my grandma. I didn't want to linger here after the sun went down, either.

CHAPTER 12

I arrived home at almost six to a frazzled Tim holding a sleepy Luca. Ella sat at the kitchen table in front of a full bowl of a creamy mac and cheese, and Jamie was nowhere to be seen.

"Where do you want me?" I smiled at him.

"Take this guy and see if you can convince his sister to eat. I desperately need a break."

I held out my arms for the baby and sank into the chair next to my niece. "That looks yummy, Ella. Is it your favorite?"

"No." She stuck out her lips. "I only like the orange mackiecheese."

I spotted the box on the counter. Jamie must feed Ella the traditional brand, not the organic one that omits the garish orange food coloring in the dry cheese packet. Belle perked up from the stool across the room.

"I only like the orange mackiecheese." The bird's imitation of Ella's voice was perfect and made me laugh.

Ella giggled. "Belle is really funny, Auntie Mac."

"She is," I said. "I'm hungry, honey. How about you feed me a bite, and then you take a bite?"

Her expression brightened. "Feed you like a baby?"

"Like a little kid, yes." I shifted Luca to my shoulder and held open my mouth.

She maneuvered a spoonful into my mouth. It was cheesy, and I wondered about her lactose allergy. Maybe she could tolerate processed and cooked dairy but not liquid milk and ice cream.

"Mmm, yummy," I said. "Now it's your turn."

She slid a bite into her own mouth. I bit my lip not to laugh at her surprised expression. She ate another spoonful.

"I think you were hungry." I smiled at her.

"I was. I didn't think I would like this kind, but it's good."

"I'm glad. Listen, I'm going to put your brother in his bed. I'll be right back, okay?"

Ella gave a serious nod. "I have Belle to keep me compady."

"She's good at keeping people company." That was the first word I'd heard her mispronounce, quite a feat for such a young talker. I carried Luca into their bedroom and gently eased him down on his back. When his eyes fluttered open, I popped in his pacifier and tapped it softly until he went back to sleep. Jamie hadn't brought a baby monitor, but the kitchen wasn't far, and all the doors were open. I'd be able to hear him if he cried.

Belle had moved to perch on the back of the chair I'd been sitting in. Ella's bowl held only two pieces of cheese-coated macaroni and her glass of oat milk was less than half full. Tim had let me know he'd bought the milk alternative today.

Where was Jamie, anyway? Tim must know, but he hadn't reappeared yet.

"Do you want more mac and cheese, Ella?" I asked.

"Yes, please. Belle wants more too."

"Did you already feed her some?"

"Belle wants more." The parrot cocked her head. "Snacks, Mac?"

"We're saving the people food for the people, Belle, but you can have snacks." I served the human girl another bowlful and gave the bird girl a portion of frozen grapes, one of her favorite snacks.

Tim came downstairs a few minutes later. When he saw Ella's empty bowl, he gave me an approving thumbs-up.

"And she had seconds," I said.

"Attagirl." Tim smiled at her.

"Uncle Tim, when will Mommy come home?" Ella asked him.

"Probably after you go to sleep, but I know she'll give you a kiss as soon as she walks in the door."

"Okay."

After I put Belle to bed, we spent the next hour hanging out with our niece. I got her into her jammies and helped her brush her teeth. Tim lay down next to her, read her a book, and sang softly to help her fall asleep in Jamie's absence. Luca blessedly stayed in slumberland in his temporary crib.

Meanwhile, in the kitchen, I exerted all my culinary skills to heat up leftover chicken stew and set the table. I sliced half a loaf of Tim's excellent sourdough bread and set it out next to good Irish butter. Two wineglasses and an open bottle of chilled white completed the spread.

Tim and I toasted the quiet.

"I know you're wondering where my sister is," he began.

I nodded, mouth full of stew.

"She said someone she knew in Seattle moved to Barnstable," Tim said. "They agreed to meet for dinner at Jimmy's Harborside tonight."

"Did you give her your car?"

"No. She walked down and said her friend would give her a ride home." Frowning, he took a sip of wine.

"And you're not sure if you should believe her."

"Right. What if she went to get wasted by herself at the bar? Maybe there is no friend."

Ugh. "I can go and see how she is if you want. You know, pretend I wanted some time with my sister-in-law. Which I do, actually."

"That's sweet, honey. No, I think we need to trust her."

"Okay. She does seem troubled, but at least she's been responsible with the kids, right? She's been taking care of the baby. She brought formula, bottles, and diapers, and Ella seems well-equipped with the right kinds of clothes."

"Totally." He nodded. "I can't fault her for any of that. It's just that Jamie doesn't have a stellar track record for staying sober and clean."

"I know."

"We don't need to obsess about my sister. She'll be home when she gets here, and if she blew her sobriety while she was out, I'll deal. Tell me about your day, my love."

"Work was work, of course." I had shared the news about the death this morning after my walk. Now, after I filled Tim in about the body's identity, I told him about the man who shared Enzo's last name.

"And you think he might be related to the victim?"

"I have no idea, but I thought it was curious. He said he was here on family business."

"I can keep an eye out at the bakery next week once I'm back at work," Tim said. "If you think that would be useful."

"Sure." I hoped by then the police would know who was responsible for Enzo's death and that it wouldn't be his blood relative. "Lincoln stopped by the shop too. Unfortunately, it doesn't seem like they know much yet."

"Too bad. How was your visit to your grandfather's grave?"

I smiled. "Pensive, as always, although I asked Abo Reba why my father never goes with us to the cemetery. I don't think I've ever asked her that before." I savored my last bite of the stew, thick and creamy and flavored with rosemary and thyme.

"And?"

"She said Pa doesn't want to think of Abo Alcindo as being underground. He wants to remember his father alive and well."

"Makes sense."

I frowned, remembering the man we'd spoken to. "Do you have an investment adviser?"

"Are you kidding? Mac, I'm thirty-four. I own a business and we co-own a house. That's all the investments I have, for the moment."

"I hear you. I'm in the same position. The thing is, we talked in the cemetery with this guy Reba knows, a Peter Zelensky, and she said he's the investment adviser for people in Westham."

From the other room came first a baby whimper followed by a wail. Tim glanced at the wall clock.

"Nine o'clock, right on schedule for his evening bottle." He stood.

"Want me to get him?"

"I'm good. But can you microwave a cup of water in the big glass measuring cup?"

"For one minute, and then pop in one of the bottles in the fridge, right?"

"Yep." He disappeared through the door.

We were getting the routine down, but still I hoped Jamie would arrive soon, preferably happy and substance-free.

CHAPTER 13

An hour later, at ten o'clock, Jamie was still out of the house. She wasn't responding to Tim's texts or calls. He'd gotten Luca back to sleep, but now he was pacing the living room. I sat on the couch with a cup of ginger-lemon tea and my feet up on the coffee table.

"I can't believe she's doing this," he muttered. "I'm not sure if I'm more mad or more worried."

"It does seem like a pretty long dinner." I didn't want to add to his being upset, but more than four hours was way too long to stay away, especially when you've left your young children with an uncle they barely knew. Yes, he was a warm and nurturing man who cared deeply for his sister and the little ones. But he wasn't Mama, and neither was I.

"I'm thinking about heading out to check on her. If Jamie's got her elbows on the bar getting sloshed, I'll have to drag her home, and it won't be pretty."

"Go, if you need to. I'll tend to the kiddos if either of them wakes up." I stifled a yawn. Ten was my bedtime.

He sank down next to me. "The thing is, I don't want to be the overpowering big brother. Is it too soon to go looking for her?"

"I don't know, sweetheart. That has to be your call. It's too soon to ask the police to search for her."

His eyes flew open in an alarmed look. "The police? Do you think something bad happened to her?"

"No, not at all." I swore silently. Why had I voiced that thought? "Maybe you should call Jimmy's, see if she's there."

"I could describe her, I guess."

"Do you know the name of the friend she was meeting?"

"Bob." Tim shook his head. "That's it. No last name. Only Bob."

I shifted on the cushions. Something was pressing into my hip. I felt around in the crack between the cushion and the arm. *No.* I pulled out a cell phone in a lime green case.

"Isn't this hers?" I asked.

He dropped his face into his hands for a moment, then took the phone.

"It must be on silent," he said. "No wonder she hasn't been responding. Who doesn't take their cell when they go out, and a mother of babies to boot?"

A troubled soul like Jamie, that's who, but I kept my response to myself. He knew the answer to his question.

"I have to find her, hon." He kissed my forehead and stood.

"Of course you do. You'll drive, yes?"

"I will. I'm sorry to leave you alone here."

"I'm fine. I might snooze a bit, but it'll be a light sleep. I'll wake up if either Ella or Luca does, and I'm sure you'll be back soon, with your sister in tow."

"May that be all it is. There's another bottle ready in the fridge for Luca, if you should need it."

I smiled up at him. "I love you."

"I love you too."

Poor Tim. I wasn't at all sure he'd be back soon, and I'd thought of several unpleasant outcomes. Jamie could be drunk. She could have run off with this Bob dude for a fling, if he even existed. She might have started walking home in the dark and gotten hit by a car. Or she could have tried to end her own life again, as she'd attempted last fall in Seattle. The last two were the worst.

Had she left her phone here on purpose?

With a sharp intake of breath, I thought of yet another bad possibility. Enzo had been murdered by parties unknown. What if his death hadn't been personal? A homicidal maniac could be looking for more victims. Who better to target than a woman with issues walking alone in the night? I swallowed. That was not a good place for my thoughts to dwell.

Still, I got up and made sure the doors and windows were all locked. The classic admonition of *Better safe than sorry* had never been more relevant.

CHAPTER 14

Jamie never came home. Tim had trudged in at eleven thirty, saying he'd driven all over town looking for her. The bartender at Jimmy's said she left at nine o'clock after he refused to serve her any more drinks. Sure enough, she'd been alone at the bar, not with the fictional Bob, and had eaten nothing more than an appetizer of Buffalo wings.

Ella had a meltdown of wanting her mama when she woke up this morning, but between Tim and me, we managed to restore her happy self, except every few minutes she asked when her mother would be home. Each time, Tim mustered a smile and said, "She's taking a little vacation."

I skipped my early walk with Gin even though the morning wasn't rainy or overly cold, but I felt terrible leaving him with both kids after breakfast. I had to open my shop. Rentals were due in and to be picked up. Orlean had a full schedule of tune-ups and repairs. There was no way I could close for the day. I'd promised Tim I would ask around and keep an eye out for his wayward sister.

Now that I was behind the counter here in my Main Street shop, my pessimism grew by the minute. I kept picturing Jamie in various outcomes, and none of them were good. How troubled she must be to not come home last night. My heart broke for her, and for Tim and the kids.

Tim could file a missing person report with the police, but maybe not yet. I pulled out my phone to check how long the person had to be missing before reporting it, and then decided there was an easier route.

I was about to text Norland to ask him when Florence Wolanski hurried in. Flo was a Cozy Capers stalwart as well as the Westham Public Library director, and her research skills were wicked awesome, bordering on legendary.

"Hey, Flo," I said. "You look like you're here to put out a fire."

"Not a fire, exactly, but I wanted to see if you were okay." She ran her hand through her spiky short white hair.

"What?" I wrinkled my nose. "I'm fine. Why?"

"Have you checked the group text thread?"

"No, I haven't had time to."

"I thought so," she said. "To go radio silent isn't like you."

"I have house guests." I would leave it at that for the moment. "What's going on?"

"Seems Tulia had a customer yesterday who was on his phone talking about Uncle Enzo."

I gave a slow nod. "Did she get the customer's name?"

"Herbert something."

"Herbert Lawrence. He was in here yesterday and rented a bike from me."

"But he doesn't live in the area, right?" Flo asked.

"He doesn't." I told her what he'd said about coming to Westham on family business. "He lives in Bedford, which is where Hanscom Air Force Base is. He looked kind of military."

"So a guy who was trained on guns shows up to murder his uncle. Interesting."

"Wait. Enzo was shot?" I asked.

"I don't know. But it's possible, right?"

"I guess. I wonder who he was talking to."

"Not a clue." She peered at me. "You look a little strained. Are you okay?"

"Not really." I let out a long breath and beckoned her closer. "Tim's sister and her kids are visiting from the West Coast. Jamie went out alone last night and never came home. I'm super worried, and Tim is frantic. At the same time, we both have to be calm and comforting for baby Luca and little Ella. It's a mess."

"You poor thing, Mac. What do you need?"

"I need Jamie to get her rear end home." I thought for a moment. "I was going to ask Norland about how long we need to wait before reporting her missing. Do you know?"

She pulled out her phone and tapped and swiped.

"For an adult of sound mind, twenty-four to forty-eight hours. Children and people with dementia are in a different category."

"Thanks. I hope the police don't push back, saying she's a person of free will and there's no need to worry."

"I suppose they might," Flo said. "Either way, we can certainly all keep our eyes out. Send the group a message. Describe her. You know, height, hair color, build, what she was wearing." She reached out and patted my arm. "Don't worry, Mac. She'll turn up. It's hard to be a single mom of little ones. I know. I did it."

"You mean Jamie might have simply wanted to get away for a bit?"

"It's possible."

"You could be right." I thought for a moment. "I'm sure it's the first time since the baby was born that she had a chance to be away from both kiddos. But disappearing like she did and drinking at Jimmy's still seems like a mean thing to do to Tim, and to Ella. The little girl was super upset this morning when she woke up and her mother wasn't there." Tim had slept on the couch all night. The couch luckily was long enough for him, or nearly.

"How old is the baby?"

"Three months."

"Your sister-in-law could be suffering from postpartum depression," Flo said. "I think you told us last year she was already prone to mental illness or at least clinical depression. The months after giving birth can make that a lot worse."

"That's no good. I doubt she's seeing anyone about it." Poor Jamie.

Orlean approached from the repair room.

"Hey, Flo. Mac, I couldn't help overhearing. Your sister-in-law's gone missing?" She wiped oily hands on a red rag.

"I'm afraid so," I said.

"Gimme a thumbnail description. I'll look around for her."

"Thanks, Orlean. Let's see. She's white, about five nine, shoulder-length dark blond hair, and she's thin. Her eyes are blue like Tim's. I don't know what she was wearing last night when she went out."

Flo nodded, tapping into her phone.

"That's good," Orlean said. "Full name?"

"Jamie . . . oh. I don't know if she's Brunelle like Tim or if she still uses her ex-husband's name. I'll text Tim and ask him." I should know her last name, but Tim was the one who corresponded with her, and it was never via snail mail.

"Lemme know."

My mechanic might keep her words short, but she was long on heart.

"Also," Orlean continued, "the two of you and the rest of that book group have got to be working on the murder. I knew Enzo from pickleball, may he rest in peace."

I laughed. "You just gave me whiplash in three directions, Orlean. You play pickleball?"

She lifted her chin. "Yep."

"And Enzo Lawrence did too?" I asked.

"Yep." Orlean turned on her heel and went back to work.

"I sent the description to the group," Flo said.

"Thanks. I'll add Jamie's last name and what she was wearing if I get that stuff from Tim." I tilted my head. "Do you also play pickleball?"

"Sure. Norland plays, and once I saw Lincoln and Delia out on the court. Who doesn't play?"

"Me, for one," I said. "Lincoln and Delia, huh? Reba told me they're seeing each other."

"Yes. Isn't it the sweetest thing?"

"Mmm." My thoughts were on the Enzo part of the last few exchanges. "Did Enzo get along with other players?"

"He hasn't played much lately. He was having balance issues." Flo widened her eyes. "Wait. You think Enzo's killer also plays?"

"It's possible."

"I never played in the same game as Enzo, but Norland might have." Her phone dinged. "Oops. Gotta run. Staff meeting over lunch. Don't forget we're going to the jail tomorrow. We have a four thirty entry time."

"Right. Thanks for the reminder."

I watched her hurry away as fast as she'd come in. With everything that had been happening, our weekly volunteer shift at the county jail library in Barnstable had slipped my mind. Flo and I always went together. Many of the men and women incarcerated there had a thirst for books, which we were happy to quench.

With any luck, Jamie would be back today, and I could leave Tim without a guilty conscience.

CHAPTER 15

The minute Flo left, the shop got busy with hardy cyclists who didn't mind the cold. I really needed to hire a helper. I barely had time to text Tim to ask how he was doing, but I squeezed it in. I also mentioned he could hit up my parents if he needed help with the little ones. Their work schedules were often flexible enough to allow for drop-of-the-hat requests like that.

Tim wrote back that he was managing, and that he didn't have any news. He also said Astra was coming by to take Ella to the playground and for lunch. Being responsible for only a baby who mostly slept and not also a preschooler would be a lot easier on him. Mom must not have too many astrological consultations scheduled for today.

I told him the book group and Orlean were all looking out for Jamie. I added XXs and OOs and sent the message.

As the morning went on, I had people wanting rentals, others looking to pick up a patch kit or a new helmet, and a couple of repair requests. A white-haired couple browsed the new bikes.

"Do you sell e-bikes or rent them?' the woman asked. "We're not as energetic as we once were, and an electric assist as we ride would be nice."

"For now, I don't," I said. "But that might be a good idea. I'll look into it." It could also be a complication I didn't need. I suspected Orlean might not want the additional learning curve on how to maintain them, either. On the other hand, I had plenty of senior citizen customers who would benefit from the boost an e-bike provides, and they might drive less if they had that option. It was something to think about.

Orlean took her lunch break at noon, disappearing outside. In a brief lull, I managed to get through half my sandwich before a man wheeled in a bike. I took a second look as I swallowed that bite. It was Peter Zelensky from the cemetery, the widower who wanted his late wife's bike made rideable.

"I am here, as promised." He removed a pair of sunglasses.

"Good morning, Peter. Or, I suppose it's afternoon by now." I wiped my mouth and came around the counter. It had been cloudy this morning, but the sun appeared to be shining now. I hadn't had a chance to go outside once since I opened the shop at nine.

The bike was a light aqua women's Sixthreezero brand

with upright handlebars, a wide cushioned seat, mud fenders front and back, and a basket on the front. Not a racing cycle, for sure, but it was perfect for running errands around town and riding on the rail trail. The bike was dusty, though, and the front wheel was flat.

"We can clean this up," I said. "Give it some oil and air, and make sure the brakes are safe. Is that what you're looking for?"

"Exactly, thank you." His breath smelled faintly of peanuts. Maybe he'd had a peanut butter sandwich for lunch.

"I'm not sure how backed up my mechanic is, and she's out to lunch." I went back behind the counter. "Fill out the top portion of this form, and we'll give you a call about when you can pick up the bike."

"That sounds good." He wrote down his information. "Quite the scandal about the homicide this week, isn't it?"

"Scandal?" I blinked. "I'm not sure it's a scandal so much as a horrific crime, not to mention a tragedy for the man's family."

"Of course, of course." He brushed the air. "I mean the perpetrator must be someone local. Will Westham's fine reputation be tainted by one of their own being convicted for murder?"

I took my time responding. "What makes you think the killer was from around here?"

"Well, the victim was from away, wasn't he? Obviously someone here on the Cape didn't like what he was doing locally."

I frowned. "What was he doing?"

"You know. Digging into other people's business. Taking over roles and expressing unpopular opinions. I'm sure lots of people are glad he's gone, may he rest in peace."

I was too stunned to say anything. It was clear that Peter hadn't liked Enzo, his rote wish for peace in the thereafter notwithstanding.

Peter checked his wristwatch. "I need to go. One never wants to be late for pickleball." He smiled. "Thanks for helping with the bike, Mac."

I swallowed. "Have fun." My impression of him had flipped from yesterday. What a cold man, to speak of a recently deceased resident like that.

Also, was I really the only person left who hadn't picked up a paddle and joined the hordes of both seniors and younger folks hitting a noisy ball around? Somehow the game didn't appeal to me, and neither did the competitive scene I'd heard about. My bum knee, the reason I'd stopped riding a bicycle, wouldn't like the lateral movement, either.

What piqued my interest even more was how other players had interacted with Enzo, and now with Peter. Norland would know, for sure.

CHAPTER 16

Before I had a chance to contact Norland, I glanced up when what seemed like an entire basketball team trouped in, followed by Harini Whitt. The tall women must be the group rental on the schedule. So much for calling the former chief of police.

"I'll be right with you all," I said to the rental group. "Hi, Harini. How can I help you?"

"There's something I'd like to talk with you about. It's not about a bicycle, and it looks like you're busy here."

"I'm alone in the shop right now. If you don't mind waiting, I should be able to help this group with their rentals within ten or fifteen minutes."

"Um, okay. I saw a bench out front," she said. "I'll wait there."

It was too bad I was such a responsible business owner. I'd rather have told the Tall Ten to wait, because

I was that curious about what Harini wanted. I shrugged. She said she'd wait. I hoped she would.

No new shoppers came in before the renters rode off, all with their seats raised to the maximum. I made my way outside and shielded my eyes. The light looked like fall, appropriate to halfway through the season, with autumn's golden tinge keeping company with the smell of dry leaves. But the air was warm enough for me not to need an additional layer over my sweater.

I sat next to Harini. "Thanks for waiting."

"One second." She finished whatever she was doing on her phone and glanced up. "It turned out to be a nice day. I didn't mind taking a Vitamin D break."

"I'm so sorry for the loss of your friend."

She whipped her face toward me. "What friend?"

"Enzo Lawrence. He told me he was friends with the costume shop owners." Or maybe he'd said owner, singular.

"Ah, yes. It's tragic, of course." She turned to look across the street instead of at me. "But he's Shelley's friend, not mine. I barely knew him." She kept her spine erect but ran her thumb back and forth across the nail of her index finger in a nervous gesture.

"Do you know when Shelly last saw him?" I asked.

"None." She gave her head a sharp shake. "I mean, no, I don't. Why should I?"

None? What a strange response. And shouldn't the reason I asked be obvious? Maybe she didn't know Enzo had been murdered. I decided not to pursue the topic.

"I suppose your shop is probably closed, now that the Halloween rush is over," I said.

"Not at all. Sure, the spooky costume side will be quiet for a while, but Shelly is big on staying open all year for custom costumes and other business." Harini relaxed her hand. "Plus, we have the dance section, and recital season will be in full force from now until Christmas."

"My grandmother said you were a professional ballerina. The dance stuff must be your area."

"It is. Who's your grandmother?"

"Reba Almeida. She's about this tall," I held my hand up to the level of my mouth, "and is often in a pink track suit."

Harini smiled. "I met her last week. Delightful lady."

"She is."

We sat for another moment, but she didn't bring up the reason she'd wanted to talk with me.

"Your name is lovely," I said. "Does it have a particular origin?" She and I had a similar skin tone. If pressed, I would guess her family was from somewhere in India, which was how the name sounded too. Maybe Whitt was a former married name.

"It means *deer* or *goddess* in Hindi, or so I'm told. I don't speak the language." She left it at that.

I did too. People's ethnic origins were their own business. When a car pulled into the shop parking lot with a bike suspended on a rack attached to the back, I cleared my throat.

"You wanted to talk about something?" I asked. "I see business approaching."

She blew out a breath. "I heard you're a detective of some kind, like a private investigator." Again she avoided my gaze.

"No, that's not true. I own a bike shop. I'm part of a book group. That's all."

She pressed her lips together.

"I'm not sure when the book group is going to meet next," I added. "It might be tomorrow or Friday. I hope you still plan to join us."

"I'll try. The candy shop lady has my number."

"Gin?"

"Yes, that's it, and I picked up a copy of the mystery at the Book Nook," Harini said.

The customer wheeled the tandem toward me. I stood.

"I'm sorry, Harini. I have to get back to work now, but let me know if I can help with whatever you wanted to discuss, okay?"

"Sure. Thanks." She rose and made her way down the sidewalk, chin high and arms graceful, for all the world as if she was still on stage.

I'd tried to develop a practice of being less nosy. Right now I really wished I'd dug into why she wanted to talk with a private investigator, and why she'd seemed so nervous at the mention of Enzo.

CHAPTER 17

"**D**id you have fun today?" I asked Ella at about six o'clock. We sat at the kitchen table with plates of pizza that Tim had called in to be delivered.

She swallowed her bite of cheese-free pizza, which instead had tomato sauce with bits of chicken. "I played with Grandma Astra. After lunch we picked up Cokey at school, and we played with Grandpa Joe and Tucker."

"That sounds fun." Of course both my parents would chip in to help.

"It was." Her sweet smile slipped away. "I looked for Mama, but I didn't see her anywhere." Her lip trembled.

"Oh, sweetie. You know how much she loves you, right?"

Ella nodded.

I thought fast about what I could say. "It's hard work

being a mommy. Maybe she wanted a little vacation, because she knew you'd be happy with Tim and me."

The girl brightened. "Like we're on daycation in Cape Cod."

"Exactly."

"Auntie Mac, what does Abo mean?"

"It means grandmother or grandfather in Cape Verdean. That's the language Grandpa Joseph's father spoke. And Bizabo means great-grandmother."

"Oh." Ella gave a wise nod. "Does Titi mean auntie?"

"It does, and Tio mean uncle. And there's Tio Tim."

He came back from settling Luca into the crib after giving him his bottle.

"I'm so hungry I could eat a little girl." He approached her with outstretched arms.

Ella squealed. "No, you have to eat pizza, not me."

"I do? Okay, you twisted my arm." He sat and loaded his plate with two slices of the mushroom, pepper, and olive order. He thumbed something on his phone before he took a bite.

My phone dinged with an incoming text. I pulled it out.

I need to go to WPD. Don't want to say it in front of her. You OK with both kids? You can give her a bath and baby should sleep an hour or 2.

I glanced up and bobbed my head. Of course he didn't want to talk about the police station while Ella could hear him. It had been twenty-four hours since Jamie left. With any luck they would let him report her as missing by now.

I texted back.

Let me know if you need Norland's help. He can pull strings.

Tim nodded.

"Mama says no phones at the table, except I don't even have a phone," Ella said.

"That's a good rule." I pocketed my phone.

"Does Mama scold herself?" Tim asked.

Ella laughed. "No, silly Uncle Tim. She told that to Papa Nick."

Tim and I exchanged a look. Luca's father, perhaps? Or maybe Ella's.

"Who is he, honey?" Tim took a big bite of pizza.

"He's Mama's friend." She sipped her milk. "But I haven't seen him in a long time because he went traveling."

Huh. A traveling friend, whom Ella called "Papa." Maybe he was the friend who Jamie went to see last night, except she'd told Tim his name was Bob.

Tim finished his third piece, wiped his mouth, and stood. "I have to run an errand, Ella, but I'll be back to kiss you good night."

The edges of her mouth turned down. "What if you don't come back?"

"I will come back." He scooped her up into his arms and held on tight for a few moments. When his eyes filled, he sniffed and swiped at them. "I promise. Auntie Mac is going to give you your bath, and I can guarantee she's the most fun ever in a bathtub." His wave of emotion over, he winked at me.

I blushed, remembering an epic hot tub session during our Caribbean honeymoon.

Tim didn't get home until eight thirty, when I was

sitting in bed reading the New England classic *Blue-berries for Sal* to Ella. When Luca began to wake up, Tim took over reading while I took the baby into the other room for a diaper change and bottle.

After both little ones were asleep, Tim joined me in the kitchen.

"The police agreed to file a report."

"I'm glad," I said. "Can I pour you a beer?"

He kissed me. "That would be perfect."

A couple of minutes later we snuggled on the couch, him with a beer, me with a glass of white wine.

"They pestered me with questions, Mac."

"What kind of questions?"

"Certain questions were to be expected. When she arrived, where she lives, her phone number, her height and hair color and all." He furrowed his brow. "But then it turned to whether she and I had argued. Whether she knows anyone else here. If she drove, and so on."

"Who was doing the asking?"

"Officer Kimuri. Wasn't she on the case last December?"

"Nikki Kimuri. She was," I said.

"The thing is, hon, I felt like she was suspicious of me. Me! We're talking about my baby sister, here."

I leaned against his strong, warm arm. "Nikki doesn't know you. She might have dealt with different kinds of families where a brother would be happy to make a sister disappear."

"I know." He let out a long, noisy breath that caught at the end.

"Of course you wouldn't hurt Jamie. You don't even swat flies, but we have to make sure the WPD understands that about you." I resolved to contact Norland and ask for his help, ASAP, or Lincoln. Suspecting Tim was beyond ridiculous.

"I'm so worried, Mac. And I have to hide it from Ella."

"We'll find Jamie, sweetheart."

"We will," he murmured.

We sat in silence sipping our drinks for a few minutes. I wasn't sure what he was thinking, but right now wasn't the time to ask.

My own thoughts were too dark to share with him. Would we find her soon? Would she be alive and well? Would she appear tomorrow, smiling, telling a reasonable story about why she'd gone away and not come back? I wasn't sure that would happen.

CHAPTER 18

When I offered to stay home the next morning, Tim said to go ahead and walk with Gin. He and Ella had hatched a plan to take the baby with them for breakfast at his bakery, and Mom was coming over to take the little girl for the day at ten o'clock.

It was a blustery morning on the rail trail. I was glad I'd worn a knit cap and a long-sleeved shirt under my windbreaker. These weeks between the fun and decorations of Halloween and the delicious gathering of the clan for Thanksgiving always depressed me. The days grew shorter and the daylight feeble. Nothing new was growing, nothing was being planted, and everything in nature was either in decline or already dead. The winter loomed, feeling longer and darker each year.

Jamie being missing only added to the darkness. Tim's impression that the police thought he might have something to do with her disappearance made it worse. A murderer at large didn't help.

Exercise always improved my mood, at least a little. I swung my arms as we kept up the pace.

"How are things with the visitors?" Gin asked. "Have you been able to spend time one-on-one with Jamie?"

"Didn't you read the group thread yesterday?" I grabbed her arm and pulled her to a halt.

"No. I had a super busy day and my phone was on its last speck of charge. Why? What's happened?"

"Jamie went out Halloween night and still hasn't come back. Flo said she sent that around to the Cozy Capers."

"You're kidding." Gin gaped.

"I'm not."

"But Jamie has babies. She left them with you and Tim?"

"Yep."

"Wow." She shivered. "Can we walk and talk?"

"Of course." We resumed our stride. "Tim's upset and beside himself with worry, as you can imagine. He's also trying to hide it from little Ella. She's shook up, too, and we're all trying to keep her happy. I think the baby doesn't have much of a clue his mama's gone."

"He's bottle-fed, I assume."

"Yes." We passed a looming tree that had been dead in the summer. Its diseased trunk and craggy, broken limbs were riddled with woodpecker holes big and small. "Which is a blessing, in this case. I can only imagine his distress if Jamie was breastfeeding and the baby had to switch to formula in a baby bottle all of a sudden."

"I hope she comes back soon."

"We all do. I only hope she's alive and not something worse."

"Right." Gin grimaced. "She has a messy history. What does she look like? I can keep an eye out."

I described Jamie. "I think her description is part of what Flo sent. Tim filed a missing person report with the Westham Police Department last night."

"Good."

"Darn. I forgot to get Jamie's last name from him, and what she was wearing when she went out. She'd already left when I got home on Tuesday."

"You don't know your sister-in-law's last name?" Gin asked.

"No, odd as that seems. This is the first time I've met her and I've never heard anyone introduce her to someone other than family. It could be Brunelle like Tim's or something else." I shrugged. "Anyway, Tim had the impression Officer Kimuri thought he might have been involved in Jamie's disappearance. Nothing could be more ludicrous."

"Nikki Kimuri?"

"Yes. It sounds like you know her," I said.

"The woman loves high-quality sweets, especially ones with caramel. She comes into the shop to buy candy all the time."

"The other day Reba and I met a man named Peter Zelensky in the cemetery. He's a widower and was visiting his wife's grave."

"I know him from pickleball," Gin said.

"He brought his wife's bike in yesterday for me to fix up for his adult daughter. He's apparently an investment adviser. Do you have investments?"

"Are you kidding? I own a business, Mac."

I laughed. "That was Tim's reaction too."

"I mean, I sock away money in an IRA when I can, and I did inherit a little bit from my grandparents, but none of it is enough to hire someone to manage it."

"I hear you," I said. "I'm in the same boat, minus the inheritance. Most of my investments went into buying and setting up my bike shop."

"Like me and the candy shop."

"I thought so. Anyway, Peter pretty much maligned Enzo's character."

"That's terrible," Gin said.

"I'll say." We strode on, nearing the halfway mark of our usual walk. "You know, I'm also worried that Jamie might have run into whoever killed Enzo."

"I haven't heard of much progress in his murder case, have you?" she asked.

"Not at all, and Lincoln hasn't been around much."

"Sounds like we need a book group meeting to work on it," Gin said. "You know, hash through everything and have Flo assign us action items."

That made me smile. The librarian was always our organizer, making sure we divvied up investigation tasks and reported back.

My enjoyment slid away. "I agree, but I'm not sure I'll feel clear to be away in the evening after working all day."

"We could meet at your house after the kids are asleep, if you want."

"Let me check with Tim." We reached our turn-around point, where we often stopped and stretched. "Okay with you if we head straight back?"

"That's fine."

We reversed direction.

"So, what do we know so far?" Gin asked.

I ticked off possibilities on my fingers. "Shelly was close to Enzo. Harini seemed nervous yesterday when I brought up his death and said he was Shelly's friend, not hers. According to Tulia, that Lawrence guy is probably a relative. Peter Zelensky might have been Enzo's investment adviser. Peter didn't think at all highly of him, at any rate. But would any of them murder Enzo? I have no idea."

"Sounds like we have our work cut out for us."

"Yes, unless today is when the able state police detective arrests the killer."

"If Lincoln and team are successful, the Cozy Capers could discuss the book of the week instead of homicide." Gin pointed at a bald eagle flying overhead, maybe one of the ones that overwintered near here.

"I had the same thought." I also thought I would text my grandma when I got home. She, if anyone, would know if Peter handled Enzo's investments.

CHAPTER 19

I was running late as I worked through my opening checklist at the bike shop. Orlean had called saying she would be delayed because of an emergency with one of her teeth. I was lucky to have strong teeth, due to genes and plenty of preventative dental visits as a kid. My mechanic wasn't so fortunate on either count. In the years since she'd been working for me, she'd had more than one painful episode where she had to get to a dentist, ASAP.

At a few minutes after nine o'clock, I brought out the cash drawer from the safe in my tiny office and got our small register set up. I locked together the display bikes outside. Unlike in the flush of summer, I didn't need to water the flower boxes in the front. They now held ornamental cabbages and other low-maintenance fall plants.

Ella had seemed cheerful at breakfast, but Tim was

looking ragged. He did say Reba was going to accompany my mom, and the two of them were also going to take the baby for the day. *Good*. Tim needed some downtime. At least Luca had slept through the night last night. Tim had inflated a single air mattress in the downstairs bedroom so he could sleep with both kids. I wished I could help more, but I'd have to close my business, and I couldn't afford to do that.

As I hung out the Open flag, the last item on my shop setup list, Lincoln ambled down the sidewalk from the direction of the police station. In previous cases, he'd set up shop temporarily at the Westham PD, since he normally worked across the Cape out of the county DA's office in Barnstable. Either way, he was the man I wanted to see. I greeted him.

"Morning, Mac." He bobbed his head as a pickup truck clattered over a pothole.

"Any news, Lincoln?"

"Nothing to speak of. You?"

Did I have anything to share with him? "I'm not sure it qualifies as news, but Harini Whitt came in yesterday. She said she wanted to talk with me about something and prefaced it by mentioning she'd heard I was a PI. I said I wasn't, but that I'd be happy to talk. Then the shop got busy, and she left without saying what it was about."

"Interesting. She has been less than forthcoming with us."

"If it means anything, she seemed nervous when I brought up Enzo's death."

"So noted."

"Also," I began, "Orlean said she played pickleball

with Enzo. Flo plays, too, and she said Norland might have played with the victim." I shook my head. "Do you play?"

He laughed. "I don't, but that might change. I understand the game is all the rage among seniors."

"You're not a senior citizen, Lincoln."

"Not yet, but Delia's been trying to convince me to take up playing." Color rose in his cheeks.

"So, I heard Delia is your lady love."

He took in a breath and let it out. "She always has been, Mac. We split up for a while. In fact, we got divorced. But I missed her terribly. I'm more than lucky that she missed me too."

"I'm glad." I was. He and I had become friendly, and we always want our friends to be happy. "Back to the case, though. I also learned that a Peter Zelensky was Enzo's investment adviser." Reba had responded to my earlier text within a minute that confirmed Peter's involvement.

"Interesting," Lincoln said. "The victim must have had funds to invest. We're still waiting on permission from the bank to access his accounts."

"Maybe Enzo wasn't paying Peter or something. Peter brought a bike in yesterday for a tune-up, and he said lots of people didn't like Enzo."

"Why not?"

"According to him, Enzo was digging into other people's business and taking over all the roles, whatever that means." I scrunched up my nose. "I was stunned when Peter said he thought plenty of folks had reason to want Enzo dead."

"That's a strong statement."

"I know. Somebody said Peter is among the pickle-ball players."

"I'll check into him."

"Have you talked with Shelly Hitchcock at all?" I watched a tiny cyclone of dried leaves scurry by in the cold breeze and was glad I'd worn a warm turtleneck. The wind brought the scent of coffee and bacon from the coffee shop two blocks away.

"I tried to, but she wasn't in," he said.

"The other day when you were here, what was it, Tuesday?"

He nodded.

"Right after you left, a man came in wanting to rent a bike. His last name was Lawrence, and he said he had family business in the area, or something like that."

"Same surname as the victim," Lincoln said. "What else did you learn about him?"

"He filled out a rental form, so I have his address. He lives in Bedford."

"Not New Bedford?"

"No, Bedford, Mass. It's near Hanscom, the Air Force base."

"Age, appearance?" he asked.

I described Herbert. "He had a military air about him, like standing with a straight spine and square shoulders. I picked up on a bit of an attitude, as if he thought he was in charge. You know what I mean?"

"I do."

"Viewing life that way might be great in warfare, but maybe not in everyday life," I said. "Anyway, I don't think I know anything else about the murder. I assume you and your team are out checking alibis and security footage and all that?"

"Naturally. And running into plenty of dead ends, I'm sorry to say."

"That's too bad." I cleared my throat. "Have you heard about Tim's sister?"

"Jamie Brunelle, missing person. Yes, I'm afraid I have. How is your husband making out?"

"He's pretty upset. Plus, we have her baby and pre-schooler to take care of."

Lincoln blinked. "She left two little children with you?"

"She told Tim she was meeting a friend for dinner on Tuesday. She never came home." I blew out a breath. "The thing is, I was thinking one possibility was that she ran into Enzo's killer. Maybe she's the second victim."

"I suppose that's possible. Let me check with the Westham PD. I can ask Chief Laitinen what they've learned."

"I'd appreciate that. I didn't want to mention it to Tim, but I've been running all the possible scenarios through my mind. None of them are good."

"No, but you're aware most murders aren't committed by someone unknown to the victim, Mac. What are the odds your sister-in-law knew the same set of people as Enzo Lawrence?"

"Slim to none."

"I imagine she went off on a jaunt, or perhaps suffered an accident."

"Or a relapse."

"She has substance issues?" he asked.

"She has had in the past—plenty of them, combined with depression."

"Tough stuff. How are her kiddos doing in her absence?" He lowered his chin and gazed at me over the top of his glasses, his voice full of care and concern.

"Ella, who's three and a half, has had a couple of weepy meltdowns. Overall, she's doing okay. Luca was born in August. I'm sure he has a sense his mother isn't around, but he gets fed and changed and held and seems fine so far. Tim is super good with both kids."

"I'm sure you are, as well." His phone buzzed. "I'll be off. Don't worry, Mac. Jamie will turn up. We'll find her."

"Thanks. Let it be sooner rather than later."

"You bet. I'll be in touch." He walked away at a brisker pace than usual.

I headed back inside. If the detective could help locate Jamie, so much the better, no matter the outcome.

CHAPTER 20

I glanced up a couple of hours later from where I was straightening shirts and shorts on the retail shelves. Orlean still hadn't arrived, but this wasn't her. It wasn't my mom and grandma with a baby and a preschooler in tow, either. Instead, a windblown Delia Haskins hurried in.

"It's gusting out there, Mac." She ran a hand through her ear-length dark hair, which was decorated by a fair number of white hairs.

"I hope it doesn't usher in a storm." I smiled at her. "How have you been?"

"Not bad, thanks. I haven't seen you in the pub much these days. You haven't popped by for a bowl of chowder for lunch." Delia tended bar part-time at the Rusty Anchor.

"I know." I gestured around the momentarily quiet shop. "I'm currently without a third employee, and it gets too busy in here to leave."

"I hear you. We're operating without enough staff as well, and my work gets wicked busy when somebody calls in sick."

I gazed at her. "Delia, were you working Tuesday night?"

"Not Halloween, right?"

"No, the night after. November first."

"I was." She nodded. "Why?"

"It's kind of a long story. My husband's sister came to visit on the weekend from the Northwest. She was only going to stay for a week, but she went out that night and hasn't come home."

"That's awful."

"I know. Plus, Jamie's a troubled person with addiction issues. The bartender at Jimmy's Harborside said she got kicked out for overdrinking at about nine. I wondered if she walked over to the Rusty Anchor after that."

"What does she look like?" Delia asked.

I described her hair and her thin figure. "She has big blue eyes like Tim's."

"Hmm," Delia said. "I don't recall seeing someone like that, at least not on a barstool. Would she have been alone?"

"Probably. She said she was meeting a friend for dinner, but that seems to have been the story she wanted us to hear rather than the truth."

"I'll ask my coworkers."

"Thanks," I said. "Tim convinced the police to file a report on her as missing."

"Good. Is Linc on the case?"

Linc. Oh, yes. They were back together. I'd never heard anyone call him by a nickname. She confirmed it by her cheeks growing pink.

"I hope so. I mentioned Jamie going AWOL to him a few hours ago," I said. Poor Tim. He'd expected to spend the week enjoying being reunited with his sister and her children. Instead, he'd had a week of increasing worry.

"I'm sure Linc'll be able to help," Delia said.

"So, the grapevine says you and he are back together."

"Small-town grapevines. Ya gotta love 'em." She shook her head, but she was still glowing. "We have been taking baby steps toward togetherness, yes."

"That's awesome. He's been looking kind of spiffed up lately."

"Falling back in love can do that to a guy."

I wanted to ask about the child they'd lost. That kind of question could wait until later—or never.

"Mac, I know you have a reputation for getting involved with certain kinds of crimes in the past," Delia said.

I lowered my voice despite the empty bike shop. "Like murders?"

She bobbed her head. "You and the book group, right?" she asked.

"Yes, we have poked our noses in here and there."

"I do have a bicycle-related reason for stopping by, but I also thought you'd want to know what I overheard this week, you know, about Enzo's death."

Ooh. "I'm all ears, as long as this place stays quiet."

"So, I knew Enzo a bit through pickleball."

"Am I the only person who doesn't play that?"

She laughed. "Maybe? I think I've convinced Linc to join in. I used to be a crack tennis player, but he doesn't play, and pickleball is much easier on the joints. Despite both of us being under fifty, the body starts griping a lot earlier than when we were younger."

"I get it."

"Anyway, I digress," Delia said. "I was hanging around waiting for a court to open up. Enzo, may he rest in peace, and this dude named Peter were going at it, bigtime."

Peter Zelensky had said he played pickleball.

"By going at it, do you mean fighting or with their game?" I asked.

"Both. The teams get matched up at random, and those two were paired for singles. Peter seemed bitter bordering on furious about something Enzo did or didn't do."

"Did Enzo return the anger?"

"Kind of," she said. "He acted arrogant, like he was right and Peter was wrong. Mac, it wasn't pretty. Usually the players are at least decent. We all want to get aerobic exercise and that's it. But I guess it's inevitable that social stuff happens on both ends of the spectrum."

"Do you mean romances sparking?"

"Sure. For example, your mechanic has a thing going with a dude from Pocasset."

"Wait. What? Orlean?"

Delia, her gaze on the door, opened her mouth and shut it again.

"I know I'm late, Mac," Orlean said from behind me, her voice different than usual. "But did you have to talk about me behind my back?"

I whirled. One of her cheeks was swollen. She patted it.

"I wasn't," I stumbled. "I mean . . ."

"Don't worry." My mechanic spoke out of one side of her mouth. "I don't care." She brushed by us. A moment later the sound of a wrench against metal came from the repair room.

"Thanks for coming in," I called after her. "Hope you're not in too much pain." I turned back to Delia and pulled an *oops* face.

"At any rate," Delia continued, but in a softer voice, "entanglements of the disgruntled sort also happen all the time, especially when players are super competitive."

"As Peter and Enzo were."

"Yes, although something else was going on there."

"Do you think Peter was angry enough to kill Enzo?"

Her eyebrows rose to her hairline. "You think he did it? What a horrible thought."

"I have no real idea," I said. "I want to know what you think, though."

She set her fists on her slender hips. "You should come watch a few games." Her voice returned to normal. "Let's see. Today's Thursday. We play tomorrow morning at seven, and again Sunday morning. Some people also play Wednesday afternoons."

"I saw Peter at the cemetery yesterday afternoon, and he said he didn't want to be late for a game." I thought for a second. "Can you check the schedule and let me know when Peter will be there?"

"I have the schedule, Mac," Orlean chimed in from yards away.

I smiled, pointed to my ear, and gave a thumbs-up to Delia. My mechanic had uncannily keen hearing.

"Thanks, Orlean," I called back.

"I will too," Delia said. "Now, can I reserve two rentals for next week? My sister and her husband are coming from San Diego, and they love riding on the local paths."

"Of course." I led her to the rental area.

The door opened to a half-dozen customers, one after another. I made a low sound that might have been a groan.

"We're shorthanded at the pub, but they won't give me any more hours. My graphic design business is only limping along right now. I can work part-time here for you, if it would help," Delia said.

"Are you serious?" This was too good to be true.

"Why not? I'm a pro at retail, and I love riding my bike. I'm sure you can teach me the bits I don't already know."

"Delia, you're hired. Want to start right now?"

She threw back her head and laughed. "I can't today, but tomorrow for sure."

I extended my hand. "You're hired. Let's get your relatives set up for next week and we can work out the details later."

She shook my hand. "It's a deal."

CHAPTER 21

My feet were sore and my stomach was a hollow pit when the store emptied at about one thirty. I grabbed a bathroom break and my ham-and-cheddar sandwich out of the mini-fridge, in that order, then sat at the retail counter scarfing down lunch.

At least I'd have someone to take half the customer load soon. Delia hadn't said how many shifts or what kinds of hours she could work. The shop's bottom line was in fine shape. I could afford to hire another employee, and I would give her all the shifts she wanted.

I hadn't heard a word from Tim or Mom. I'd texted her to bring the kids by the shop if she wanted. So far she hadn't acknowledged my message. As soon as school let out, Ella would be happy playing with Cokey.

The question persisted about where Jamie was. Surely if she was in an area hospital, someone would be able to find her. The same applied if she'd died or been killed, as awful as those prospects were. Bodies don't vanish. If she'd left town, alone or with someone else, it could take longer to find her, especially since she wasn't wanted for a crime.

I called Tim, all of a sudden wishing I could touch him, even if through fiber optics or a satellite. He didn't pick up, and I left a quick voicemail instead.

"Thinking of you, my love. Call me if you want to." I disconnected with a heavy heart.

Harini pushed through the door wearing a tentative expression. "Good, you're not busy."

"We aren't, at the moment. How can I help you?"

"Well," she began, then stopped when noises came from the repair room. "Is someone else here?"

"Yes, my mechanic."

She pulled her brows together, glancing left and right. When she spoke, she used such a low voice I could barely hear her. "What I wanted to ask is what you know about Enzo Lawrence. His, uh, death." She kept her gaze on a corner of the room, not my face.

"I don't know anything except what I've heard on the news." Or, rather, through the grapevine, but I'd keep that part to myself. "Somebody found Enzo's body, still in a Halloween costume, on his deck. For reasons I don't know, the police think the death is suspicious. That's it."

"Are you sure?"

"Yes." I tilted my head. "Why?"

She whipped her head toward the door when it opened. "Never mind."

"Hey, Mac." Norland sauntered in, hands stuffed in the pockets of his jacket.

"Norland, have you met Harini Whitt?"

"Only briefly." He stepped forward and extended his hand. "Norland Gifford, Ms. Whitt."

She shook his hand, but her smile seemed perfunctory.

"You're one of the new costume shop owners," he said. "Welcome to town."

"Thank you. Do you also own a Main Street business?"

"Not I." He gave a low chuckle. "But I was formerly in charge of keeping the streets safe."

"He's the just previous Westham police chief," I explained.

Harini's eyes flashed and she stiffened for a brief moment.

"I'm a hundred percent retired," Norland said. "Nothing to worry about. These days my job is being a doddering and adoring grandfather, with the occasional volunteer gig thrown in."

"You're the furthest thing from doddering I can imagine," I told him.

"My, my. Flattery will get you everywhere." He winked at Harini. "I've been impressed by the costumes, Ms. Whitt, and what you've done with the shop. Do you and Ms. Hitchcock co-own the building, or are you leasing it?"

She blinked. "Shelly is the sole property owner, but we co-own the business."

"And you're housemates as well, someone told me," Norland continued in a casual tone that didn't fool me for a second.

"Yes, we share the apartment in back, at least for

now." She raised her chin. "I'll be moving out when I find a better situation."

"You can't beat that commute to work." I avoided Norland's gaze.

"Not at all. Well, I'd better get back to the shop." Harini relaxed her shoulders. "Good to meet you, sir. See you around, Mac." The door swung shut after her.

"You were up to something there," I said, my gaze on the door.

"A guy I know mentioned that the two might have an imbalance of financial equity."

"Interesting. Is this guy anybody I know?"

"Nope. But you caught her reaction when you said I'm retired police?" Norland asked.

"You bet. She couldn't hide her fear, or maybe it was distrust, at hearing you were in law enforcement."

"Did she bring a bike to be fixed? Or want to rent one?"

"No." I gave my head a shake. "She stopped by yesterday and seemed to want to talk, but things were too busy, or maybe she couldn't work up the nerve. Today the shop was quiet. She asked what I knew about Enzo's death."

"And?"

"I only said what I believe is public knowledge about him being found in costume on November first. And that the authorities seem to think something was suspicious about his death. She refused to say why she wanted to know, other than that she thinks I'm a private investigator." I put on my best Mona Lisa smile.

"To which of course you said you aren't."

"Of course. Here's a story for you. An older woman

I met in Bangkok when I was in the Peace Corps had a mouse pad for her computer. She wouldn't say where she got it, but we were all pretty sure she worked for the CIA. The mouse pad had a cartoony drawing of a dude in a fedora and belted trench coat. Under his picture was a list of five things to do when confronted. Number one was, *Admit Nothing*, followed by, *Deny Everything*." I shrugged. "Comes in handy from time to time."

He chuckled again. "I should say."

"But seriously, Norland, time's moving along. Shouldn't Lincoln or somebody be making an arrest by now? He came in earlier to pick my brain but didn't offer all that much."

"I'm sure he'd like to have the bad guy behind bars, but you know full well that investigating murder can take time, Mac."

"I know." I let out a sigh. "Is there any bike business I can help you with, or did you stop in to chat?"

"I did want to pick up a patch kit, but don't you think we need a book group meeting? Except not about the book."

I tapped the countertop. "Gin suggested the same thing. I think tonight is too soon for me. I really need to stay home and support Tim, but tomorrow evening could work, as long as we meet at my house after the kiddos go to bed, and only if it's okay with Tim."

"Of course," he said. "What if we see if anybody can gather for a quick, impromptu meeting right now?"

"You're kind of brilliant." I nodded. "You're already here, and the store is quiet. Flo usually takes a late lunch. I'll call her, and you try to reach Gin and Tulia."

"Deal." He set to work on his phone.

I called Flo, who said she'd be over in ten minutes. I gave a quick glance at the rental book. No bikes were due in today. I moved to the repair area.

"I'd like to close early," I said to Orlean. "You want to take your sore mouth home?"

"That'd be great, Mac." My mechanic laid a hand on her cheek, wincing as she did. "Thanks." She stripped off her purple gloves, tossed them in the trash, and headed to the sink to scrub her hands.

I bustled off to the front door to take in the Open flag before any new customers waltzed in.

CHAPTER 22

Gin and Tulia also agreed to show up. Fifteen minutes after Norland's brainstorm, three of the group perched on stools, with Norland on the desk chair I'd wheeled out from my office. I sat on the seat of an adult tricycle.

"You and Flo seem to be our conduit to the pickleball world." I gazed from Norland to Flo. "Maybe you can dig into Enzo's interactions there, especially with Peter Zelensky."

Flo, true to form, had brought her yellow legal pad. "Action items for Norland and me."

"You seem to know both of the costume shop owners," Norland replied to me.

"I'll figure out a way to talk more with Shelly, or Gin, you can." I pointed my chin at her.

"I'll do it," Gin said. "Shelly is another one with a major sweet tooth."

Flo jotted down Gin's item.

"And there's the mysterious possible nephew, Herbert Lawrence." Gin raised her eyebrows.

Tulia raised her hand. "I'm the one who overheard him at my shop. Maybe I can find a way to track him down, figure out where he's staying while he's in town."

"Good," I said. "I didn't get that information, only his cell and his home address."

"Item for Tulia," Flo said. "What about Harini? If Enzo was Shelly's beau, surely Harini knows something about him, or them. Norland, was it you who invited her to the group?"

"No, but I told her about it when I was in the costume shop looking for a hat for my grandson," he said. "I told her several area merchants were in the group, including Gin and Mac. When she was in here a little bit ago, she didn't seem to remember me."

"I invited her," Gin said. "She came into Salty Taffy's and mentioned that she loved gentle mysteries and wanted to meet others in town who do, but said she didn't know how to contact Norland."

"Makes sense." Norland tapped a note into his phone. "I'm happy to speak with her about Enzo if I can."

"Do that," Flo said. "And I'll handle Zelensky."

"Among all of us, we should be able to work up the research," I said. "I mean, I don't want to get in Lincoln's way, but if we can help while staying safe, so much the better."

"Speaking of Lincoln, Mac," Norland began, "you mentioned earlier you'd spoken with him."

"Ooh, do tell," Flo said.

"Yeah. I told him things, and he basically told me nothing." I grimaced.

"It's ever thus, isn't it?" Tulia asked.

"Sometimes, for sure," I agreed. "Lincoln said he and his team were checking alibis and security footage and such. He told me he hadn't been able to reach Shelly and that Harini had been tight-lipped, or something to that effect. After I told him Peter Zelensky said he'd been Enzo's investment adviser, Lincoln found it interesting that Enzo had enough money to invest. The police haven't gotten permission to access his bank accounts yet."

"I wonder if Enzo's phone has anything useful," Tulia said. "Not that we'd be able to do anything about it."

Gin slid off her stool. "I need to get back to my shop."

"Same," Flo said. "Everybody's got their assignments. Mac, you'll just keep following up with Lincoln, yes?"

"As best I can, yes."

CHAPTER 23

After everybody left at three thirty, action items in hand, I puttered around finishing my closing checklist. I straightened the retail shelves, put in a couple of pending merchandise orders, and checked my payroll app.

Coming up soon, as in three days ago, was my quarterly tax payment to the town. I usually paid ahead of time, but this period got away from me, big-time. I was pretty sure they gave residents and businesses a few days' grace, except nobody wanted to test the policy, especially not me.

I wrote the tax check, slid it into the envelope, and grabbed my bag and coat. Town Hall didn't close until four thirty, but I had plenty of time. I wished I could pay online, but the Westham town administration was a bit behind the times in that regard.

I had my foot on the ramp going up the side of the

three-story brick Town Hall building when a woman's voice called from behind me.

"Mac, can I have a word?"

I groaned to myself as I turned to see Westham Police Chief Laitinen hurrying toward me. Otherwise known as Victoria, she'd treated me as a rival when we were in high school together. Sure, we both got good grades and happened to share an interest in debating, but it wasn't like we were competing for the same anything, and I never knew what I'd done to provoke her all those years ago. Although I'd done my best to be cordial and polite and patch things up in recent years, I wasn't sure it had worked.

"I can talk as soon as I drop off my tax bill." I waved the envelope. "I'll be back in one minute. Two, tops."

"Go." She waved me on with an impatient gesture. "I'll wait."

Inside, the high ceilings and original woodwork of the doors and wide, tall windows had been preserved, but the plumbing and wiring were all updated, tech functionality was as current as it could be, and insulation had been added. An elevator and the ramp outside were part of a decade-old addition, bringing the facility into ADA compliance.

As promised, I was out in under two minutes. When I emerged, Victoria was leaning against the ramp's railing, swiping through her phone. She didn't see me for a moment, and I studied her. The petite woman looked more tired since she'd given birth to her first baby in the late spring, but her white-blond hair was pulled back in her usual disciplined bun, and she wore her preferred police-issue uniform. If you asked the citizen on the street to draw a chief of police, the resulting picture was unlikely to resemble Victoria. Still, she was good at her job, as long as "somewhat prickly" came with the job description.

"That addition is awesome." I approached her. "Were you involved in the renovation controversy?"

I'd been out of the country and had missed all the local brouhaha about adding the new section and updating the rest. My parents had kept me informed about the minority of town voters who'd opposed our municipal offices catching up to the current century. I was glad most people had seen the sense in spending the money now to provide accessibility to all and enable us to reach into the future.

"I sure as heck was," she said. "I was up for sergeant at the time. Part of the reason I passed muster for promotion was keeping my cool among the hotheaded factions." She straightened and slid her phone into her pocket. "Now, then, Mac, I assume you and your little group think you're going to get involved in the current homicide investigation."

I flashed her a wide-eyed look of innocence that would fool no one, especially not her.

"Just don't, all right?" She jammed her fists onto her hips. "Your habit of poking around and putting yourself and others in harm's way has got to stop, as of now."

"Yes, ma'am." I made a mock salute. "I appreciate your concern for my safety. If you'll excuse me, I have a hot date with a bunch of incarcerated readers, but don't worry. I won't be in harm's way. A guard will be there."

She shook her head in exasperation, or maybe it was

disgust, and turned on her heel. I had to smile to my-self. She should know by now that if my fellow sleuths and I could help bring justice to our sweet town, we would. Of course we tried to stay safe. Who in the world wanted to be confronted by a killer?

I began moseying back to my shop, which was where Flo would pick me up for the drive to Barnstable. I slowed in front of Greta's Grains. Harini stood with an-other woman, who was peering into the dark windows.

"Hi, Harini." I smiled.

She glanced over at me. "Hello, Mac."

The other woman turned her head. She pushed her glasses up. "Mac isn't a real name. It's a nickname." She spoke carefully and tilted her head to one side, then the other, studying me. Her features were indica-tive of someone with Down syndrome, and her open, intent expression was childlike. From the gray in her hair, it was clear she wasn't young at all. "What's your real name?"

"You're right. It is a nickname." I smiled at her. "My real name is MacKenzie, but I prefer being called Mac."

"Mac, this is my sister, Alisha," Harini said.

Was she saying Alicia? "Nice to meet you, Alicia." I pronounced the name with four syllables, as I usually did.

"My name is Alisha. A-L-I-S-H-A," Harini's sister spelled. "It means 'protected by God' in Hindi."

"What a lovely name," I said.

"I like the pastries here." Alisha returned her focus to the window.

"My husband Tim is the baker."

She turned her head again to stare at me. "He's nice to me. You're lucky, Mac."

I smiled. "I know. Listen, I have to get going. Take care, now."

"Okay."

"We have to go too. Come on, sweetie." Harini took her sister's arm and led her away.

As I watched, Harini looked back for a moment and shot a quick worried glance in my direction. *Why?*

CHAPTER 24

I always found the process of entering the correctional facility grueling. I'd done nothing wrong, and Flo and I were here to provide a service welcome to the inmates and wardens. Nevertheless, my heart beat double time at the sight of fierce police canines straining at their leashes as they patrolled the perimeter with their guard handlers. My throat thickened to see the shiny coils of razor wire atop several layers of high fences. Having to lock my phone, purse, keys, and jacket into a locker in the visitors' waiting room made me nervous, and a female correctional officer, or CO, patting down my already empty pockets never failed to give me palpitations.

The jail also had rules about how visitors should dress, especially women, with a goal of not provoking male inmates' imaginations. Flo and I made sure to wear modest pants, loose layers on top, and flat shoes, which was pretty much how both of us usually dressed, anyway.

Tim hadn't called me back or texted. I shot him a quick message before we went in, reminding him that I was doing my volunteer gig at the jail and hoped to be home by seven for dinner. I added that he should let me know if I could order or pick up a takeout meal for the two of us. He loved cooking for me, but doing that with two littles on his hands wouldn't be easy.

As Flo and I carried our paper bags full of books into the library, my heart rate began to slow back to normal. I'd never had anything but positive experiences in this carpeted room. The inmate residents of the facility were generally in on short sentences for nonviolent infractions. Those awaiting trial for more serious crimes stayed on their units.

The warm-colored oak bookshelves lining the walls of the library were full of books arranged alphabetically by author within each genre. All the books were required to be paperbacks. We'd been told hardcovers could be used as weapons, and inmates had been known to carve the cover itself into something sharp.

The nonfiction sections were primarily law books and biographies, but incarcerated people here seemed to prefer the escape of fiction, and who could blame them? Novels far outnumbered the volumes about real life.

The residents of the facility got twenty minutes a week to browse the shelves and pick out their reading for the next seven days. Having an organized selection was important with such limited time for them to find the books they wanted. Interestingly, the library didn't have a checkout system. Inmates could take as many books as they wanted and then either return them on their next visit, or the books would be picked up when the librarian visited the units.

The director of a library in a neighboring town had begun to volunteer here after the paid prison librarian position was eliminated during the pandemic. He was happy to have Flo step in to share the load.

She and I got to work shelving the new donations, cross-checking them against the list of books inmates had requested and setting those aside. I glanced up when a buzzer sounded. A female CO escorted in a young white woman with gorgeous curly hair that fell below her shoulders. She'd told me she was twenty-one and, due to hanging out with the wrong people and driving home after having too much to drink, was in for vehicular homicide.

"Hi, Cat." I smiled. "Here for more classics?"

"Yes, please." She was reading her way through American novels like *Catcher in the Rye* and *Of Mice and Men*, books that she'd somehow managed to avoid in high school. She kept a running list of the books she'd read in a rounded script on lined paper, adding notes here and there about content or her thoughts.

She selected a few volumes and was escorted out. A male CO then brought in a half-dozen men, including a tall, thin Black gentleman named Xavier. Well-spoken and polite without acting deferential, he never missed a library visit and read everything from Egyptian history to Gestalt psychology dream analysis, although he preferred fiction.

"I like to make the most of my time inside," he'd said. "Why let it get you down when it can lift you up?"

Today he sported a pair of red reading glasses perched on his narrow nose.

"Those look helpful," I said.

"You bet, ma'am. Every time I'm incarcerated, the first thing I do is go to the nurse and ask for readers."

I nodded, not quite ready to ask how many times he'd been in before now. Flo and I busied ourselves passing out requested books, answering questions, and shelving when we had a couple of minutes free. I glanced at the clock, which indicated the first twenty-minute period would be over in two minutes.

"Ma'am." Xavier spoke quietly to me. "You both come over here from Westham, correct?"

"Yes."

"A woman I formerly knew opened a costume shop there not long ago. You should be very careful around her. I've rarely met someone more unscrupulous."

I stared at him. "Do you mean Shelly or—?"

The buzzer sounded. The CO stepped forward. "Session's over. Inmates out, now."

Xavier grimaced and hurried to get in line without a backward glance—or an answer.

CHAPTER 25

Due to a major traffic snarl-up between here and Barnstable, Flo didn't drop me at home until seven thirty. I walked into a quiet kitchen, with Tim sitting at the table staring at his phone. A half-full glass of beer was in front of him.

"The babies are asleep?" I asked after I leaned down to kiss him.

"They are. Ella got teary again about her mommy, but I read her *Blueberries for Sal* three times until she fell asleep halfway through the third set of 'kerplink, kerplank, kerplunk.'" Tim's smile was not his usual beam, and his face was haggard.

"You're the best uncle, ever."

"Not good enough to locate my sister." He sank his face into both hands and rubbed. He glanced up at me. "I ordered Chinese, including crispy fried chicken, and had it delivered. Ella ate that with white rice, but there's plenty of grown-up food left, sweetheart. Let me heat up a plate for you." He set his palms on the table as if to stand.

"Don't you dare." I laid my hand on his shoulder. "Even I know how to use a microwave." A couple of minutes later I brought my plate of beef with snow peas over rice and a glass of pinot noir to the table.

"How was jail?" he asked.

"Interesting, as always. It's impressive how many inmates want to check out books."

"They don't have much else to do, I'd guess."

"Right. One man today said something about why let the time inside get you down when it can lift you up. I like that attitude." I washed down a bite with a sip of wine. "And then he mentioned that every time he's incarcerated, he asks for a pair of reading glasses."

"Meaning he has a habit of doing things that get him put in prison." Tim shook his head. "I'm glad that's not part of our world, Mac. Jamie's lucky she never ended up in jail. I think having the kids motivated her to try to stay out of trouble."

"She's been a good mom to them."

"Until now. It's been forty-eight hours. I don't understand where she is." His voice broke as his eyes filled.

I scooted over and wrapped my arms around him. I waited to speak until his shoulders stopped shaking.

"I asked Lincoln to help us find her," I murmured.

Tim straightened and wiped his eyes. "Thank you, hon. Tomorrow I'm going to start calling shelters and hospitals."

"Good idea. Let me know if I can help. Flo suggested Jamie might be suffering from postpartum depression, on top of everything else."

"I read up on that. She would be extra-prone to it."

"Have you told your parents?" I asked.

"I wasn't going to until I had news, but then I thought she might contact one or the other. Except she hasn't. Dad offered to come out. I told him to hold off." He gazed into my face. "Do you think that's the right decision?"

I'd never seen Tim so unsure, so broken up. "Yes. She'll probably surface soon, although he could help with the kids." Tim's father had dropped everything to drive from Southern California to Seattle last year to watch Ella and the two older children after Jamie had to be hospitalized. My mother-in-law lived in St. John in the Caribbean, and it was harder for her to get here at a moment's notice, although if asked, she would come if she could. A retired professor, she now did a lot of international consulting. "Did Ella have fun with my family today?"

"She did." He smiled. "She said Cokey wanted her to sleep over, but Derrick nixed the idea because it's a school night. Maybe they can do that on the weekend."

"Good. And little Luca?"

"He really focuses on my face. Mac, I think he's starting to smile."

"Who wouldn't smile at you?"

He snorted. "It's about time for him to smile, developmentally." He leaned over to the counter and sat back with a parenting book about what to expect in the first five years. "Between all my calls and my worrying today, I took myself out for a run to destress. I checked this out from the library on the way home. I figured it couldn't hurt to pick up a few tips about babies."

"Good thought."

"Anyway, the little guy seems to like my voice, and I'm getting the hang of how to rock him to sleep."

"I'm not one bit surprised." I glanced at the black-and-white video screen of the small baby monitor on the table. We'd decided a simple monitor would be a good thing to have around, and Tim had picked one up. "He's moving around in there. Do you want me to get him?"

Tim peered at the monitor. "He isn't due for a bottle until about nine. We can wait and see if he settles himself. If he doesn't, I've found patting him in place usually gets him back to sleep."

Almost immediately a wail came from both the monitor and the bedroom. I started to stand.

"No, I'll go," he said. "Finish your dinner." He hurried out.

I munched and sipped and leafed through the book with my clean left hand. Someone like me, who had never cared for a baby, had a lot to learn. Tim seemed to have such a knack for the little ones. I couldn't remember if he'd spent time with Jamie and her older children when they were tiny. It would have been well before I knew him.

After finishing and wiping my hands, I glanced at the monitor. Luca wasn't in the portacrib. Tim wasn't visible, either, but all was quiet.

On our way back from Barnstable, I'd told Flo about

Xavier warning me against the costume shop owner. Neither of us had a way to figure out if he'd meant Shelly or Harini. Now I brought up the Cozy Capers thread about the murder on the phone. I checked to be sure Harini wasn't part of it, and her name wasn't in the group.

She didn't seem to be champing at the bit to discuss the book, which was fine. As far as I was concerned, we could postpone that kind of meeting until after a killer was locked up.

Flo hadn't texted the group about what Xavier told me, so I did. I added another quick message.

Any thoughts about that?

Tulia responded first.

No idea which owner he could have meant.

Norland added a note.

I'll see if I can find out anything.

My hummingbird metabolism meant I was still hungry. I heated up the last piece of crispy chicken with some rice and poured a splash more wine. While I ate, I scrolled back through the thread until the last message I'd read. There weren't that many, and nobody seemed to know anything new. I'd hoped somebody would have encountered Herbert Lawrence.

No sightings of Herbert the apparent nephew?

Gin wrote back: **Not by me.**

I waited, but my phone stayed quiet. Everybody else must have become busy with their lives tonight. We really did need to get together again in person soon. I had cleared with Tim having everybody gather here.

Let's meet at my house tomorrow at eight. Quietly.

I added a message only to Gin.

Am going to watch pickleball tomorrow A.M. instead of walking. Sorry.

She responded in a few seconds.

Norland convinced me to play. See you there!

Gin planned to join the ranks of pickleballers? She'd better not put an end to our morning walks. I valued them for the friendship we shared as much as for the exercise.

I blinked. My eyes were tired. It was time to take out my contact lenses and think about bed. I cleaned up the kitchen, put my phone on mute, and peeked into the downstairs bedroom. Tim sat leaning back in the easy chair in the corner, baby on his chest wrapped in his strong arms, uncle and nephew both off in dreamland. Ella was also sound asleep, thumb in her mouth and curled up with the stuffed seal we'd sent her for last year's birthday. Jamie had said Celine had become the girl's favorite stuffie.

I'd go up and relieve my eyes, then come down and stake a place on the couch to read. I wanted to be sure we got the baby fed at nine, a half hour from now, and that Tim didn't get so deep into sleep he was at risk of dropping the wee one.

Who knew? Maybe Jamie herself would wander in, pretending nothing was wrong with abandoning her children for two days and causing her brother no end of grief. Somehow I doubted that would happen, but I'd be delighted to be surprised by an unexpected surprise.

CHAPTER 26

I'd told Gin last night I wouldn't be walking this morning because I wanted to go observe interactions on the pickleball court. But when a sweet girl in a nightgown flung herself into my arms in the kitchen at seven o'clock, the pickleball plan also went out the window. My niece was a much higher priority than me playing at being a detective.

"Good morning, Miss Ella," I said into her dark curls as she snuggled in, clutching her stuffy with one arm, her thumb in her mouth. She was warm from bed, her solid little body a comfort to hold.

"Uncle Tim is still asleep, Auntie Mac. So is Luca."

"That's good. Boys need their rest. Did you have a good sleep?"

"Mm-hmm."

I stroked her silky hair. "Tim said you had fun with Cokey yesterday."

"We did!" She sat up straight. "And we're going to have a sleepover in the lighthouse on the weekend. Is it the weekend now?"

"Not quite yet. Today is Friday, and the weekend is Saturday and Sunday." I didn't want her to get her hopes up about spending Friday night with her cousin if that wasn't in the plans. "A sleepover sounds like fun."

"Do you have to go to work today?" she asked.

"I do, but not for another hour or so."

"I'm hungry, except Uncle Tim said you don't know how to cook."

I laughed. "I don't usually cook dinners, it's true. But I'm hungry too. Let's see what we can come up with for breakfast, okay?"

We settled on oatmeal, which didn't take long to prepare. I shot Gin a quick text that I wouldn't be at pickleball and to see what she could find out. Soon enough, Ella and I sat in front of bowls topped with chopped apple, a sprinkle of cinnamon, and a little brown sugar. I added a dose of cow's milk for me and oat milk for her.

"Isn't that yummy?" I asked her.

She nodded. "When will Mommy come home?"

Whoa. "I'm not sure, honey." I wanted to tell the poor thing it would be soon. But getting her hopes up about that would be worse than disappointing her about a sleepover. Jamie had been gone over forty-eight hours. Tim and I needed to check with the police today and figure out what else we could do. "What do you and Uncle Tim have planned for today?"

"He said we can go to the playground, and then we can get a snack at his bakery again. Did you know it's named after my grandma?"

"I did. Your grandma Greta, right?"

Tim's mother had taught him to bake, and he'd named his bakery Greta's Grains to honor her. Tim's Bread and Pastries didn't have the same ring.

"Yes," Ella began, "but she lives on an island, so I don't get to see her very often. I told Mommy I want to go visit, and she said maybe next year."

"That sounds like fun."

"You and Uncle Tim can come too." She tilted her head, regarding me. "I didn't know you wore glasses, Auntie Mac."

"I do, but during the day I wear contact lenses."

"What's that?"

"They're like little pieces of glasses I put in my eyes that let me see better." I'd never had to explain contacts to a kid before, and that explanation sounded ridiculous. "I'll show you after breakfast."

"Okay."

Belle piped up from under her cage cover at the far end of the kitchen. "I'll show you after breakfast. Snacks, Mac?"

Ella laughed.

"Oops." I stood. "I usually get her up earlier than this." We'd taken her cage upstairs after Jamie got upset about Belle being near her children, but yesterday I'd brought the bird back down. It was much easier to care for her down here.

A minute later, Ella squatted on the floor feeding Belle grapes and chatting with her. I poured more coffee, dosed it with milk, and sat at the table again. My phone pinged three times in succession with incoming texts. My eyes went wide at new messages on the group thread. The first was from Norland.

Near fistfight on pickleball court btwn Zelensky and newcomer.

The next message was from Delia, not part of the thread.

Happy to work today if you want.

Today would be perfect. I typed a response.

Great, thx. I open at nine.

She wrote right back.

Crazy dustup on pball court just now.

Too bad I hadn't seen it, but between Delia and Norland, I knew I'd get a detailed report on what went down. I added a question.

Is Lincoln there?

No, but Chief Gifford broke up the fight.

I went back to the group thread. Three messages had originally come in. I tapped the one I hadn't read, also from Norland.

Newcomer is H Lawrence.

Curiouser and curiouser, as Alice would have said. Even though we'd talked about meeting, I added a confirmation about our in-person gathering.

Remember, we meet tonight my house at 8, but sans Harini.

Tim wandered in holding a blinking Luca in one arm. Tim, also blinking, ran his hand through his bed hair with the other. I held out my arms for the baby. Tim handed him off and kissed me at the same time.

"Morning," he murmured.

"Uncle Tim, Auntie Mac knows how to cook oatmeal!" She ran to the table and showed him her bowl. "It was very good. And she put apples and cinnamon on it, and sugar too."

I rolled my eyes. "It was a tough assignment, but I managed."

He ruffled my hair. "Good job."

Bella gave her wolf whistle and imitated his voice. "Good job. Good job."

Tim knelt and opened his arms to his niece. "How's my favorite Ella this morning?"

"Good. Auntie Mac's going to show me the little glasses she puts in her eyes."

"Wow. I'd like to see that too." Tim hugged her and stood. To me, he said, "I'll be right back. Thanks for covering for me here. That little dude was up several times in the night." He covered a yawn.

"Who needs to watch pickleball when you have a girlie to hang out with? Do you want to go back to bed?" I checked the stove clock. "I don't need to leave for another hour."

"No, I'm awake. I'll fix the baby's bottle when I come back." He disappeared through the door for what

I expected was a bathroom break and likely also checking for news about Jamie.

Luca seemed content for now to sit with me and
watch his sister interact with a big parrot. I wouldn't
check my messages while I had charge of two children.
Even though I was dying to know more about the
dustup, as Delia put it, kiddos came first, every time.

CHAPTER 27

I finished showing Delia around the shop by nine thirty. "Why don't you handle retail and I'll focus on rentals and other stuff? If you can't find anything, please ask."

"Sounds good," she said.

"Between Orlean and me, we can handle questions people have about repairs and how bikes work." I raised my voice. "Right, Orlean?"

"Yup."

"I really appreciate your being willing to take some hours with us, Delia." I explained the pay and how I preferred to do direct deposit. "We can figure out a regular schedule as we go. At least I have a reliable weekend crew now, so neither Orlean nor I have to be here on Saturday and Sunday."

"Good, because those are my longest days at the pub. And the best tips come in then too."

A pair of lean men in their twenties pushed in through the door.

"Want to take over?" I asked her.

"Sure."

I sidled away to the rental area, where I could still hear but not appear to be overseeing. Delia did fine.

After she sold matching Mac's Bikes cycling shirts to the pair from New Jersey, she handed them a trail map and pointed out the nearest access to the Shining Sea multiuse trail.

"The path used to be a rail line that ran south to Woods Hole and north too," she explained. "Daily laborers and society people alike took it."

One of the men paid her, and they both thanked her for the mini-history lesson. Delia was a local, and she served tourists drinks and food all the time at the Rusty Anchor. Of course she knew the history.

I moseyed back after they'd left.

"How'd I do?" she asked.

"You passed with flying colors and then some." I smiled.

"Good. I love letting people in on what the past was like around here. I think I'm a frustrated history teacher."

"You could still do that, couldn't you?"

"Uh, if a district didn't want me to show them a teaching certificate and a master's degree, sure." She batted away the suggestion. "It's fine. I wear my amateur badge with pride, and I volunteer at the historical society when I can."

A shiver rippled through me. A bad actor associated with the historical society had tried to kill me last year.

Luckily, that person was now behind bars for a long, long time.

"Cool," I said.

"Speaking of history, I heard about what you found behind a wall in your house last winter. An imprisoned skeleton? That's crazy stuff."

"It was stunning, I have to admit, and I'm glad it's all behind us." I cleared my throat. "While it's quiet in here, can you tell me what you witnessed on the pickleball court this morning?"

"That was something. I mean, sure, certain people are super competitive players. There's this guy, Scott, and he'll argue about a ball being a quarter-inch onto the line. He intensely wants to win."

"I won't play with that one," Orlean chimed in from the repair area. "What a jerk."

"She's right. Scott is eighty and pretty fit for that age, but man, can he ever get irate." Delia gave her head a shake. "I have to say, most players are reasonable. They're out there to get exercise and have fun, maybe make a few friends. That's it, but not this morning. This new dude showed up, name of Herbert. He and Peter seemed to know each other."

"Peter Zelensky," I said.

"Yes. I was playing on the next court, so I didn't get all of it, but they seemed equally disgruntled with each other. I heard the word *cheated* from one side and *unethical* from the other. They stopped playing and stood there shouting at each other. Norland finally got between them and told them to take it off the court. Instead, Herbert stalked away and Peter disappeared somewhere."

"Wow. And you don't know what it was about?"

"No, I missed how it began."

Orlean sidled in. "Definitely something about money, about finances. I didn't catch specifics, either."

"Thanks," I said to her back as she returned to the brakes she was working on.

"By the way, Mac," Delia said. "I checked with my coworkers at the pub last night. I'm pretty sure your sister-in-law wasn't in the Rusty Anchor that evening."

Additional information was good, but my heart broke a little more for Tim.

"Thanks so much for checking," I told her.

The store got busy after that, with a steady stream of customers of all shapes, sizes, ages, and needs. I barely had time to think, despite Delia helping. When I did have a moment free, all I could dwell on was that both Peter and Herbert also had ties to Enzo.

CHAPTER 28

By twelve thirty, Delia seemed at ease working in the store, and right now it was empty of customers. I grabbed the bank bag and slung my EpiPen bag across my chest.

"I'll be back by the time you have to leave," I told Delia. "Two o'clock, right?"

"Yes, thanks. I need to run home and tend to my pooch before my pub shift starts at three."

"Call me if it gets busy here or there's something you don't know. I'll be done with my errands in plenty of time. Do either of you want me to pick up lunch for you?" I raised my voice to include Orlean, but both declined the offer. I'd been so far out of my routine this morning, I'd forgotten to pack my usual ham-and-cheese sandwich.

Business was quiet at the Lobstah Shack too. On a Friday in the summer, you could barely get in the door before two o'clock. Now? Only one customer was ahead of me, and owner Tulia Peters seemed to be doing all the work without the benefit of her usual counter employee.

"Mac, I'll be right with you," she said.

Five minutes later I sat at one of the few small tables in the mostly takeout restaurant with a cup of the best fish chowder on the Cape and a luscious crab cake in front of me. Tulia sank into a chair opposite me.

"I might close up early today," she said. "Westham is dead at this time of year, at least when it comes to people wanting a seafood lunch or takeout dinner."

"I hear you. I've had a surprising number of customers, but maybe they're all eating at home. And my business could dwindle to a trickle the minute it gets really cold."

"I can deal with quiet," Tulia said. "What I put away in the summer months compensates for a few slow ones. We get plenty of tourists starting before Thanksgiving and on into New Year's too."

I could only nod as I savored another spoonful of the thick, savory soup.

"I can't stop thinking about the dude who referred to 'Uncle Enzo' on the phone in here," she said. "I haven't found out anything else about him so far. Last night Gin texted that she hadn't seen him."

"Right. Maybe I didn't share it with the group. When Herbert rented a bike from me this week, he listed his address as in Bedford, and he shares a last name with the victim. Herbert has a kind of military posture, if you know what I mean."

"I noticed that."

"I wondered if he might be in the service at the base in Hanscom up there."

"Good thought." Tulia narrowed her eyes. "I might be able to check into that, and he's my action item, anyway."

"Are you connected with the base somehow?"

"In a way. I'll let you know. Maybe I'll have news tonight when we meet."

"Awesome." I finished the soup and dug into the crab cake. With a crispy fried exterior, the inside held big chunks of sweet crabmeat, a hint of dill, and some kind of binder. "Mmm," I murmured around a mouthful.

"Hey, any news of your sister-in-law?"

"Unfortunately, not a speck. So far, the police haven't found her, and she hasn't shown up at home, either."

"Tim must be out of his mind," Tulia murmured. "Not to mention the kiddos."

"The little ones are all right. Tim, not so much."

"I've been asking around," she said. "So far, crickets for sightings, but I'll keep it up."

"Thanks, my friend. I'm not getting a good feeling about whatever happened to her or where she went, but you never know."

"True words."

A group of rosy-cheeked fiftysomethings in hiking boots and outerwear trouped in.

"Duty calls." Tulia stood. "See you tonight."

"It's a date."

I savored my last bite of crab cake and tossed my

paper dishes in the trash before heading out. Having friends on the case, whether it was personal or homicide-related, always brightened my outlook.

The brightness faded fast. Victoria strode along the sidewalk on the other side of Main Street. She wore uniform navy pants and a Westham PD windbreaker but otherwise looked like a small, thirtysomething blond woman who liked clothes in dark blue. When she spotted me, she set out to make her way over to where I was, despite not being at an intersection or in one of the occasional midblock crosswalks. I had no desire to tangle with her, but I had no plausible escape route.

An older-model sedan approached going too fast. Victoria halted in the middle of the street. She faced the car, widening her stance, and flipped her palms out with straight arms. The driver stepped on the brakes, a wise move, if I knew Victoria. Which I did, for better and for worse.

A half-balding man with a thick head and close-trimmed white hair stuck his face out the window. "What are you doing in the middle of the road, lady? Get over on the sidewalk where you belong."

I swear I could see the smoke rise out of her ears. She took three long steps toward the dude's vehicle and crossed her arms over her chest, again with the wide stance. This guy had no idea who he'd tangled with. Despite not wanting to talk with the chief a minute ago, I perched on the closest bench. This was going to be good.

She flashed him her badge. "You, sir, are going to pull to the curb. You are going to show me your license and registration. And if you ever accost a pedestrian again, I can guarantee you'll have a lovely little vacation admiring the wallpaper in the Westham jail." Glaring, she pointed to the side of the road. "Now."

The man opened his mouth as if to argue but seemed to think the better of it. "Yes, ma'am." He pulled over and switched off the engine.

Victoria glanced over at me. I stood.

"I wanted to have a word with you," she called.

"Sorry, have to get on with my errands and then back to work." I smiled sweetly. "Rain check?"

She frowned. "Yeah, sure, whatever."

I moved along before she could change her mind.

CHAPTER 29

After I made a sizable deposit at Westham Cooperative Bank, I paused on the sidewalk. I itched to find out if it had been Shelly or Harini whom Xavier had spoken of, and Cape Costumers was only a few doors down Main Street. It occurred to me that, while I'd talked to Harini, I hadn't interacted with Shelly since last Friday. She was Gin's action item, but more information never hurt.

Before I reached the costume shop, a small group of loved ones came toward me from the other direction. Abo Reba held Ella's hand, with Pa next to them holding Luca in a familiar-looking soft carrier strapped to his chest. I smiled and waved, waiting for them.

"Auntie Mac, I got to eat lunch in the parsonage," Ella announced. "Grandpa Joseph made sandwiches."

"That's awesome. He makes yummy sandwiches. What kind did you have?"

"Um." Ella wrinkled her little brow. "Tuna and peanut butter."

"On the same sandwich?" I asked.

"Yes." She nodded. "I liked it."

Pa shrugged. "I offered a choice, and she asked for both on one sandwich. It's actually not bad."

"You should try it, Auntie Mac," Ella piped up. "It's very good."

I smiled at her. "I'll give it a try."

"Apart from lunch, we thought we should give Tim a break," Reba said.

"I'm sure he appreciated that." I patted the baby's back through the carrier. His knit hat was the only thing visible as he slept.

"I carried you in this same Snugli, MacKenzie," Pa said in his low baritone. "Until you were big enough to ride in a backpack."

"Seriously?" I took another look. The carrier did appear a bit worn.

"I remember that," my grandma said. "You always fell right to sleep when your father carried you."

"Derrick can carry their baby in it after he or she is born." I expected Pa had saved the soft carrier, imagining I could use it for my baby too. I hoped that would happen.

"Are we going to the candy shop now, Grandpa?" Ella tugged on his sleeve.

"Yes, sweetheart, we are." Pa winked at me.

She squealed and clapped her hands.

"Say hi to Gin for me," I said. "She owns Salty Taffy's."

"She owns a whole candy store?" Ella's big dark eyes grew bigger.

"She sure does. Do you know what a bestie is?" I asked her.

"It's a friend who is your bestest one."

"Exactly." I gave her a high five. "It's what Gin and I are, besties."

"My bestie at home is named Nicholas, but Cokey is my bestie here."

"Perfect. Hey, I'll see you later, alligator." I had a whole routine of those phrases with Cokey.

Ella repeated it before taking Reba's hand. Ella skipped down the sidewalk, with Reba walking briskly and Pa ambling behind. I could teach the girl the rest of the phrases later, unless Cokey beat me to it.

A minute later, I meandered into the costume shop. I didn't have a single valid reason to be in there, though. I thought fast. I could pretend my niece was taking a dance class, except she wasn't. I hadn't been invited to a masquerade party or have any need for a fancy costume, not that I would want to wear one. If Harini was working, I couldn't pretend we'd scheduled a book group meeting to discuss *Nine Lives and Alibis*— because we hadn't.

Shelly waved a hand from the dance outfits area. "Welcome back, Mac."

I greeted her as I approached. "How's business?"

"A bit slow, but that's to be expected after the Halloween season ends." She was dressed far more casually today than she had been last week, in a black cardigan over a green turtleneck with black knit pants.

"What did you go as for Halloween?" I did my best to make the question sound offhand.

"My favorite dark character, of course, Morticia Addams."

Bingo. That had to have been Shelly in the bank drive-through.

"You're perfect for that," I said. "You already have the dark hair. Add a black dress and white makeup and you're all set."

"Indeed, although I find it interesting you know so much about her. Most young people have no idea who Morticia is."

"I used to watch *Addams Family* reruns with my grandmother when I was little. She's a big fan of the series."

"I see. So, how can I help you?" she asked.

"I was out at the bank and realized I hadn't offered my condolences on the loss of your friend."

She folded her arms over her chest. "What friend is that?"

"Enzo Lawrence, of course. He told me you two were special friends." I crossed mental fingers at stretching the truth with the added adjective, but anything goes in the pursuit of justice. "I'm so sorry."

She lifted her chin. "Thank you. His passing is a great loss to everyone."

"I heard he was found on his deck, still in costume. It must have been quite a shock to the person who saw him like that."

"Of course." She looked away and straightened a tidy pile of leotards that didn't need it.

"You must have met Enzo in New York. How long had you two been friends?"

She tilted her head and frowned at me. "So it's true."

"What is?"

"You're a detective. A PI."

"Not at all." *Ugh.* I had gone too far with my questions. Would I ever learn? "I run a bike shop. I'm a small business owner, like you."

"Of course." She pulled her phone out of the pocket on the side of her thigh. "If you'll excuse me, I have an appointment soon."

"Of course. I'll be off." I turned to go but pivoted to face her again. "I forgot. Xavier said to say hello."

Her eyes flashed in what looked like alarm. "Where do you . . . isn't he . . . what now?"

"I ran into him yesterday. When he heard I was from Westham, he sent his greetings to you." *Sort of.*

Shelly blinked. "Thank you. I think."

"Want me to return the greetings?"

"Whatever." She pocketed her phone and strode toward the back of the store.

"You have a good day," I called after her.

She raised a hand without turning round. I walked to Mac's Bikes, my thoughts on her reaction to the news that I'd spoken with Xavier, which I found interesting in the extreme.

CHAPTER 30

By three thirty, I was eying the clock. Delia left after I came back, and the shop had been quiet since. I couldn't close before five because I had rentals due in and Orlean had to leave at four, but I wanted to. I should be helping Tim with the kids or looking for Jamie. Or pursuing a murderer. Probably all three.

I perched on a stool behind the retail counter. I was caught up on orders and bookkeeping, and all the merchandise was in good shape. Maybe the internet could help me with a bit of murder digging.

Shelly Hitchcock was a mystery. She, or maybe Harini, had a connection with an incarcerated man who knew something bad about one of them. Shelly knew Enzo from New York. Had that also been where she'd met Harini? Shelly owned a building and co-owned a business. And she believed in astrology. She'd told me she'd had a consultation with Astra, aka my mother.

Mom might have insights about Shelly. Unless . . . would telling me violate confidentiality or something? Were astrologers bound to the same rules as therapists and doctors? I knew I had to find out.

Alas, she didn't pick up when I called. I tapped out a text, instead.

Have a question for you. Come by the shop before 5 or call? Thx, XXOO.

What else could I check into? Xavier had said one of the costume shop owners was unscrupulous. Shelly was a co-owner of the business, according to Harini, but a sole owner of the building. Maybe I could access the property records online, either through the county offices or Westham's, and see if she was on solid footing there.

I struck out with the county's records, but the town's assessment division showed back taxes due on the building going back two years. I stared at the screen. It seemed Shelly had owned the property well before she opened the shop. I tapped the counter, trying to remember what had been in that space before this fall. During the winter holiday season last year, a children's clothing store had been near there, but it had closed in the new year. Had it been in the Cape Costumers storefront?

I shook my head. I couldn't picture that stretch of Main Street. Maybe the place had stood empty for two years. If so, buying commercial real estate and not earning money from it for over a year was an expensive project. No wonder Shelly couldn't pay her taxes. Did Harini know? As usual, I had too many questions and not enough answers.

Speaking of Harini, I should see what else I could learn about the dancer. Even if she was talented enough to dance with the New York City Ballet, which few were, she was far too old to have held a recent position with them, unless it was that of teacher. With a unique name like hers, it shouldn't be too hard to learn about her past.

Perhaps I could dig more deeply into Peter Zelensky. I ticked off what I knew about him. Widower. Father. Financial adviser. Lived in North Falmouth. Norland had said Enzo had seemed angry with Peter, and today he and the mysterious Herbert Lawrence had gotten into it on the pickleball court. I began to dig.

Peter's LinkedIn profile listed an MBA degree from a university in Ohio. I didn't see a police record for him, always a good sign for someone dealing in other people's finances. He appeared to have a son, who had graduated from a private high school three years ago. Peter seemed squeaky clean from what I could see. So, why was he arguing in public with Herbert Lawrence this morning?

I hadn't really investigated Herbert yet, either. It still annoyed me he'd left his street address blank on my rental form. I'd have to remind Delia and my weekend staff, not to mention myself, to check over the form to make sure it was complete before customers left with their rentals.

I first searched for Herbert Lawrence in conjunction with *United States Air Force* and hit gold right away. He was an independent contractor for the Air Force in something called *Information Services*. Was he an IT guy for the Hanscom base, or was that code for intelligence work? Maybe he wrote software, which could run the gamut from controlling automated systems to programing attack drones.

I couldn't tell whether he'd been active duty in the past. I dug further, pairing his name with Enzo's. A leaner Herbert appeared in a news photograph with Enzo from thirty years ago. It was a celebration for an acting award Enzo had won; not a Tony, but something more regional. In a quote in the article, Enzo said how proud he was that his only nephew had taken a break from his training to come help him celebrate.

Military training, most likely. Either way, the two men were plainly related. So why hadn't Herbert acknowledged Enzo's death or shown any sorrow about it?

Noises came from the back. A minute later Orlean passed by with scrubbed hands holding her insulated lunch bag. She shrugged into her coat. "See you Monday."

"Have a good weekend," I said as the door closed on my words. I groaned. It was now after four and still too early to close up with rentals due in. Even though we'd been fairly busy, a slower season like this presented a different energy than full summer or earlier in the fall, when bikes were in high demand. I dug back into my research but finally gave up. I was getting nowhere.

"Hey, sweetheart." My mom swept in and hurried over to embrace me. She stepped back. "I'm reporting in that your father and I put up posters all over town."

"Posters?"

"Yes, with Jamie's picture on them. I took her photograph last Sunday and we copied it. Joseph checked with Tim today to make sure he didn't mind. The posters ask for information on Jamie and to call the police nonemergency number if people know anything."

"Wow. Thank you. Thank Pa for me too."

"It's not a problem. She's family, after all, and you both are too busy with those sweet children and your work."

"I really appreciate it." Why hadn't I thought of plastering the town with a missing poster?

"I'm also checking the Westham town group on social media." She cocked her head, gazing at me. "Are you all right?"

"I'm fine." I gave her a frowny smile. "Am I not supposed to be?"

"It's that transit you're going through, honey. I worry."

"Please don't." Whatever transit she thought I was experiencing, real life presented a ton more for me to go through right now. "Speaking of astrology, Shelly said she's been having consultations with you."

"Oh, yes. A lovely woman, isn't she?" Astra glanced toward the back of the shop.

"Don't worry, Orlean isn't here."

"The thing is, Shelly has a dark side, at least according to her natal chart. The influence of Scorpio is strong. You know Scorpios can be secretive, and with her Pluto and Saturn in aspect to Mercury, well . . ."

"Well, what?" I had no way to make sense of what sounded like gibberish.

"I would be careful around her, my dear. Extra careful."

CHAPTER 31

After Mom left, I returned to my online searches but glanced up when the door opened. A woman who'd arranged a four-bike rental for her and her friends stood there. Their bikes weren't due back until tomorrow at the end of the day, but this woman's cheeks were flushed and she wore an annoyed look, her lips pressed into a crooked line.

"Hi," I said. "Is everything all right?"

"The bikes are fine. But one of my friends said she absolutely must get home tonight, not tomorrow, so we're leaving. The bikes are all out back by your rental container." She placed her palm on the doorjamb and began to turn.

"Hang on a second, please. Let me pull your paperwork. I need to check the bicycles before you leave."

She blew out a breath, but she consented to accompany me until I'd made sure all was in good order.

"I can't believe she doesn't want to stay through to-morrow," the woman said. "The weather's going to be perfect."

"You'll have to come back." I smiled and gestured at the four bikes. "You're all set with these. Safe travels home."

She thanked me and hurried away. Unless she and her friends were flying home out of Hyannis on Cape Air, they were doomed to hit bad Friday afternoon traffic no matter which way they headed. I was grateful to be able to stay right here in Westham at the start of pretty much any weekend.

By four forty-five, the final rentals had been returned and I was getting ready to close up shop. I wiped down the counters and locked the day's cash in the safe, leaving minimal opening cash in the open drawer. I stepped outside to bring in the Open flag.

A mild breeze was blowing from inland and the slanting fall light, legendary on the Cape for its beauty, was lovely now an hour before sunset. We would revert to standard time tomorrow night, which meant the late afternoons would instantly become a lot darker and grow steadily colder. In the meantime I planned to soak up the good weather tomorrow.

I was furling the flag when the familiar whir of bicycle wheels approached. Herbert Lawrence braked to a stop in front of me and set one foot on the ground. In lieu of a helmet, he wore a blue ball cap labeled Boys and Girls Club. His windbreaker had the same insignia.

"Mac, the front brake is loose," he said without preamble.

"Let me take a look." I set the flag pole against the

building. I pressed the brake level a couple of times and squatted to check the mechanism. "It is. I'll get a tool from the shop."

"Should I wheel it in?"

"No, that's okay. I'll be right out."

Herbert might be innocent, but if he'd had anything to do with Enzo's death, being alone with him inside was a supremely bad idea. I made sure the door lock clicked behind me when I went in. I grabbed what I needed from Orlean's tidy tool bench, plus a rag for my hands, and headed back out.

"There you go," I said after fixing the problem. "Good as new."

"Thank you. I trust I'll receive a discount on the rental rate?"

As if. I gave him a level gaze. "Sir, bicycles are made of moving parts that get a lot of impact from the terrain they are ridden over. We charge a fair rate and stand by it. If you'd like to turn this one in early and rent a cycle elsewhere, you are free to."

He blew out a puff of air. "It's fine. I'll keep it. I did ride over a couple of rough areas. One time was when I had to dodge so I didn't hit a bunny." He smiled. "I confess I have a soft spot for small furry things. Cute little buggers, aren't they?"

"As long as you don't have a vegetable garden." I pointed my chin at his hat. "Do you work for the Boys and Girls Club?"

"No, but I volunteer for them. I teach chess and lead a fitness class."

"The kids must appreciate that. I hope your visit to the Cape is going well. Besides those brakes, I mean."

"It's fine." His smile disappeared.

"Were you related to the man who died this week? You have the same last name. If so, let me offer my condolences."

"Thank you, but that isn't necessary."

A group of couples paired up on a half-dozen large motorcycles came down the street at a soft roar, thankfully in possession of better mufflers than some. Still, I waited until they passed.

"I heard you joined the ranks of local pickleball players," I said.

He narrowed his eyes. "Who told you that?"

"A friend who plays." I kept my voice casual.

"It's important to stay active." He put a leg over the bike and tested the brake lever for himself. "This seems fine now."

"I'd have to agree with you about staying active. So, how do you know Peter Zelensky?"

"What?" He glared at me, nostrils flared and eyes glittering.

"My friend said the two of you got into a bit of a fight on the court. She told me it didn't sound like the kind of disagreement that happens between strangers." I lifted a shoulder and dropped it. "I wasn't there."

"You certainly weren't. And you can tell your friend to mind her own . . . business." He turned the bike and rode away.

I could swear he had choked back an obscenity at the last moment. I watched him go, then grabbed the flagpole and headed back inside. My questions had shaken up Herbert Lawrence's cozy snow globe, and he hadn't liked it. He also hadn't denied he was related to Enzo.

It was a conversation to share with the Cozy Capers when we met tonight. I was looking forward to hearing whatever they might have learned and their take on Herbert's defensiveness.

The sooner we solved this homicide, the better. As often happened, the police seemed to be moving too slowly for anyone's taste.

CHAPTER 32

"Is there any way we can find out who inherits Enzo's estate?" I asked the Cozy Capers that evening at a bit after eight o'clock. Gin, Flo, Norland, and Tulia sat around the kitchen table with me. The door to the living room was closed, but I'd still reminded them to keep their voices down, as two little ones slumbered two rooms away. Tim was upstairs on his laptop with the baby monitor at hand.

Three of us sipped white wine, while Norland nursed a beer and Tulia, as usual, was enjoying a ginger ale.

"Enzo's estate." Flo tapped her ubiquitous yellow legal pad. "Probably not. Herbert might not even be related to the victim. You know? Some people use *Uncle* and *Aunt* loosely."

"True, like for close family friends who aren't actually related," Norland agreed.

"Except they are." I described the photo I'd seen of the awards ceremony.

"Why do you ask about the estate, Mac?" Gin asked.

"Before he died, Enzo came in and bought an adult tricycle for cash. He didn't hesitate to hand over the money, and it seemed like he was well-situated in terms of money." I gazed around the group. "If so, I'm curious about who might inherit."

"Because motive, right?" Tulia asked. "There can't be two Enzos around here. That dude I overheard must have been referring to the victim. But is he the next of kin? No idea."

"I can try to get the information about other next of kin he might have had from Shelly next time she comes into Salty Taffy's," Gin offered. "I haven't seen her all week, which is a long stretch without candy for her. I'm sure she'll be in soon and hopefully tomorrow."

"Action item for Gin." Flo jotted it down on her yellow pad. "Okay, my friends, what do we know for sure?"

"For sure? Maybe not, but this morning Peter Zelensky and Herbert Lawrence seemed to know each other beyond the pickleball court," Norland said.

"I spoke to Herbert this afternoon," I said. "I told him I'd heard about the fight during the game and asked him how he knew Peter. He totally got his back up."

"Did he answer?" Gin asked.

"He did not, although he added that the friend who told me should mind her own business. I think he was about to use stronger language and thought better of it."

"Good luck with that," Flo said. "We are all about

not minding our own business when it comes to murder, and rightly so. What else we got?"

"I called my cousin Jackie," Tulia began. "She's a captain in the Air Force at Hanscom. I asked her if she knows a Herbert Lawrence." She looked at us like a cat who'd had a live mouse under its paw.

"And?" Flo made a rolling motion with her hand.

"And she says the dude spends money like it's going out of style. He drives a new Tesla. He wears a super expensive watch. His off-duty clothes look like they either came straight from the designer or is sportswear created for rich people."

"Does whatever job he has pay that well?" Gin asked.

"No way." Tulia shook her head. "Jackie has no idea how he pays his bills. He's retired from active duty but works on base as a civilian consultant. Before he retired, she ranked above him, and she lives in a modest condo and drives a decade-old car."

"Anything else?" Flo asked.

"Not from Jackie," Tulia said.

"Mac, what about what Xavier said about Shelly at the jail?" Flo said. "I saw that you shared it in the group thread last night."

"I did." I repeated Xavier's warning. "But it might have been about Harini, since she's a co-owner of the shop."

Norland frowned. "You didn't find out how he knows her?"

"No," I said. "It was right before the inmates' time in the library was up and they were escorted out. I didn't get a chance to ask whether he was talking about Shelly or Harini. He only mentioned the costume shop owner, but I stopped by and spoke to Shelly this afternoon. I'll tell you, she looked alarmed when I said Xavier said to say hello to her."

Flo raised a finger. "I looked into him a bit, which wasn't hard, with a name like Xavier Casbohm."

"No kidding." Gin laughed. "That's way more unique than Enzo Lawrence."

"You are aware that the word unique—" Flo began.

"Yeah, yeah, yeah." Gin rolled her eyes. "It can't be modified. Something is either unique or it's not, but you have to admit that you know what I mean."

"At any rate." Flo cleared her throat. "Casbohm also lived in New York City and apparently was peripherally involved in the theater."

"Is he an actor?" Tulia asked.

"Only if you mean a bad actor," Flo replied. "He has sometimes worked as a guard, a bouncer, or a bodyguard. But when he runs short on funds, he seems to think it's fine to rob a liquor store—or a box office."

Norland, who had bent his head over his phone, glanced up. "With suspicion of Shelly Hitchcock's help in one case."

I whistled.

"Tell us more," Tulia said.

"They couldn't come up with enough evidence to convict her," Norland said.

"How did Xavier get nabbed on the Cape?" I asked.

"He was apprehended for attempting to rob a convenience store in Hyannis," Norland said.

"Maybe he followed Shelly up here," I said.

"Or Enzo," Tulia added. "At least he's not our killer if he's been inside at Barnstable for a while."

"He's been incarcerated there since last summer." Norland gazed at me. "Have you spoken with Lincoln recently?"

"Not since yesterday morning, which I told you all about. It seems like ages ago."

"We could have invited him to join us tonight." Gin grinned.

"As if." I joined her in the smile. "He would have politely declined and also told us to butt out of the investigation."

"What about Harini Whitt?" Flo asked. "She must have also known Enzo in New York. Do we know if she had a reason to kill him?"

Nobody offered anything more than a headshake or a shrug.

I raised a finger. "The only thing I know is when I first met Harini at the costume shop, she said she shared the apartment behind the shop with Shelly. She mentioned that she was planning to move out as soon as she found something better. Maybe the two of them don't get along as well now that they're both working and living together. It might not have anything to do with the murder, though."

"Do you think you can dig a little deeper on that, Mac?" Flo asked.

"I can try." I was hoping to relax with Tim and the kids tomorrow, but our schedules were flexible.

Norland pointed his beer bottle at me. "When Harini dropped by your shop yesterday, Mac, remember how fast she left when she heard I was former police?"

"Right, there's that too. She came in and asked how

much I knew about Enzo's death, but I never learned why she was asking. I'll see what I can find out."

Flo noted my action item on her list.

"It seems like we really need to know more about Enzo himself," I murmured. "Who was he? How did he treat people? Did he have secrets?"

"Everyone has secrets." Flo kept her gaze on the pad of paper.

"And the dude was eighty," Tulia said. "That's a pretty good run right there. Nobody gets through that many years without making a few enemies."

"I'm sure I never have." Norland folded his hands under his chin and batted his lashes over wide innocent eyes. From a seventysomething former police chief with gray hair framing a lined face, the expression looked funny enough to make us all laugh. "But seriously, I can check into his past. See if he has a record and look into his past employment and financial affairs, as far as I'm able."

"So noted," Flo said. "For my part, I'll see what I can learn about Peter Zelensky. I witnessed that argument this morning, and I think I might have a contact who can help us."

Tulia raised her hand. "I'll get back to my cousin and work with her to see if she can learn where Herbert gets his big bucks."

"Would I be correct to think you don't have any news about Jamie?" Norland asked me, his tone as soft as Luca's little cheek.

"Unfortunately, that's right, but my family has put up posters all over town, and Mom is monitoring social media." A mini-wail came from the bedroom. "And I'm going to kick you all out right now. The baby needs his bottle."

Everyone hurried to stand, and I got four quick hugs before my friends slipped out the back door. I switched off the overhead light, leaving only the undercounter light strip on, and turned my focus to family.

CHAPTER 33

We had a flurry of activity the next morning, which included breakfast and reading picture books to Ella and everybody getting ready for their Saturday. Derrick and Cokey were expected any minute to pick up Ella for a day of cousin play and the promised sleepover. Tim had whipped up a batch of cinnamon scones to go with scrambled eggs and bacon, making the house smell like heaven. Ella approved, eating an extra half scone after she'd finished her plate.

Now our niece hopped up and down with excitement, holding her little Cape Cod backpack full of several changes of clothes, her nightie and toothbrush, and her stuffed seal. I threaded her curly ponytail through a pink Seattle ball cap and helped her put on matching pink sneakers.

"We call them tennies, Auntie Mac, not sneakers."

"That's because you're from the West Coast, sweetie. Here the word *tennies* means you're going to play tennis in them. But you can call your shoes whatever you want."

After Derrick left with two thrilled little girls, Tim strapped Luca into the stroller to deliver him to my parents for the day.

"I'm going to spend time at work after I drop him off," Tim said. "The bakery needs my attention. I don't know what I'm going to do next week if . . ." His voice trailed off.

"We'll figure it out, sweetheart." I held out my arms. "Between us, we can figure out anything." I squeezed him in close.

His shoulders relaxed as he squeezed back. "You're the best, MacKenzie Almeida."

Luca piped up from the stroller. Tim laughed and planted a kiss on my lips.

"I'd better get walking," he said. "I expect the little guy will fall asleep, or at least be entertained enough by the wind and trees and cars not to complain."

"You've got the diaper bag and bottles and everything?"

He pointed at the backpack-style diaper bag he'd stashed in the stroller's bottom compartment.

"Love you, boys." I leaned over to kiss the baby's forehead, pulling his tiny Mariners knit cap down over his ears. "You be good for your abos, *queridinho*."

And just like that, I was alone in a quiet house and it was only ten o'clock. I barely knew what to do with myself. I wandered through the downstairs. I picked up a couple of Ella's books in the living room and tidied a stack of magazines.

I paused at the door to the bedroom that was normally Tim's and mine, aghast at the mess. Setting to work to straighten it, I began by closing Jamie's suitcase in the corner. If she came back, she wouldn't appreciate anyone having gone through it. I tossed a couple of baby suits in the clothes hamper, followed by the leggings and shirt Ella had worn yesterday.

I pulled the sheet and comforter up and smoothed them. As I grabbed a pillow to fluff, it knocked a mostly empty baby bottle to the floor, which rolled under the bed. Kneeling, I bent over to see how far it had gone on the hardwood floor. It wasn't the only bottle under there.

I sat back on my heels holding five vodka nip bottles, all empty. Poor Jamie. She'd said she was staying straight and sober, but it clearly had proved too hard a challenge for her to accomplish.

Had she brought these nips in her suitcase? If not, we'd gone out without her more than once. She could have dashed down to the convenience store and stocked up. If I searched the room, I imagined I'd find more, whether full or empty.

It didn't matter now. My own challenge was deciding if I should tell Tim what I'd found. I hated to add to his worries, to make him even sadder than he already was. We both tried to be open and honest in our marriage, but sometimes talking about hard things was a matter of timing.

I gathered up the bottles, small and larger, and headed to the kitchen. The baby bottle I rinsed out for now. The nips went into a paper bag, which I folded over and stuck into a corner of the hutch. I'd deal with those later.

CHAPTER 34

Belle was oddly quiet as she sat on her roost. I poured the last half cup of coffee and dosed it with milk before warming it up in the microwave. I added a spoonful of sugar as an indulgence after it was warm.

I puttered around, doing the breakfast dishes, wiping down the counters, and putting Jamie out of my mind for the moment. If I knew how to cook, I could plan a nice grown-up dinner for my man and me, except the last time I tried to make dinner, Tim had to rescue my pad Thai.

In lieu of another disaster in the kitchen, I decided that ordering Japanese takeout for dinner and serving it on pretty dishes alongside a pair of lit tapers would be good enough. Attempting to eat out at a decent restaurant with an infant at his bedtime wasn't a brilliant idea in anybody's playbook.

As I showered, I thought about Tim's sadness that

none of his inquiries about Jamie yesterday had yielded information. Area shelters and hospitals had either not seen her or refused to give Tim any information. Maybe Lincoln had had more luck.

I ran through what we'd talked about at last evening's Cozy Capers meeting. My task was to find out more about Harini Whitt. I could stay here and search the internet, but I would also stroll by the costume shop. Either she or Shelly should be working. We had a Chamber of Commerce social event coming up. I could use inviting them to it as an excuse for stopping in.

Good. I liked having a plan. I wasn't so sure Shelly would welcome another visit from me. If I kept my tone light and businesslike and stuck to my story of inviting her to the Chamber gig, I should be safe from her suspecting me of more sleuthing. Maybe.

Clean, dressed, and with contacts in, I settled at the kitchen table with my tablet, another scone on a small plate, and a glass of water. I picked up the scone with my left hand and leaned over the plate to keep the crumbs and sugar contained as I munched. I swiped into searching with my right hand.

Luckily for me, nobody else in the universe seemed to have the same name as Harini's. I found a relatively recent article featuring her teaching dance to a class of mostly kids of color in New York. I saw a photo from twenty years earlier of her at the Met gala. Dressed in a tasteful and flattering dark floor-length gown, she was on the arm of a man whom the caption identified as James F. Whitt. When I searched on that name, I came across his obituary from seven years ago.

That answered one question I'd had—whether she

was divorced or widowed, or whether her family from childhood had the surname of Whitt. I kept digging. She'd taught at the Boston Ballet School for about ten years. Not so surprising for a person who'd made dance her life, but that rabbit hole led to an announcement of her engagement to James, listing Harini Mukherjee as a rising star in the ballet world.

All interesting, but none of it answered questions about her ties with the unfortunate victim. I'd give it one more stab. I first paired her married name with Enzo Lawrence but got zip. When I changed his name in the search bar to Shelly Hitchcock, things picked up. I found a squib in the local news reporting on the opening of Cape Costumers.

Then I found something that made me sit back and think. About a decade earlier, a theater-oriented gossip column included a juicy tidbit: "Favorite off-Broadway silver fox seen with still-graceful ballerina, HW. Will hunky older EL break up another marriage or break another heart? Watch this spot for all the latest hot sightings."

Ooh. Harini and Enzo had apparently been a number, and while she was still married, to boot. I flipped back to the Whitt obituary and nodded to myself. James had been a decade older than his wife, and he had died "due to complications from dementia."

As recently as last week, Enzo had been the special friend of Harini's business partner. "No wonder she wanted to move out," I said aloud.

"No wonder she wanted to move out," Belle piped up in my voice. "No wonder."

"Seriously," I agreed.

"I can't do this." Belle shifted her voice.

I stared. She sounded exactly like Jamie.

"I can't do it anymore." Belle continued her perfect imitation. "I can't do it anymore. I can't. I just can't."

My scalp turned to goose bumps, and the chill ran down to my toes. Jamie had to have uttered those words when she was alone with Belle.

"Seriously." The bird reverted to my voice. "Seriously. Seriously. Snacks, Mac?"

I let my shoulders drop. "Sure, Belle."

With the parrot happily munching on frozen carrot bites, I considered what to do. I didn't want to dash Tim's hopes. Jamie could have been referring to how hard it was to stay straight and sober. Judging from the nip bottles, she'd done something about that. Or she could have been thinking about her life. I hoped Belle wouldn't repeat those phrases in front of Ella or Tim. I wasn't going to share what the bird had said if I didn't have to.

And if she did speak in Jamie's voice saying that again, I'd meant what I said to him before he left. We'd figure it out. Together.

CHAPTER 35

On my way to Cape Costumers half an hour later, I neared Westham Town Hall. Belle's mimicking Jamie's voice and her words still bothered me, but I couldn't think of a thing I could do about it. All we could do was wait.

What I'd read in the gossip blurb about Enzo pushed its way to the front of my thoughts. The article had mused on him breaking up "another marriage." How many breakups had he been part of? It could have been plenty if he was a serial philanderer. Recently he'd apparently been romantically involved with Shelly, but I didn't know how long that had been the status quo. Maybe whatever had happened between him and Harini was enough for her to murder him. But why now, and why share an apartment with a woman who had broken up their relationship?

Rhythmic thwacks reached my ears. I paused on the sidewalk in front of the recently renovated municipal building. Several public tennis courts sat behind the building, but a tennis ball being hit sounded more like a thud. This was a sharper noise. I turned right along the drive leading to the parking lots until I rounded the corner.

A municipal bulletin board was shielded by an overhang. One of Mom's posters about Jamie was front and center, along with dozens of other smaller notices about fundraisers, yard sales, and sign-ups for winter youth basketball. Would the missing poster get the attention of someone who had seen something? I could only hope it would elicit new information.

Inside the high tennis court fence, two sets of doubles hit yellow balls back and forth over short nets, while a dozen others stood nearby looking on and chatting. The men and women on the sidelines generally wore nylon or stretchy long pants with windbreakers or fleece hoodies. A few on the court were dressed in shorts and long-sleeved T-shirts, despite the blustery fall day.

I approached but watched from outside the chain-link fence. The solid flat paddles were bigger than a ping-pong paddle and smaller than a sheet of paper. The ball had holes in it but looked thicker and maybe a bit softer than the kind of ball little kids played with. Delia played on the same side as a man with short, thin white hair ringing a mostly bald pate. Both were about my height, but the man was stocky where Delia was wiry. Despite appearing almost twice her age, he was holding his own on the court.

I peered at him. This was the guy Victoria pulled over for not respecting a pedestrian—her—yesterday.

Playing opposite them was Peter Zelensky and a woman I didn't know, and I also didn't recognize any of the four players on the other court. No Flo, no Orlean, although neither worked on Saturdays. Orlean was in my shop every weekday. My weekend guy, Edwin, could handle repairs and maintenance as well as the rest of our business.

Peter glanced over at me while awaiting a serve. I smiled and gave a little wave. He frowned and looked away, focused on the game. I couldn't imagine he didn't recognize who I was.

I turned when someone hurried up, breathless, next to me. Harini wore a navy track suit and carried a sports bag over her shoulder.

I greeted her. "Looks like you're on trend."

"Hi, Mac. I don't know about trends, but I've always loved racquet sports. You're not playing?"

"Me?" I laughed. "No way. Did you play in New York?"

Her bouncy stance stilled. "No."

"I wonder if Enzo did."

"I wouldn't know." She kept her gaze on the game.

"Oh? I heard somewhere you two were going out for a while."

Harini swiveled her face to stare into mine. "You can't believe everything you hear." She strode around to the open gate and entered the court to stand on the sidelines. She drew a paddle from her bag and swung it with one arm, then the other, to warm up her arms, I guessed.

"That was a fair ball." Delia's partner stalked to the net, his lips pressed into an unpleasant line.

"No." Peter wiped sweat off his forehead with his sleeve. "It was out."

"I saw it land," the man insisted. "I get the point."

Peter glanced at the woman he was playing with.

"Nope. Peter's right," she said. "Clearly out."

"Scott," Delia said. "Relax. They're right. And, you know, what does it matter? It's Saturday. We're playing a game for fun and exercise."

Scott gave his head a shake but resumed play. Still, the next time he got a shot on the ball, he slammed it so hard into the other side of the court the woman simply stepped aside.

This Scott guy seemed to have anger bottled up inside. It might be worth asking around if he'd had disputes with Enzo. I sniffed, catching a whiff of aftershave.

"Some people don't know how to have fun," a deep voice beside me said.

"Lincoln." I patted my heart. "You're the second person to sneak up on me."

He chuckled. "Mac, one of the first things they teach in the academy is to always be aware of your surroundings."

"I guess that explains it, then, since attending police academy has never been on my bucket list." I took a second look at him. Along with sweat pants and sneakers, he wore a pullover sweatshirt with a word in a language I didn't recognize on the front. "You're in exercise clothes. Are you joining these maniacs?" I gestured toward the court.

"Afraid I am." He kept his gaze on the game, but a little smile played on his lips. "Delia twisted my arm. I've played a couple of times, and I'm sure I embarrassed her, but I figured, why not give it a shot?"

"Good luck. What does your shirt say?" I asked.

"It's 'Hello' in Wampanoag. You know I've been studying the language."

"I do, and I think it's awesome."

The game seemed to end. The four players met at the net and touched the handles of their paddles together.

"Do you know anything about the man who was playing with Delia?" I asked. "His name is Scott."

"I don't. Why?"

"He's super competitive and seems angry."

"And you wondered if he knew our recent victim." Lincoln looked over the top of his glasses at me.

"It did cross my mind."

"I'll see what I can find out." He shifted his gaze back to the court. "Coming," he called to Delia, who was motioning him inside. "You take care, Mac."

"I promise," I said to his back. "Have a fun game."

He raised a hand in acknowledgment. As he entered the gate, Peter Zelensky whipped his head around. Why would he look alarmed at seeing Lincoln?

CHAPTER 36

The front windows of Cape Costumers now featured Thanksgiving decor on one side of the entrance, complete with a mannequin wearing a turkey costume. A printed sign I hadn't seen before in the corner of the window advertised custom costumes for any occasion as well as tailoring.

The window on the other side of the store was devoted to dance wear of all kinds, from tutus to tap shoes, leotards to leopard-print leggings, ballet tights to pink toe-shoe bags.

Halloween was over and they'd moved on. Would that include decorating for Christmas before Turkey Day?

I'd wait and see. I was firmly in the camp of giving every holiday its season but no more, which was what I did in Mac's Bikes. We'd taken down the Halloween decorations on November first. Christmas and Hanukkah stuff wouldn't appear until the weekend after Thanksgiving. And so on throughout the year. I knew other retailers felt differently, and that was their choice.

The black cat glared at me from atop the hay bale on the sidewalk. *Ugh.* It arched its back and hissed.

"Good kitty?" I murmured, giving it a wide berth before I reached for the door. I sneezed, despite the distance. Sometimes it felt like pets shot their dander at me on purpose. My allergic immune system maintained there were no good kitties or doggies, at least not for me, except for Cokey's hypoallergenic pup. Tucker had hair instead of fur, which made it possible for me to be around him occasionally.

Inside, the store was quiet. Nobody stood behind the counter at the back. No shoppers browsed the costume aisles or the dance area. I cocked my head and listened.

When I was a girl, I'd spent time at Abo Reba's side while she sewed quilts for premature babies and Halloween costumes for Derrick and me, plus summer shirts for him and dresses for me. She'd hemmed lengths of West African and Indonesian batik fabric for tablecloths and made matching cloth napkins.

If that wasn't the sound of a sewing machine coming from the far end of the store, I'd have to get my hearing checked. I moseyed to the back. I was almost to the open door behind the counter when the whirring stopped.

"You're completely off base," Shelly's voice muttered. "That's not true, and you know it."

"Yes, it is," a man insisted. "And you owe me."

I squinted, trying to place the voice. It was familiar, but the name attached to it remained elusive. The machine started up again. Whoever the dude was spoke louder. Too bad his words were masked, to me at least, by the sound of a needle zipping in and out of fabric at high speed.

The whirring ceased, followed by the familiar *fwap* of the little lever flipping up, which released the cloth from being secured under the presser foot.

"I need you to leave, right now," Shelly said. "You can talk to my lawyer if you have anything more to say."

"I can guarantee you, I will," he snarled.

I didn't dare circle around behind the counter to peek in. In fact, I should probably clear out of the store before either of those angry people came out and caught me eavesdropping. I slid toward the exit as quietly—and fast—as I could.

"Besides," he added, "I know things about you you're going to wish I didn't."

"Listen," Shelly said, her voice growing louder. "You need to get on your horse and ride, buddy, preferably back out of town. You're not getting what you mistakenly think you're owed, ever, unless it's over my dead body—or yours."

"Are you threatening me?" he growled.

I crept the last two yards to the exit in record time, and I'd never been so relieved a store didn't have a bell on the door. I walked two stores down the street and paused, pretending to study the display in the Book Nook store window but keeping my peripheral vision alert to where I'd come from.

A moment later a man pushed out of Cape Costumers. Herbert Lawrence glanced in both directions, then headed straight for me. My heart rate competing for an Olympic sprint event, I steeled my gaze on the window. He stormed by, with the smoke coming from his ears nearly visible, but kept on going.

Whew. My shoulders slumped. My breath rushed out as the questions rushed in. What did he know about Shelly? What did he think he was owed? Both of them had sounded furious and desperate. I might have to make my way back to the pickleball courts and slip Lincoln a word. Westham didn't need any more dead bodies. Not Shelly's, not Herbert's.

CHAPTER 37

Lincoln could wait. Anyway, he would be busy lob-
bing a ball with a paddle to his reignited love about
now.

I cautiously reentered the costume shop. The sewing
had resumed, but this time it seemed prudent to an-
nounce myself.

"Hello?" I called when I neared the counter.

The noise stopped. The lever again went *fwap*. Shelly
appeared in the doorway, eyebrows drawn together and
the corners of her mouth downturned. The scent of her
perfume came with her, a floral but peppery aroma. I
hadn't noticed the smell previously. Maybe too many
other people had been around.

"Mac?" She cleared her throat and smoothed out her
expression. "What can I help you with?"

"I happened to be passing by and thought I'd stop in.
The Westham Chamber of Commerce is having a so-

cial next week for local business owners. I hope you and Harini can make it."

"I can't answer for her. I might be out of town, but thank you." She looked over my shoulder when she spoke instead of at me.

"Okay. In case you decide to join us, it's this Thursday at six thirty in the credit union meeting room. First Citizens' is a little way down the road on the other side of the street from the bookstore."

She jotted down the information on a small pad of paper next to the register. "Thank you."

"But you know where it is." I gave a little laugh. "I think you bank there, don't you?"

She swallowed. "I know where the credit union is."

"The cat out front was a nice Halloween touch." I smiled. "Is it yours?"

"Harini adopted it. I told her it couldn't be in the shop, though. Too many people are allergic."

"I would be one of them." I tapped my sternum. "Were you sewing in the back?" I wanted to keep the conversation going.

"Yes." Shelly tensed. "Why?"

"No reason. I grew up around my grandmother sewing, so I know the sound of the machine. It brings back fond memories." I smiled.

"How lovely for you." She didn't sound one bit sincere. "I have a custom costume to finish by Monday and I was trying to take advantage of the lull in business in here."

"Makes sense. I'll let you get to it, then." I began to turn away, then faced her again. "By the way, a guy pretty much stormed out of here when I was about to

come in. He didn't look happy. Actually, he appeared
to be furious. I hope you're okay."

"I'm fine." Her frown returned. She folded her arms
on her chest. "You were in here yesterday trying to get
information out of me. I hope you'll figure out how to
mind your own business instead of acting like the Main
Street snoop." She spun on her heel and closed the
door to the back behind her.

All righty, then. I knew when I was dismissed. I
made my way back to the sidewalk. Now what?

It was twelve thirty. I considered the action items
the Cozy Capers had volunteered for. Tulia's name was
next to Herbert's, and lunch from the Lobstah Shack
was always a good choice.

Right now Shelly was on my mind more than the
man from out of town. Gin had signed up for finding
things out about the costume maker. Who didn't love a
piece of fudge? True, I hadn't eaten lunch yet, but the
extra scone I'd had at home would tide me over for a bit
longer. I headed for Salty Taffy's.

Unlike Cape Costumers, the candy shop was full of
customers. Maybe everyone's Halloween candy had
gotten scarfed up in short order. Or it could be that
these shoppers wanted quality sweets, not something
mass produced and extracted from a giant plastic bag
of two hundred minis, not that there was anything wrong
with that. I'd eaten my share of chocolate wrapped
around caramel and nuts and yummy peanut butter cups
from Ella's Halloween candy haul.

Either way, I nearly swooned at all the delectable
smells in here. Chocolate, toffee, and peppermint all

flavored the air. Giant spiral lollipops in green and pink were displayed on a stand. The glass-fronted case next to the sales counter was full of slabs of fudge in various flavors and ingredients. Another section held hand-rolled truffles, and one wall had nothing but clear bins holding wrapped saltwater taffy in thirty flavors and colors. It was one of my favorite sweets and also made an attractive display.

Gin wasn't at the counter, though. When the young guy handling retail had a minute free, I asked if Gin was in, saying she was a friend. He leaned to the side and pushed open the swinging door a few inches.

"You got a friend here, boss," he called.

An apron-clad Gin, her hands in latex gloves, poked her head through without touching the door.

"Come on back, Mac."

I followed her through. I'd been here once when the big red machine was pulling taffy. Today it was clean and quiet, but another time when she and I had been threatened by a killer, Gin had used the machinery to our advantage.

She now stood at the big stainless-steel table forming chocolate truffles bigger than a marble but smaller than a ping-pong ball.

"Want one?" She gestured toward a line of misshapen blobs. "Those are the seconds, otherwise known as the ones I messed up. Have as many as you want."

"Thanks." I picked up the end one, careful not to touch any of the rest, and let it melt in my mouth. All I could say was, "Mmm."

"Good, aren't they?"

"Yes, they are good, which is the most inadequate description ever used for a taste of the divine."

She cocked her head. "It's your day off and you have no husband or borrowed children in tow. If I had to guess, I'd say you might be out and about investigating."

"Trying to, but I'm not getting too far." I recounted what I'd read about Harini and Enzo.

"And recently he was romancing Harini's business partner? Awkward."

"Yes. Also, I dropped by the pickleball court an hour ago."

"As we do." Gin squinted at me. "Except not you."

I laughed. "Hey, I heard the noise behind Town Hall and wanted to see what it was. As I watched, Harini arrived to play. When I alluded to her and Enzo being a number in New York, she didn't like it and told me not to believe everything I heard. Delia and Peter Zelensky were playing, along with that unpleasant guy you or someone referred to."

"Scott? Sounds like everybody who's anybody was there."

"Lincoln showed up to complete the roster, except he didn't tell me a thing. On the other hand, Peter looked alarmed to see our detective friend arrive."

"You've been busy, girl." Gin scooped out the last little ball, rolled it in cocoa, and laid it carefully on the parchment paper–covered pan.

"Wait until I tell you what happened after that."

"Ooh, dish." She took the big bowl to the sink and ran water into it.

"I know Shelly is your action item, but I was walking by and thought I'd invite her and Harini to the Chamber social next week."

"As we do." She grinned over her shoulder at me.

"Exactly." I related overhearing the heated argument. "It ended with Shelly saying something about over her dead body—or his—and telling him to get out."

"So he thinks she owes him something. Interesting."

"Very."

"Who was the dude?" she asked.

"I didn't know when I was listening, but I thought the voice sounded familiar. I made it outside before either of them saw me and hung around to see Herbert Lawrence storm out."

"The elusive and possibly suspicious nephew." Gin finished her washing up and stripped off her gloves.

"The same. I was a hundred percent relieved he didn't recognize me staring into the windows of the bookstore. I went back and invited Shelly to the event."

"And?"

"And she was cold and distracted, or maybe she just didn't want to see me. I said I'd seen an angry man storm out and asked if she was okay. That pushed her over the edge. She accused me of snooping and gave me her back. I left, because of course she's right."

"In other words, I'll have to tread very carefully when I get a chance to talk with her."

"Probably a good idea."

"Boss?" the young guy called from the front.

"He must be swamped out there," she said. "Good to see you, my friend. Take care, okay?"

"You too." I swiped another misshapen truffle and popped it in my mouth.

"I can box up all of those for you if you want."

I laughed. "Please don't. They wouldn't make it home."

But before I left, I bought a small spiral lollipop for Ella, and one for Cokey. Little girls needed a treat now and then.

CHAPTER 38

My two bites of chocolate had not satisfied my appetite, no matter how heavenly they were. Where better to have both lunch and maybe a chat than the best seafood takeout place on the Cape? Even though I'd eaten at the Lobstah Shack only yesterday, there was no such thing as too much good food.

I passed Greta's Grains on the other side of Main Street. I contemplated a stop to see Tim but decided not to. He had his plate—and brain and heart—full. If he was working out business details with his staff, I didn't want to interrupt him. If he had news about Jamie, he would let me know.

An onshore wind had picked up in the last hour. It brought a chill along with the salty smell of the sea, and I pulled my red knit Red Sox hat down over my ears. With hair as short as mine, my head got cold easily.

Tulia's place was beyond Mac's Bikes with only one storefront in between our two places, but I stayed on the other side of the street walking there. I never liked to intrude on Edwin and Sofia. Both of them were excellent with customers and bikes, and I didn't want them to think I was checking up on them. They'd call me if they needed me.

I had an ulterior motive for my lunch choice. Witnessing Herbert and Shelly's altercation a little while ago made me eager to find out if Tulia had gotten any more intel on him from her cousin on the base.

I crossed over and pulled open the door, encountering a different set of divine aromas. Lightly fried fish, rich lobster bisque, and the tang of lemon greeted me, plus bread toasting and a hint of sour dilly pickles. A sight as welcome as the smells was my tiny grandmother seated at one of the few tables of this mostly takeout restaurant.

She raised a hand in recognition but held her other hand over her mouth as she chewed. I pulled up a chair opposite and pointed at her paper-lined plastic basket, which held about a quarter of a toasted bun with something fried inside, accompanied by lettuce and tomato. A half-eaten pickle spear also nestled into the basket and a bottle of orange soda was half empty.

"Fish sandwich?" I asked.

She nodded and swallowed. "Haddock. And perfectly done, I might add. It's today's special. How are you, sweetheart?"

"I'm all right, but I'll be better after I get one of those into me." I stood. "Save my seat."

Like the candy shop, business here was bustling with

weekend diners. I was fourth in line to order. Tulia's counter helper, a skinny boy still in the awkward braces-and-pimples stage, was working as fast as he could, as was Tulia behind him, assembling orders. So much for my thought of talking with her.

When I ordered a fried haddock sandwich, with coleslaw and a lemonade, for here, Tulia turned.

"Thought that was your voice, Mac," she said. "I have something to tell you, but it'll have to wait."

"Not a problem." I paid and thanked the young man.

"The name is Mac?" His voice cracked.

"Yes, thank you." I resumed my seat with my grandma.

Reba leaned in. "Are you hard at work following clues and checking alibis?" She kept her voice low, but her eyes sparkled.

"You like homicide cases way too much, Abo Ree," I murmured. "But, yes, I am looking into a couple of things."

"Ooh, do tell."

My gaze was on the door, which I faced. I raised my eyebrows when Herbert himself pushed through, followed by Pickleball Scott. I shifted to look at Reba. "I'll tell you later, okay?"

She swiveled her head. "Good afternoon, gentlemen."

Rats. I'd been hoping to overhear their conversation. I didn't expect Scott would remember me, and if I stayed quiet, Herbert might not recognize a bike shop owner out of context. But of course my grandmother would know Scott. Being her, by now she'd probably already met Herbert too.

I pulled my phone out and pretended to swipe through

whatever was on it. I hadn't taken off my cap. If I could stay under these dudes' radar, so much the better.

Scott turned toward us. "If it isn't Miss Reba, the prettiest lady in all of Cape Cod." The skin around his small eyes crinkled as if he was smiling, but his mouth didn't keep up. Or maybe that was what he thought a smile looked like. "Have you met my friend, Herbert Lawrence?"

"Why, yes, I have." She beamed. "Remember, Herbert? I directed you to where to find something in our little Westham Food Mart."

His shoulders tensed and tendons stood out on his neck. "Ah, yes, Ms. Almeida. Good to see you again."

"Are you enjoying your stay in our lovely town?" she asked.

"How could I not? I am riding a bicycle all over. It's a rental, but it's not too clunky."

I didn't quite kick her, but I gave her a nudge and a tiny headshake.

"That's excellent." She gave him an innocent smile. "How long will you be visiting?"

"Not for long. My business here is about wrapped up."

"And how do you know my friend Mr. Scott?" she asked.

I'd thought Scott was his first name. Live and learn.

"We had several negotiations to work out." Scott raised his chin.

"Well, I'll let you two get to your lunch," Reba said.

"Let's get in line, man," Scott said to him. "We have a game in an hour."

"Mac?" The counter boy called to me. "Your haddock sandwich is ready."

I glanced up from my faked phone business to see Herbert staring at me with pursed lips.

"Hi, there, Herbert." I smiled as I stood. "I'm glad the rental isn't too clunky. If you'll excuse me, my lunch is ready." I wove around both men, picked up my basket of lunch and the lemonade, and left several dollar bills in the cup labeled Tips.

Tulia turned to me. She glanced over my shoulder, then said, "I'll come sit with you two in a minute. Looks like things are quieting down in here."

I understood what she meant when I got back to Reba's table. Scott and Herbert had departed instead of waiting to order food. Nobody was left in line.

Reba stared at the door. "Well, if that don't beat the bugs afightin'."

"Where'd they go?" I asked her.

"I think hearing your name spooked Herbert. He said he'd changed his mind, and that a burger at the Dairy Barn sounded better. Scott gave him a look like he was nuts, but off they went."

"How do you know Scott, anyway?" I bit into my perfect sandwich.

"I heard that." Tulia strode past at the same time as Reba spoke. She flipped the sign on the door to Closed. and pointed at Reba. "I'm closing early. Don't answer Mac until I come back with my lunch. We three have some talking to do."

CHAPTER 39

By the time Tulia sat next to me with a plate towering full of fried odds and ends, I had only one bite left of my sandwich and another of coleslaw. In the back, her young employee ran water and clanked pans.

"What, do you eat up all the leftovers?" Reba pointed to Tulia's platter.

"Pretty much, after the kid has helped himself to what he wants, including a heaping lobster roll, like he did today."

"Keeping the help happy?" I asked.

"Absolutely." Tulia lowered her voice. "He's going through an awkward phase, but he's golden. Polite, on time, knows how to make change, loves seafood, and doesn't complain. He's every business owner's dream. You can bet your sweet patootie I want him to keep working for me. If the boy is hungry for the most expensive thing on my menu, he gets it."

"I hear you," I said. "I have a super reliable weekend crew, which means my Saturdays and Sundays are my own, finally. I hold my breath neither of the two decides to go work elsewhere. I can't give them a lobster roll, but I always say if one of them needs to leave early on a Sunday for a family celebration or to visit an ill friend, I can sub in."

"Now, then," Tulia said. "What happened in here a few minutes ago? Those two were perusing the menu and getting ready to order. And then, bam, they're gone. What'd you do, Reba, threaten them?"

"Who, me?" Reba's laugh was an infectious cascade of tiny bells, as always. "No, it was when Herbert Lawrence realized that the woman in the cap hiding in her phone at my table was Mac. He instantly found himself allergic to lobster, or so it seemed. I mean, who decides a burger is a better choice than a lunch from the Lobstah Shack?"

I gave them a helpless look. "Herbert brought his rental in for a brake adjustment the other day, and I might have been asking him one too many questions about Enzo, as well as about his fight with Peter Zelensky."

"As we do." Tulia smiled before dipping a morsel of fried clam into tartar sauce and popping it into her mouth. A trio of French fries got the same treatment, except in ketchup.

"Actually, it was yesterday Herbert was in Mac's Bikes," I said. "Didn't I talk about it last night, Tulia?"

"Maybe not in so much detail," Tulia said. "Reba, Mac had just asked you how you know the Scott fellow."

"I have a friend who is his ex-wife. I'm sure I've heard more about Scott than he would like generally known." Reba raised an eyebrow. "He's her ex for a reason. Has been for twenty years, and as far as I know, he's still single. But I also see him at the Y when I go for the old folks' aqua aerobics classes. The man is, shall we say, rather manic about his fitness."

"He was charming toward you, though." I savored my last bite of sandwich. "Even though I witnessed him being scathing on the pickleball court."

"He acted like that toward my friend, too, during their marriage, and especially ever since. Scathing, insulting, and manipulative. Scott and I have remained distant but friendly," Reba said. "But isn't that the mark of the sociopath or of a narcissist? They can turn on the charm and then as quickly turn it off."

"I don't suppose you have any idea how he knows Herbert?" I asked.

"No, I don't," Reba said.

"Scott and Enzo must have met on the pickleball court," Tulia pointed out.

"Yes, and I share the age group with them," Reba said. "But Herbert is considerably younger."

"Abo Ree, you called him Mr. Scott. What's his first name?" I asked.

"It's Dayton, like in Ohio. I don't know, maybe it was a family surname. He tells folks he prefers to be called Scott."

Dayton Scott. I filed away that bit of information. "Have we found out for sure if Herbert was Enzo's blood relative?"

"We have." Tulia grabbed a napkin, wiped her mouth

and hands, and pulled out her phone. "I heard back from my cousin."

"Cool," I said. "And I saw that picture of a younger Herbert with Enzo. The newspaper described him as his nephew."

Reba shot a glance at me. "Was there doubt?"

"Of course," I said. "You know how certain people use kinship terms like *uncle* or *auntie* for folks who are family by choice or friends of their parents or whatever."

Tulia snorted. "Listen to you, using words like *kinship terms*—you sound like an anthropologist or something."

"That's because it was always my dream to study and do anthropology." I smiled wistfully at my former aspirations. "I went into finance because I was good at it, and I knew I'd make a heck of a lot more money than if I were an itinerant academic. Plus, keeping numbers tidy and balanced satisfied my need for order."

"Your OCD, you mean." Reba smiled to soften calling my need by what it probably was: obsessive compulsive disorder.

"Exactly." By now I was comfortable with who I was, a neat freak of the first order and then some. "But I was always attracted to the messy world of people."

My Peace Corps years in a Thai village had been a personal challenge for sure, but also rich in a way that fed me. I stretched my brain around a new language and alphabet. I stretched my heart around new friends, including a family who watched over me. And I stretched both my world view and my personal tolerances to encompass a joyous, traditional, delicious rural culture in a tropical climate. It was definitely messy at times, but I wouldn't erase those three years for anything.

"Earth to Mac," Tulia murmured.

"Sorry." I shook myself and rejoined the present. "So, what did your cousin say?"

She read from her phone. "Lawrence applied to the base credit union for a loan. They denied it, citing his credit record. He went into the office and objected, claiming something about how he was about to inherit from his uncle, Enzo Lawrence, in Westham."

I stared at her. "When did he say that?"

"Couple weeks ago. Or maybe last month. Pretty recently, anyway."

"But not since Tuesday," I said.

"Not that recent." Tulia shook her head.

"Does your cousin work in the credit union?" Reba asked.

"No. She's active duty, but her BFF works there as a civilian."

I carefully maneuvered the last bits of coleslaw onto my fork. "Tulia, is it okay if I share with Lincoln what you told us?"

"My cuz said that would be all right."

"Good, and thank you." I stood and cleared my trash and Reba's. "Sorry to desert you both, but I have a detective to find."

Reba laid her hand on my arm. "No news about Jamie?"

I let out a noisy breath. "Not that I've heard. Lincoln said he would look into her disappearance if he could, so that's another reason for me to locate him."

"You go along," Tulia said. "I hold Jamie with God." She opened her forearms and palms to the side and closed her eyes.

Reba blew me a kiss. "Me too."

My eyes filled as I made my way out. I felt helpless to do much else but hold Jamie in some kind of blessed space.

CHAPTER 40

Out on the sidewalk, I sent Lincoln a text, asking if we could talk soon. When he didn't reply, I thought for a moment about what to do. He might have temporarily set up shop in the police station. Or maybe, judging from his presence on the pickleball court this morning, he had the day off and was spending it with Delia. It was more likely he was off pursuing a new lead in the still-active homicide case, at least I hoped he was.

I might as well check the station. It wasn't far and, like almost everything else in Westham, was located on Main Street. As I neared my shop, I broke into a smile. Riding toward me on the sidewalk was Cokey in a pink helmet. Next to her in the street rode Derrick, with a helmeted Ella strapped into the bike seat behind him. I waved as they turned into the parking lot.

"Titi Mac!" Cokey put her foot on the pavement. "We're going for a bike ride."

"I can see that." I smiled. "Hi, you three."

"This is Cokey's old seat, Auntie Mac," Ella said. "From before she learned to ride by herself. I don't know how to ride a regular bicycle yet." She wore the purple helmet I'd given Cokey when she was smaller.

"I'm sure you'll get there soon," I said. "Hey, Derr."

"Hiya, sis."

"Neli wasn't up for a bike ride?" I asked.

"No. She didn't think it would be safe to try to balance a bike and a baby bump at the same time."

"She's probably right."

"You're not working today, are you?" Derrick asked.

"No, I was just walking by. Looking for Lincoln, actually."

"Any news?" He spoke in a low murmur.

"Unfortunately, no." I glanced back at Ella, but she was chatting with Cokey and didn't seem to be listening to us. Still, I kept my voice soft. "Tim's pretty broken up about all of it."

"I'd be that way if you disappeared," he whispered. "So don't you even think about it."

"No worries on that front, bro." Not a chance I would vanish. Why would I want to walk away from all the people and work I loved? I wouldn't, but the thought brought home how unhappy Jamie must have been, how unloved she might have felt, at least back in Seattle.

"Daddy, let's go," Cokey urged.

"Yes, ma'am." To me, he added, "Good luck. See you in the morning."

"Where are you headed?" I asked Cokey.

"We're going to ride one section of the trail," my niece said. "I'm big enough now."

"You sure are. Have a fun ride," I said. "Love you guys." I was still smiling as I continued my path, Cokey's *love you* echoing in my ears.

CHAPTER 41

When I reached the bakery, it was dark inside and locked up, as it always was by midafternoon. I hoped Tim was home napping, or better, out for a long run, which was a kind of therapy for him. I didn't think we had to retrieve Luca from my parents until five o'clock.

The next side street led down to the small harbor where the appropriately named Jimmy's Harborside perched at the beginning of the pier. I'd been part of more than one Cozy Capers gathering at Jimmy's bar during what we called Happy Hour, despite the Commonwealth of Massachusetts having a law against discounted drinks during certain hours. We'd already discovered Jamie hadn't been at that bar after nine o'clock Tuesday night, but I still wanted to see the site myself. I knew it would be through a new and sadder lens. I could hit up the police station afterward.

I walked at a brisk clip down to the water. I bypassed the restaurant itself and headed out onto the pier. This harbor was relatively shallow, and the pier allowed larger boats to dock at the end. Not cruise ship larger, but the occasional luxury yacht or sailboat would park here for a few days. People loved fishing off the pier, too, and taking a stroll along its length was a popular tourist activity on summer days and evenings. A long breakwater stretched into the Atlantic, sheltering the harbor.

Today the damp air blowing off the ocean made traversing the pier a lot less fun. In fact, only a few brave souls trudged or jogged on the wide, sea-weathered boards. The pier had room for me and my thoughts. I put my head down against the wind and headed toward the end.

When I glanced up, a runner I'd seen from the back at the far end now ran hard toward me, his heels kicking up in the back, his arms pumping. I stopped. I'd know that form anywhere. That blond ponytail swinging, that Mac's Bikes–branded windbreaker, those strong legs and pink running shoes. As Tim recognized me, he slowed to a jog.

Seconds later I had my arms around him. I felt his sobs.

"Come sit down, my love." I led him to the nearest bench overlooking the sea.

He squeezed me tight, then sat. "I'm sorry, Mac. It's . . . so hard." He wiped tears and sweat from his face with his hand.

"I know." I stroked his knee and kept my hand on it.

We sat in silence for a minute. A fishing boat putt-

putted past us on its way into harbor. A small gull with black tail feathers landed on the nearest piling. It proceeded to strut back and forth on the railing, regarding us. When no food was forthcoming, it flapped away.

Tim twisted to gaze at me. "What are you doing out here, anyway?"

"I imagine for the same reason you are." I made a wide gesture that encompassed the pier as well as Jimmy's. "This is the last place we know for sure where Jamie was. I wasn't out to learn anything new in particular, but I thought an idea might come to me, just being here."

"I know. I mean, I needed a run, but for me it's also feeling her presence. That sounds nutty, but it's true."

"You're a sensitive person. It's not nutty, and I'm not surprised."

He shivered. "I need to get moving." He stood and extended his hand to me.

"You're sweaty. Of course the wind would chill you. Run home."

He swept me into an entirely satisfactory public display of affection, then murmured loving things into my ear and released me.

"See you there?" he asked.

"Eventually. I really need to find Lincoln and tell him a few things first."

"Okay. I'm picking up Luca at five at the parsonage."

"Do you want me to get him?" I asked.

"Thanks, but that's okay. I'll do it."

"I'll see you at home after that, if not before, and I'm ordering takeout sushi for our dinner."

He smiled. "I love it when you cook."

I laughed. "And I love you."

Tim headed away at a run, while I headed back at my usual knee-coddling pace. I stopped, frowning. What if he found the bag of nip bottles before I got home? I should have told him. On the other hand, he would be busy showering and going to pick up Luca. I doubted poking around in the hutch would be on his agenda.

I reached the restaurant's back deck, now empty of umbrellas, chairs, and customers for the season. I gazed upward. Were there security cameras out here? Had anyone asked? Maybe footage of the time period after Jamie left the bar would indicate if she'd left the premises for solid land or had taken a nighttime stroll on the pier. Peering up, I couldn't see the eye of a camera, but it could easily be disguised as something else. Perhaps they took cameras down until spring so they didn't suffer a battering by winter weather.

I contemplated venturing inside to inquire about a camera, but surely Lincoln already had, or maybe Tim had asked. I resolved to keep going with my plan to find the detective. Asking him about footage from Jimmy's Harborside could be the first item on my growing list.

CHAPTER 42

I approached the police department dreading that I'd encounter Victoria in action. She wouldn't approve my going in search of Lincoln. But I had to find him. I'd set my foot on the first granite step of the station when Lincoln himself pushed through the door, and he was alone. Whew.

"You're the very person I was looking for," I said.

"Afternoon, Mac. Did we have an appointment?" He trotted easily down the stairs.

"No, but I texted you a few minutes ago."

"Ah." He pulled out his phone. "I put it on mute for a meeting with your favorite chief of police." He glanced at my message and back at me. "I haven't eaten. Have you?"

"Yes."

"Come with me to the Rusty Anchor, anyway. We can talk there."

"It's a deal." Seeing Delia at the pub might be part of the reason he'd chosen it as our destination, but I didn't care. I wasn't on the clock, and I'd be happy to put distance between me and a possible encounter with Victoria. Sipping a draft beer or a hot toddy on a cold Saturday afternoon might be just the ticket.

Soon enough, I was doing exactly that in a booth near the fireplace.

"Delia isn't working this afternoon?" I inhaled the comforting smells of hops on tap and burgers on the grill.

"No." His cheeks grew pink. "Her shift begins at five. So, what do you have?"

I swallowed the first sip of my oatmeal stout, a thick, dark ale I drank only in the colder months. "I ate lunch today at the Lobstah Shack with Tulia and my grandma, and a couple of things happened I thought you would want to know."

"Please dish." Lincoln sipped the black coffee he'd ordered to go with his Southwestern chicken wrap.

"Herbert Lawrence and a man named Dayton Scott came into Tulia's restaurant together. Scott's the hyper-competitive guy from pickleball."

"Yes, I witnessed that this morning." Lincoln raised a single dark eyebrow.

"The two seemed to be friends, or at least they came in together. Reba knows Scott."

"Of course she does."

"Yep." I smiled. "She said her friend was married to him for a while, but he was awful to the friend, and they have been divorced for years. Reba described Scott as a narcissist or a sociopath."

"Strong language."

"It sounded like he deserved it," I said. "Charming one minute, scathing and insulting the next, and to his own wife, of all people."

"So noted. That description comports with what I saw of him on the court a few hours ago."

"I kind of tried to stay under their radar so I could listen to what he and Herbert were saying, but when the counter kid called my name to pick up my sandwich, Herbert realized I was there and seemed to go on high alert. By the time I was back at our table, the two had left in favor of a Dairy Barn lunch."

"You have to admit, they make a mean burger, not that I eat them any longer."

"Agreed. But anyway, several other things came out of talking with Tulia and Reba. First, Tulia's cousin is active duty at Hanscom. She knows Herbert, and her friend who works at the base credit union does too." I relayed what Tulia had said about Herbert's loan application and credit rating, and that he'd stated plainly he was Enzo's nephew.

"Interesting. We're onto the blood relations part. I can contact this cousin?"

"I think so," I said. "You'd have to ask Tulia, because I didn't get the cousin's name, but she said it was okay to tell you both bits."

"Got it. Thank you."

A purple-haired server with multiple piercings set Lincoln's lunch in front of him.

"Thanks," Lincoln said. "Hot sauce?"

"Absolutely." The server pulled a bottle out of their apron pocket and flashed Lincoln an approving smile."

Lincoln thanked them. To me, he said, "Anything else you want to share?" He bit into his wrap, which bulged with spiced chicken, cheese, jalapeños, tomatoes, and more.

"Herbert Lawrence got around today." I told Lincoln about overhearing Herbert and Shelly's argument and seeing him storm out. "And when I went back in and tried to ask Shelly about him, she told me to mind my own business."

"She's got a point there, Mac."

"Maybe." I thought back on the day. "How did your pickleball game go, by the way?"

He cocked his head. "Fine. Why?"

"You might not have seen it, but when you walked onto the court this morning, Peter Zelensky gave you a look.

"What kind of look?" Lincoln asked.

"I thought he looked alarmed. Do you have any idea why?"

"Nooo." He drew out the syllable. "But his name keeps popping up. I have a team member checking into his background other than his association with the deceased. He might have had past dealings with law enforcement that didn't go well. That's why many citizens don't care for those in my profession."

"I see. Let me know what you find out?"

"Possibly. Anything else?" He took another big bite of his lunch and made a contented sound.

"Let's see," I began. "Before you got to pickleball, I chatted with Harini for a minute. I asked if she'd played the game with Enzo. Do you know they used to date in New York?"

He shook his head.

"She didn't like me asking, not at all." I took a sip of my beer.

"You've been busy, Mac, but Shelly's right. You really need to stay out of the investigating business, you and your group. I've told you before. It's dangerous."

"We're staying safe."

He gave me a look over the top of his glasses. It didn't have the same effect as when he'd worn the heavier black rims, but I got the message.

"Okay, okay." I held up a palm. "I will retreat to doing online searches in the safety of my home." I was pretty sure he knew I was crossing the fingers of my other hand in my lap, but I had to make the effort. "To change the subject, I don't suppose you've found my sister-in-law."

"Sadly, no, but inquiries are out there. You'll be the first to know if I do."

"Tim and I were out on the pier an hour ago. I couldn't tell if there were security cameras outside. I hope Jimmy's Harborside has some. The footage could at least tell us which direction Jamie went when she left, and if she got into a vehicle or met someone—or both."

"Inquiries are ongoing."

"That doesn't sound very encouraging, but thank you, Lincoln," I said. "That's all I can ask."

What I could hope for was considerably more, although the chances of that hope being realized seemed to be dwindling by the hour.

CHAPTER 43

It wasn't until half an hour later, after Lincoln had gone back to work and I was moseying homeward that I realized Lincoln hadn't revealed a thing about the case. Why hadn't I asked about the method of death, and what he and his team had learned so far?

All I'd done was provide information. Admittedly, that had been one of my goals, and I hoped what I'd told him would further his investigations. Still, learning was always a good thing too.

How had Enzo died? Why was he outside on his deck still wearing the skeleton costume he'd been seen in the day before? Had he felt ill and crawled out there for a lungful of cold fresh air? Had his killer deposited him on the deck during the dark of night?

Too many questions. Zero answers. I thought hard about how I could get some. I sat on one of the many

Main Street benches. Norland might have picked up answers about the death by now, or he could have dug something up about Enzo's past. I composed a text to him.

Wondering re how Enzo died. Know anything?

I waited a moment, snugging my scarf closer around my neck. Our former chief of police was probably making cookies with his grandson or watching a movie with the boy and his big sister. Norland could be in his basement wood shop creating beauty, out grocery shopping, or having a beer with other retired friends. The possibilities were endless on a Saturday afternoon. What he wasn't doing was replying to my message.

As the breeze rustled the last remaining leaves on a tupelo tree and flapped the Open flag hanging from the Sand Dollar, a nearby gift shop, I idly checked for other messages and emails. The group thread had zilch for news. Same with the actual news. Interest in a Westham homicide seemed to have dwindled to barely noticeable. I might as well head home. I glanced up and blinked, surprised, to see Norland a few feet away.

"I might know a few things." He smiled as he sat next to me.

"You saw my text."

"I did, at about the same time I saw you sitting here sending it."

"Where were you headed?" I asked.

He cleared his throat and smoothed down his khaki slacks. "Meeting someone for a drink."

I took another look at him. His hair was neatly trimmed and the oxford shirt under a tweed sports coat was neatly pressed. Leather shoes finished the outfit.

Norland wasn't a slob, but his usual attire was a more relaxed, casual style, as in weathered blue jeans, sweaters or sweatshirts, and sneakers. I inhaled. Yep, that was aftershave, the applying of which was another practice Norland wasn't known for.

"Are you on your way to a date?" I gently elbowed him.

"Gah." He groaned. "Is it that obvious?"

"It's just that you look, um, more cleaned up than usual. There's nothing wrong with going out with someone, by the way. What's the lucky lady's name?"

"Uh-uh, Mac." He shook his head. "Too soon. It's only our second date."

"But you're hoping for more." I kept my voice gentle.

"I confess I am. I'm pretty sure Maireth wouldn't mind. In fact, she told me outright I should find someone else when I was ready."

Norland's beloved wife had died three years ago. After his initial grief, he'd settled into the life of a retired police chief, grandfather, and cozy mystery book group member. I'd thought he wasn't interested in finding romance and intimacy again, and I was happy to be proved wrong. It was funny that both Norland and Lincoln had spruced up their appearance in the name of love. I was all for it.

"Anyway, I'm early, and you have questions," he said.

"I do, but first let me say how happy I am for you." I smiled. "Now, back to the questions. I shared a few bits from my day with Lincoln in the pub not too long ago. After I left, I realized I hadn't asked if they've figured out how Enzo died, and how and why he was outside on his deck still in costume. Do you know?"

"I've heard through the grapevine that he appears to have had an allergic reaction to something."

I frowned. "Like a beesting? I suppose he could have been injected with whatever he was allergic to." Why wouldn't he carry an EpiPen like I did?

"Not sure it was from being injected."

"That's odd, isn't it? I mean, they think it was homicide. So the killer would have had to rub something in Enzo's face or make him inhale whatever he was allergic to, which must have been a substance most people don't have a reaction to. Or maybe it was a poison."

"Exactly," Norland said. "As to where his corpse was found, do you know what livormortis is?"

"Um, no."

"After someone's heart stops beating, their blood stops circulating. The blood in the body pools in a downward direction, because of gravity, and it stains the tissues and skin." He glanced at me.

"I'm with you so far."

"The staining generally doesn't start for about two hours after death, but it can indicate if a corpse has been moved. For example, if you find a body lying on their stomach with staining on the back, you know the deceased has been moved."

"Hmm. Lincoln said a few days ago there was something odd about the position of Enzo's body."

Norland nodded. "I believe they found staining that didn't correspond to the position of the corpse."

"But why in the world would he be wearing a costume on the day after Halloween?" I asked.

"I'd say all signs point to him being killed the evening before. What time did you say you saw the skeleton in the bank drive-through?"

"It was around six o'clock." I caught movement out of the corner of my eye and turned my head. "Uh-oh."

"Oh-oh what?" he asked.

"Your successor is headed in our direction and she doesn't look happy."

Victoria strode toward us with her brisk, short-legged gait. A moment later she stood in front of the bench, feet slightly apart in a stance many police officers seemed to favor. Instead of swinging a fist into the other palm—also favored by police—she jammed her hands in her uniform jacket.

"Good afternoon, Victoria," Norland said in a mild tone.

"Chief, Mac."

"How's the baby?" I knew she'd been out on maternity leave in the summer, but I'd never heard if she'd had a girl or a boy. Whichever it was, her baby would be a month or two older than Luca.

My question seemed to throw her.

"What?" She blinked.

"I asked how your baby's doing."

Her voice softened. "He's fine. Putting on weight like nobody's business. And smiling."

"A baby's smile is all it takes," Norland said. "It's the best thing in the world, at least until they laugh. No heart is immune from that."

I expected he was referring to the heart of the usually hard-nosed, diminutive woman standing in front of us. She'd had to fight hard for recognition and promotion in the nearly all-male police department. I knew from experience that having sharp edges was nothing new to Victoria Laitinen.

"So I've heard," she said.

"What's his name?" I asked.

"Miko. It's Finnish." She cleared her throat. "Now, then. I've had complaints about you, Mac. You need to cut out your amateur efforts at solving this homicide, you understand?"

"Who has been complaining?" I asked.

"Several residents and visitors. You have to stop. You could be putting yourself and others in danger."

I smiled up at her. "Thank you for the warning." I expected *visitors* meant Herbert Lawrence.

"Honestly." Frowning, Victoria shook her head. "Norland, can't you talk some sense into her?"

"I'll see what I can do."

The current Westham chief of police turned on her heel and nearly stomped away, muttering as she went.

"Why do I get the treatment from her and you don't?" I asked. "She must know you're in the book group too."

"Because I'm so handsome, maybe?" He preened, then laughed.

"Seriously, though. You don't get in trouble from former colleagues for your amateur sleuthing?

"Not so far, which is fine with me." Norland stood. "I've got to get along, but you know she's right, Mac. It's dangerous to be asking questions of anybody who even remotely might have wanted Enzo out of the way."

"Yes, sir." I gave him a mock salute and then stood. "Have a fabulous date."

A soft look came into his eyes. "I plan to."

All this love going around—for babies, for new lovers, for former spouses—was extra important with a killer also on the loose. It made me want to get home to my own beloved as fast as I could.

CHAPTER 44

I gazed down at a milk-laden Luca at about seven o'clock that evening. I'd fed him his bottle, half of which he'd sucked down with his eyes closed. Was the poor little guy now an orphan? I didn't dare voice the thought aloud.

I didn't imagine Jamie had been murdered, but the same rule of thumb about elapsed time had to apply. The longer a case went without developments, the lower the likelihood that the truth would come out. In a homicide, every day that went by without an arrest reduced the chances that the guilty party would be charged.

For a missing person, it was one more day for any of the possible scenarios. Jamie could be farther away and had hardened her resolve not to return. She could be more and more ill. Or, if she was deceased, her body must be somewhere unlikely to be discovered if it hadn't been by now. None were what we wanted, but one scenario was the actual one. Unfortunately, I didn't think there were any others.

We hadn't gotten any hits from the posters we'd put up, and the last time I checked the Westham social media site, nobody had reported spotting Jamie.

I stroked the baby's silky hair and waited for Tim to come back from picking up the sushi order I'd called in. Was Victoria stroking her own son's hair right now? I'd been shocked last spring when I realized she was pregnant. I'd known she was married, but her personal life was otherwise unknown to me. She'd always presented herself as rigid and cool, and it was hard to reconcile that with her having a home life happy and functional enough to want to bring a child into it.

I set the baby's empty bottle on the table and took a sip of the chardonnay Tim had poured me before he left. Thinking about Victoria brought me to what Norland and I had been talking about when she showed up. Enzo had been killed by something he was allergic to. That was a new piece of information to fit into the puzzle. But what was the allergen, and how had it been administered?

Norland hadn't shared that news with the group, which surprised me. Maybe his date went so well it hadn't occurred to him to communicate with us about murder. His budding romance made me smile all over again, that is, until I checked the clock. Where in the world was Tim? Yoshinoya was at most a ten-minute drive into town.

I brought my free hand to my mouth as my breath

rushed in. What if he'd had an accident? Was he okay? I swallowed down the lump in my throat. I'd lived for years as a self-sufficient single person. Now? I couldn't imagine life without him. What should I do? I could put the baby in his portacrib and make a few calls.

No. I needed to get a grip. It was Saturday night. The restaurant was probably backed up, and the estimate they'd given me for a pickup time had been way off. Maybe he'd had a flat tire. Or, best case, he'd seen Jamie and was convincing her to come home. I wasn't sure why my thoughts always went to the worst possible thing that could have happened, but I knew I needed to work on changing my reaction.

Luca stirred and whimpered. *Oh.* I was transmitting my tension to him. I relaxed the hand gripping him, along with my shoulders, and began quietly singing a Portuguese lullaby Pa had sung to me when I was little. The lyrics were something about telling the bogeyman to get lost and let the baby sleep. The song worked its timeless magic, putting the baby in my arms back to sleep and keeping me as unstressed as possible under the circumstances.

Five minutes later, Tim bustled in carrying a bag smelling faintly of the sea, tangy sushi rice, and deliciousness, plus another bag. He kissed my forehead, giving both me and the baby a loving smile, then popped the second bag into the freezer.

"Sorry, sweetheart," he said in a low voice. "The place was overbooked and understaffed." He set down the bag and washed his hands, then held out his arms. "I'll put him down and be right back."

I did not mention the terrors my imagination had conjured, nor my thoughts about the prospects for finding his missing sister.

As I waited for him to return, I lit the planned candles and transferred the sushi to a pretty platter. Miso soup got poured into small enameled bowls, and I laid a pair of nice chopsticks on each napkin near tiny shallow soy sauce bowls. I didn't like to eat off of the cheap wooden chopsticks the restaurant provided. By the time Tim returned, I was setting down the cruet of soy sauce. I held up an empty wineglass.

"What's your preference tonight? A fine California chardonnay or a Cape Brews pilsner?"

"Wine is fine." He sank into his chair and rubbed his face with his hands.

"Are you okay?" I filled his glass and sat.

He straightened, taking my hand. "Yes. Let's enjoy our time together." He poured soy sauce into each dipping bowl.

And we did enjoy our time. He filled me in on Mom's report about Luca's day. I told him of meeting Derrick and the girls on their bike ride. Tim related a few things about plans for the bakery for the coming week, and I mentioned learning about Norland dipping his toe into the senior dating scene. We both left facts and fears about homicide and missing persons out of the conversation.

"One thing Astra told me was that we can slide Ella into the church preschool if we want," Tim said.

"That could be really helpful. What about Luca?"

"They also have a slot that opened up in the baby

care program." He maneuvered a piece of sushi topped with salmon into his mouth.

While it wasn't great that we had to make plans for childcare until Jamie returned, I was glad Tim was facing the reality that both of us were small business owners. He had to be on the job as much as I did.

And if his sister didn't return, well, Tim was already named as the children's guardian in case anything happened to her. Would he and I morph into de facto parents overnight?

I dipped the last piece of cucumber roll into soy sauce and savored it. Tim finished the remaining maguro sushi and sipped his wine. I nibbled on a pickled ginger slice. He covered his mouth halfway through a big yawn.

"I'm sorry, Mac. I really should get some sleep. The little one is going to want another bottle in a couple of hours. The schedule and the stress are both taking a toll on me."

"I can do the night shift if you want."

"I'll manage it, but I wondered if you would take care of the baby in the morning. My Sunday baker asked for the day off weeks ago, and I need to go in early until about ten."

"Of course. You do what you have to do. I'm happy to pull morning shift with Luca." I leaned over for a kiss. "Go sleep."

"I will. Also, a quart of green tea ice cream is in the freezer for you."

"What?" I exclaimed. "That's my favorite."

He smiled as he stood. "I happen to know that. Don't forget, tonight is the time change."

I groaned. "It's fall, so we fall back an hour. I wish they would pick a time and stick with it all year round."

"I should say something clever about wishes, but I'm too tired to come up with an appropriate adage."

I blew him a kiss as he left the kitchen. I couldn't come up with a saying, either. At least these days our phones and devices adjusted to the change from daylight to standard time automatically, but the shift always gave me a case of jet lag without the benefit of travel.

CHAPTER 45

I cleaned up, including Luca's bottle, and started the dishwasher, which blessedly was a super quiet model. When it was only Tim and me, we often did the dishes by hand, but it seemed important for the bottles and nipples to get the extra treatment, even if the machine wasn't full.

Smiling, I scooped out a bowl of ice cream. Tim was a darling to remember how much I loved the delicate flavor. Green tea ice cream wasn't widely available in markets, but the Japanese restaurant made their own and sold quarts to interested customers. It was a treat of the first order.

I settled in at the table with the bowl and my phone, savoring the treat as I swiped through the news and a bit of social media. I ended up at the Cozy Capers text thread and summarized to my friends what I'd learned during the day, investigation-wise. I first relayed the gossip column I'd read, which linked Enzo and Harini. She was my action item, after all. I added that she hadn't been happy with my asking her about knowing Enzo in New York.

I then mentioned the pickleball game and the man named Scott. I told them about seeing Herbert and Shelly arguing in the costume shop, and Shelly telling me to butt out. I added what happened at the Lobstah Shack, including Herbert and Scott knowing each other, and that the two split after Herbert realized who I was. I didn't message that I hadn't picked up one thing from Lincoln, because this was about stating what I *had* learned.

Should I include what Norland told me? I went ahead and added it. He wouldn't have shared the information about Enzo's death with me if it was a secret.

And Victoria told me to stop snooping too.

Gin replied, **As if! And of course she did.**

I laughed softly. Speaking of action items, Flo's was Peter Zelensky, and we hadn't heard a peep out of her. I texted about his reaction to seeing Lincoln this morning, then added a question.

Flo, any info about Peter?

She didn't respond. In fact, nobody but Gin seemed to be paying attention to the texts.

My phone, which I'd set to mute, vibrated with an incoming call from Gin.

"Hey, what's up?" I asked, keeping my voice low.

"Can I stop by?"

"Of course. But Tim and the baby are asleep, so come to the back door, okay?"

"Sure."

Five minutes later I let her in. "Wine, tea, Scotch? Or Scotch in your tea?"

She eyed my squat glass holding a half inch of whiskey. "What you're having, but only a finger."

I poured, adding a flick of water, and set it on the kitchen table in front of her. I took the chair opposite.

"Cheers." She lifted her glass.

I clinked mine against it. "Cheers, and here's to getting answers sometime soon." I tasted mine.

Gin took a small sip, then set down her glass. "I know you don't have to drive anywhere, but I thought you were drinking less alcohol because of trying to get pregnant."

"In general, yes. But since I got my period yesterday . . ." I pulled a rueful smile.

"You have a week or two to indulge. I'm sorry, Mac."

"Eh. What can you do?" I shrugged. I would be more than happy to abstain from drinking for the next nine months. I could always hope for next month, and it was a topic I would discuss with my nurse practitioner at my next physical in January. "So, where's your man tonight?"

"Eli's off at a conference in Minneapolis, along with a few hundred other ocean-researcher nerds." She smiled. "He asked if I wanted to come along. Go to a place colder than here and have to socialize with science geeks? I said thanks, but no thanks."

"I'm not surprised."

"I told him I'd rather stay home and make candy." She smiled. "And speaking of candy, I might have a small answer with respect to the case."

Ooh. "Dish, please."

"Shelly came into my shop at the end of the afternoon. She said she needed reinforcements."

"Because sewing is hard work?"

"What?" Gin asked.

"When I was inside Cape Costumers today, she was busy making a custom outfit."

"I get it. Anyway, I pointed out the new peanut butter fudge," Gin went on. "Shelly got the saddest expression on her face. She looked like she was about to cry."

"Peanut butter fudge is tragic? I don't understand," I said.

"Hang on and hear me out. I asked her what was wrong. She said her boyfriend had been violently allergic to peanuts."

"Her late boyfriend, otherwise known as homicide victim, Enzo."

"Exactly." Gin took another sip. "And when you texted that thing Norland told you about how Enzo died, I figured you'd want to hear what Shelly said."

"You could have texted it to the group."

"I know. But isn't this more fun?"

"Absolutely." I bobbed my head. "Do you think Shelly knows Enzo died from an allergic reaction?"

"I'm not sure. If she killed him, you can bet she does."

I made a sound in my throat. "You mean she could have faked the weepy stuff."

"Isn't that what murderers do? Fake the emotions? We've seen it before, Mac."

"We have, many times."

"Somebody killed him. It could have been her."

I tapped the side of my glass. "If it was peanuts he died from, I wonder how the killer forced Enzo to ingest them. I mean, you can't force-feed someone peanut butter, right?"

"No. And I would think it'd be hard to disguise the taste." She got a dreamy look in her eyes. "For those of us who love the stuff, the taste is part of the pleasure. When I was growing up, the ice cream place in my town had a chocolate–peanut butter milkshake on the menu. Mac, it was to die for."

I shuddered.

"Gah," Gin said. "I shouldn't have used that phrase. But." She tapped her glass. "What if the murderer offered Enzo a milkshake that had so much dark chocolate in it he couldn't detect the peanuts?"

"Maybe," I said. "The only allergies besides beestings that I know about are my own violent sneezing and hives when I'm around cats and dogs. Anyway, I would think you'd need a lot of peanut butter in a dish or a milkshake to have a fatal reaction to it. But anaphylactic shock is scary."

"I remember that time the bee stung you when we were out walking. If you hadn't had the EpiPen with you, things would have gone down a lot worse."

"Exactly. I wonder why he didn't have one, unless he was careless about it."

"Could be."

"You're going to let Lincoln know what Shelly said, yes?"

"Of course." Gin tilted her head. "Except, if the police already know Enzo died of an allergic reaction, they've probably also requested his medical records."

"True. Still, more information is always good." I suppressed a yawn. "Sorry. It's been a long day."

"I'll let you get your beauty sleep." She drained her glass and stood. "I know I need mine."

"Thanks. I do have to get to bed. I landed the early shift with Luca tomorrow."

"Have fun with babykins. You don't have both kids?"

"No, Ella was invited to sleep over at Cokey's. Derrick and Nelinda are the ones with two kiddos tonight."

"Thanks for the drink and the company." Gin gave me a hug. "I'll text Lincoln the minute I get home, and I'll share it on the thread. Sweet dreams."

"You, too, and drive safely." I locked the door after her.

But it was only nine thirty, and I didn't go straight up to bed. Instead, I poured a whisper more whiskey and fired up my tablet. I felt an urge to dig more deeply into various allergic reactions and what caused them.

CHAPTER 46

I managed my morning one-on-one with the baby quite nicely. Luca was sweetly cheery when he woke up, and with more light in the early morning, I was in a better mood than if it had been dark. The murky late afternoons were a different story, but at least today we'd be in the well-lit, warming embrace of family dinner at the parsonage.

After a clean diaper and a bottle, we sat and cuddled. I read him a couple of Ella's picture books and one I'd brought back from Thailand, thinking I would read it to my own baby. When Luca began to get cranky, we walked laps in the house as I sang the few lullabies I knew. When I ran out of those, I switched to Christmas carols. He didn't care what the words were.

When I got to "Jingle Bells," Belle began imitating the refrain, except all she sang was, "Jingle Belle, jingle Belle."

"It's *bells*, Belle." I laughed. Truly, how would she know? There were no other Belles in her world, or any other most likely. I didn't correct her version again.

By nine thirty, Mr. Luca was back asleep in his temporary crib. This wasn't so hard, really.

I had switched off even vibrating notifications on my phone for the night, with exceptions set for Tim, my parents, and Derrick. Doing so meant I'd missed a flurry of activity on the group thread.

Wow. I grabbed another cup of coffee and headed back into the living room so I could hear the little guy when he awoke. I put my feet up on the coffee table to read.

Flo wrote that her contact hadn't gotten back to her about Peter, but that she would keep pinging her. Norland said he'd checked into the Cape theater company Enzo had acted with.

E had reputation for being pushy when it came to roles he wanted. Caused bad feelings with other actors incl Peter Z.

Peter had alluded to exactly that, although I hadn't known he acted too.

I now saw that Gin had told the group what she'd learned from Shelly about Enzo's peanut allergy. With any luck Gin had also communicated the information to Lincoln. I thought about yesterday in the Lobstah Shack and added a message to the thread.

Might need to look into ill-tempered Dayton Scott, how he knows Herbert. Anybody know him beyond pickleball?

Norland chimed in.

I can take him on. Only person on my list is dead.

I smiled and shot him a quick thanks. Flo added a note.

Didn't you say Reba knows him, Mac? Ask her?

Duh. Why didn't I think of that?

Will do, at dinner tnite.

My thoughts went back to Shelly and what Xavier had said about her.

Flo, can we go to Brnstbl tomorrow? I want to ask Xavier more re Shelly and also check her property info at courthouse.

She replied right away.

No. Can't vary regular day at prison. I'll check on-line.

I texted her a thumbs-up emoji. Whatever Xavier knew about Shelly would have to wait.

Gin didn't seem to be online at the moment, and Tulia hadn't popped in, either. Well, it was Sunday morning.

A message pinged into the group from Zane.

Just popping in to say hi! The twins say hi too.

He added a photo of him holding his children. The baby in a pale green sleeper slept in the crook of his left arm and the one in yellow in his right. I wrote directly back.

Adorable! No blue and pink for them?

No. Trying to avoid gender stereotypes as long as we can.

I studied the photo. The kiddo in green had a sweet face and long dark eyelashes. The one in yellow had a bigger head and less hair. I tapped out a question.

Boy in yellow, girl in green?

Haha—see? No, the opposite!

I laughed softly. *Touché*, Zane.

My bad, LOL. They're both beautiful.

I added a heart emoji and sent it. Norland did the same, and Tulia sent a string of little symbols, including a thumbs-up, a heart, a unicorn, a rose, praying hands, a teddy bear, and a smiling face surrounded by hearts. Flo sent an open book emoji as well as a message.

Let me know when you need more baby books. Library has a slew.

I knew reading books to babies and children of all ages was one of the best things the adults in their lives could do. For myself, I couldn't remember a time when I wasn't surrounded by books.

Zane said goodbye and left the conversation. I finished my coffee, wondering what else the group and I could look into without putting ourselves in danger. I might not have promised Lincoln to stay away from investigating, but nobody wanted to be assaulted, least of all me.

At a sound from the kitchen, my shoulders tensed. It was followed a second later by Tim in the doorway, a smudge of flour on his cheek.

"I'm home, hon." He spoke softly. "He's out?"

I relaxed as I nodded and put away my phone. "Fell asleep about an hour ago."

"Awesome, and thank you." He kissed my forehead and ruffled my hair. "I'm going to grab a quick shower. Fresh sourdough boule in the kitchen whether you've eaten or not. It's still warm, and I also made rolls to bring to family dinner."

"You're right. I did forget to eat, and you're an angel."

"Takes one to know one." He disappeared into the bedroom.

The sound of running water filtered in a minute later from what I sometimes thought of as our skeleton bathroom. Not that it wasn't fully equipped and lovely, but because of the decades-old skeleton we'd found in the wall last winter as we'd begun demolition prior to building out the space.

Me, I pointed myself toward a slice of warm, chewy, crusty bread slathered with good butter. If I was an angel, Tim's bread was pure heaven. As was the prospect of spending the rest of the day with him. Derrick would bring Ella to family dinner at the end of the afternoon, so today was me, my favorite man, and my new favorite baby.

CHAPTER 47

So much for making plans. Sunday at one thirty found me at Mac's Bikes. Edwin had called my cell saying he seemed to have contracted either food poisoning or a vicious stomach bug. Sofia had asked long ago for the day off, so I had no choice. I'd changed my clothes and hurried down there.

"You go home this minute, my friend," I said.

Edwin's face was pale and his voice shaky. "Thanks, Mac. I'm sorry, but . . ."

"Don't worry. Just go."

He rushed out and drove away. In case whatever he had was infectious, I grabbed a few disinfecting wipes and cleaned the counter and the pens in a can near the register. I also wiped off the exit door handle, the one to the bathroom, and the handle on the mini-fridge.

One couldn't be too careful, especially considering we had children at home with us.

I perched on the stool behind the counter and considered the rest of the day. Family dinner at my parents' began at five, but any of us was always welcome to show up earlier. I'd told Tim I would meet him and Luca there. At the moment, my shop was empty and quiet. If it stayed that way, I could close early, unless rentals were due in.

Pulling the rentals book toward me, I flipped it open to today. And groaned. Rental contracts for four bikes expired today, and the renters had until five o'clock to bring them in. I'd be here for the duration. Not only that, but because of the time change, it would be dark when I locked up, as it would be every day at that time for the next couple of months. I'd forgotten to change the due-back time to four o'clock. On the spot I added a note to the book to change that going forward.

I wasn't totally comfortable with being in the shop alone, especially in the dark, particularly not with an unsolved homicide in town. It couldn't be helped. With any luck, the returners would show up early or call and ask for an extension. At least the parsonage was only a five-minute walk away.

The shop's *empty and quiet* status changed a minute later. I sold a tire patch kit and a bottle of chain lubricant. A woman dropped off a tandem scheduled for a tune-up tomorrow. A couple ordered two pedal-less balance bikes, one in pink, one in blue, for their twin grandchildren. These were not people interested in avoiding gender stereotypes, and I didn't try to talk them out of their color choices.

A couple returned their rentals at about three thirty, but that left two returns outstanding. I puttered around as the shop emptied. I straightened merchandise and answered a call about buying an adult three-wheeler, which we had in stock now that I'd canceled Enzo's order. I checked the shipping status of an overdue order for helmets. I showed a few lean twentysomethings our array of customized biking shirts and jackets, then happily sold to all of them.

As suddenly as it had gotten busy, my shop was empty and quiet again. I glanced at the group thread, but nothing new had come in. My gaze drifted to the wall clock, which was made from bike gears, with a brake lever and a spoke as the hands.

Wait, what? The spoke that was the minute hand pointed to six, but the lever representing the hour hand sat at a little after five, not four. It couldn't already be five thirty, could it? I checked the time on my phone.

Doh. I smacked my forehead. This was an analog clock that required adjusting twice a year. I lifted the timekeeper off the wall and brought it into the current era, that is, Eastern Standard Time. The door opened again as I was rehanging the clock.

I turned to see Dayton Scott clomp in wearing biking shoes, stretchy long pants under a bike-cut jacket, and a helmet. I didn't think he'd ever come in before, unless it had been on a weekend when I wasn't here.

"Welcome to Mac's Bikes, sir. I'm Mac. How can I help you?"

"I think my pedal's broken. If you'll hold the door, I'll bring the bike in."

"You can show me outside." Once again, I had no desire to be indoors alone with a man well-known for being ill-tempered. I grabbed a small toolkit from under the counter.

"All right," he said.

He opened the door and went through but held it for me, flashing me what he must think was a charming smile, except I couldn't decide if it was a leer or he'd tasted something rotten. Outside, the sky was already growing dim, and I was glad for the motion detector light. I squatted to examine his pedal, which hung at a tilt from the crank arm.

"I think it's simply loose." I fished out the correct wrench and applied it to the problem. I pressed on the pedal, which held firm, then pushed up to standing. "You're all set, Dayton."

"What do I owe you, ma'am? Wait a minute." The corners of his mouth drew down and he curled his top lip. "How did you know my name?"

"Aren't you Dayton Scott?"

"Yes, but . . ." His voice trailed off. He squinted at me. "You were in that seafood joint yesterday."

"I was." I smiled. "I was sitting at a table with my grandmother when you came in with your friend, Herbert. You both left so suddenly, you didn't have a chance to order."

"Herb, ah, had an appointment he'd forgotten about."

"I hope he's doing okay after the death of his uncle. How do you know Herbert? I mean, I know he doesn't live around here because he rented a bike from us last week."

"He and I have done some business together." He lifted his chin and avoided my gaze. "And Herb's fine, by the way."

"I'm glad to hear it. Did you know Enzo?"

His nostrils flared and his lips squeezed, as if he'd tasted rotten lobster. "If you'll excuse me, I need to get going."

"Of course. Anyway, if you referred Herbert to my shop, I appreciate it."

"I didn't. And I asked you before, *Mac*." He stressed my name as if he didn't believe a woman could be named that. "What do I owe you?"

"No charge, *Dayton*." Two could play at that game. "Enjoy your ride. You have a light, I hope?"

"Thank you, I do." He climbed on the bike. "I prefer to be called Scott." He rode away into the dusky afternoon.

He hadn't switched on a light of any kind, not on the bike, not on his helmet or sleeve. I shook my head. His choice, his life.

Right now my choice for my life was to carry out my closing routine in a fully lit shop. I brought in the outside display bikes and went back to take down the Open flag, locking the door behind me. Rental returns could knock if they happened to show up in the next fifteen minutes.

I wished I'd been able to weasel out of Scott more details about how he knew Herbert, about the business he said they'd done together. I would next time, if there was one. I halfway wondered if Scott had loosened the pedal himself. All it needed was a simple tightening. Had he known I was there alone and wanted to get inside my shop? But why?

CHAPTER 48

"**M**om, these are fantastic." I popped another crispy, chewy crab appetizer into my mouth in the parsonage kitchen. As fate would have it, my rental returns had shown up at four fifty-five. I didn't make it over here until five twenty, which was two minutes ago.

"Thank you, darling. It's a new recipe I found called Crabbies. They're easy to make, and if you double the recipe, they freeze well to serve at the next occasion."

"Will you send Tim the recipe?"

Astra laughed. "Spoken like a true Virgo."

"And a woman whose mother never insisted she learn to cook."

"That too." She lifted her jelly jar of red wine. "Cheers."

I clinked my own with hers. I sipped, then inhaled. "Cheers. It smells fabulous in here." Something baked, something fried, something savory, and possibly also something made of apple: all those scents filled my nose.

"Doesn't it? Besides the Crabbies, dinner is your father's homemade oven-fried fish sticks, plus my winter squash soup and Tim's rolls, and Neli baked an apple crisp. Your grandmother brought fresh apple cider too."

"Almost all of which both girls should like, am I right?"

"You got it." She lowered her voice. "What sweet children Jamie's Ella and Luca are. You can tell their mama did her best." She swiped at her eyes.

"She did, and with any luck, she'll continue to." I reached an arm around my bighearted mother and squeezed her shoulders. "Is everybody here?"

"Indeed they are. The girls are in the playroom with Tucker getting up to who knows what, and a handsome man is giving a baby boy his bottle."

"Tim?"

She laughed. "He fits the bill, but so does your father. Joseph insisted on doing the feeding."

She was correct. My husband and my dad were both handsome in entirely different ways, and both also adored children of any age.

"Can I do anything to help?" I asked.

"No, honey, I think we're good. Derrick set the table. Actually, you can see if Neli wants more cider or if anyone needs their wine topped up or another beer."

"I'm on it." I grabbed one more appetizer and my glass.

In the living room, Neli leaned toward Reba in adjacent chairs and showed her something on her phone. Derrick and Tim bookmarked Pa on the couch, where

Luca was eagerly drinking his liquid dinner. Girl giggles and doggie yips filtered in from the family room in back. I loved that my parents had never turned the room into anything fancier than a child-friendly den, which it always had been.

What was missing from the scene was Jamie. She'd been here last week. Did Mom's tears mean she had a sense Jamie wasn't coming back? I had to admit, I was feeling that way, too, although I wouldn't say so to Tim. He was suffering enough as it was.

"Does anyone need a drink top-up?" I asked the assemblage.

Hearing only a chorus of "No, thanks," and "I'm good," I headed to the den, which had fallen quiet.

"Hey, girls," I began, but when I saw Cokey sitting in the play corner with her arms around a tearstained Ella, I hurried over and knelt in front of them. "What's wrong, honey?"

Ella turned and buried her face in my lap.

"She misses her mommy," Cokey said.

My own eyes welled up. "Of course she does." I boosted Ella up to sit on my lap and wrapped my arms around her, smoothing her hair off her forehead. "Of course you do, sweetie."

"I told her it would be okay," Cokey added.

"Everybody here loves you, Ella." I couldn't bring myself to say that her mother would be coming back. "Uncle Tim and Cokey and me and everybody. You know that, right?"

She nodded without looking up, but her sobbing stopped. Tucker lay his paw on her leg. Ella reached out a hand to stroke his head.

"Do you want to play with my new stuffie?" Cokey proffered a cheery green creature that might have been an extra round mouse. "Abo Joe brought her from a trip he went on."

"What's her name?" Ella asked.

"She's Koko, Totoro's sister." Cokey picked up a well-loved stuffed osprey I'd given her a year or two ago. "And I'll play with Ossie. Let's pretend they're cousins, like you and me."

"Okay." Ella slid off my lap, her anguish disappearing as fast as it arose.

I left them to play happily, thanks to Cokey's big-hearted empathy and Ella's young resilience. Back in the living room, Abo Reba sat alone on the couch. I sank down next to her and took a sip of wine.

"Everything okay in there?" she asked in a quiet voice.

I glanced at Tim. "Everything's fine."

"Any news about the you-know-what?" Her gaze was as intense and curious as ever.

"Not really." I twisted up a knee to face her. "Can you tell me any more about Dayton Scott?"

"You mean, as in would he have done the deed to Enzo?"

I nodded.

"I wouldn't put it past him, but he would have needed a good reason," she said. "I can't imagine what that would be."

"Motive is one of the all-important things. Scott was in the bike shop this afternoon. He sure didn't like me calling him by his first name. I asked him how he knew

Herbert Lawrence, but all he would say is that they had business together."

"Maybe the nephew did it and this so-called business of Scott's was aiding and abetting him. Had you thought of that?"

I stared at her. "I had not."

Reba shrugged. "Seems like it could be possible."

"It absolutely could. I was also thinking about Peter Zelensky. Do you—?"

Mom emerged from the kitchen and set a platter of food on the dining table, which was at the other end of the room we were in.

"Soup's on, darlings," Astra announced, then raised her voice and called toward the den. "Girls? Dinner's ready. Run and wash your hands. Derrick, help me with the rest?"

He stood and followed Mom into the kitchen.

"I might have something on Peter," my grandma murmured to me. "Give me a call tomorrow if we don't get a chance tonight, yeah?"

I gave her a nod. Right now, investigating a murder rightly needed to take a back seat to family.

CHAPTER 49

I raced through my opening checklist at nearly nine o'clock the next morning. At home, I'd been responsible for both children. Tim had gone off to the bakery at his usual early time, and somehow I'd managed to get both Ella and Luca fed and ready for the day. Belle had actually helped, singing "Jingle Belle" and sending Ella into peals of laughter.

We walked over to the parsonage at a brisk pace, with Ella standing on the back of the stroller. I'd dropped them off to my parents a few minutes ago. My little sports car didn't have a back seat, where child car seats belonged. The weather was fair but not particularly warm, so I'd made sure both children were bundled up. I'd packed up diapers and bottles for the day for the baby and a couple of changes of clothing for Ella. Mom and Pa were going to take over and deliver the little ones to the day care and preschool she'd found them spots in, and my mother had also said she would supply formula as well as Ella's lunch.

But now I was running late on my own day and felt frazzled. I was sure that was how most parents felt on a daily basis. If Jamie didn't return, this would be our weekday routine for the foreseeable future. I'd better get used to the schedule and the demands on my skill set and patience quotient. It also occurred to me that I'd have to trade in Miss M for a much more practical ride.

In addition, I was coming to realize that being obsessed with tidiness in all aspects of my life simply wasn't going to fly if Tim and I had to take over permanent charge of our niece and nephew. Kids weren't neat. They made messes, and life threw up unpredictable obstacles. Children got sick. They had minds of their own. They grew and changed. I faced steep personal challenges if I was going to become an instant auntie-mom to those two. Was anything more worth it? I didn't think so.

I hung out the Open flag, the last item on the list, and stood looking up and down the street for a moment. Would Jamie come sauntering up, taking a drag off a cigarette as if nothing had happened, as if she hadn't been missing for nearly a week? We would welcome her with open arms—and possibly a therapy appointment—if she came back.

A cold wind rustled through the few remaining leaves on the big swamp oak guarding the parking lot and made me shiver. I cut short my fantasizing and headed inside.

Delia reported for work at nine thirty, the time we'd agreed on for her shift. Orlean pushed through the door a moment later. My mechanic, as usual, muttered a greeting and pushed straight through to the repair area. Delia hung up her coat.

"Where would you like me this morning, Mac?"

I was pleased how well Delia integrated into our team. She'd quickly picked up a lot of the jargon about bikes, tossing off terms like crank arm and adjusting barrel. She'd learned the store layout in short order and seemed to enjoy chatting up customers. As far as I was concerned, she could work here full time if she wanted, but I would confirm with Orlean before offering.

We had a steady stream of shoppers, renters, and folks seeking repairs until about eleven. When the place was empty except for the three of us, Delia sidled up to me behind the counter.

"I heard something interesting last night at the bar," she began.

"You were working?"

"I was. Tending bar and serving, like always." She glanced around, but we were still alone in the main shop, and Orlean whistled as she worked in the repair room. "Those costume shop ladies were having a drink, but they also were arguing while they were there."

My eyebrows flew up. "Harini and Shelly."

"The same. They came in after dinner, maybe eight o'clock, and sat on barstools. I served one a Cosmo and the other wanted a chocolate martini."

"Which actually bears no resemblance to a martini."

"Totally, but to each her own, right?" She laughed. "So, which is the one with the perfect posture, even at her age?"

"That's Harini Whitt. She used to dance ballet professionally."

"She looks the part," Delia said. "Anyway, she was telling Shelly that she wasn't doing it any more. Harini said she didn't care what Shelly told anyone, including the police."

"That's more than interesting," I said. "I mean, they're business partners, but I wonder what else is going on that might involve the police?"

"Seriously. What is it that she doesn't care if Shelly reveals?" Delia leaned closer. "Don't you think it has to be about the murder?"

"That's the feeling I have, but feelings aren't evidence. At all. Did they say anything else?"

"I was back and forth a lot with other customers. I thought I heard Shelly talk about cleaning up oil. Or peanut butter. Something like that." She narrowed her eyes, thinking. "And there was something about a camera."

"That all sounds so random. A camera? Oil? Peanut butter? Wait." My eyes went wide. "Enzo was apparently deathly allergic to peanuts. My friend Gin found out."

"He must have been killed that way," Delia whispered.

"Shelly and Harini wouldn't have any reason to clean up peanut oil, if that's what they were arguing about, unless they were the ones who gave it to him."

"No wonder they were talking about the police. And if they were involved in Enzo's death, the camera might have been a reference to a security camera."

"Good point," I said. "I haven't looked behind their store, for one." I could take a little stroll down the alley behind Cape Costumers on my way home today. The police probably wouldn't have asked Shelly about security cam footage. Why should they? Enzo's body was found at his home, not at the costume shop—unless that was where he was killed. "Have you told Lincoln what you overheard?"

"Not yet. I haven't had a chance."

A wave of customers arrived. I grew too busy to dwell on Harini and Shelly arguing about camera footage, cleaning up oil, and police.

CHAPTER 50

The shop was quiet at one o'clock, and I had a plan for my lunch break. After clearing my absence with Orlean and Delia, ten minutes later found me pedaling on Short Sand Road on one of my own rental bicycles. Bicycling was not one of my usual activities.

I'd had a bike accident in New Zealand while traveling after my Peace Corps stint in Thailand. The person-over-handlebars incident had wrecked my knee, and I'd never gotten the joint repaired because I was basically terrified of surgery and all the mess that it would entail. This kind of ride I could manage, though. Pedaling slowly on a level surface during my lunch break didn't aggravate the old injury, and riding a bike was the quickest way to get to my destination on this fact-finding mission.

I passed the Bay State Light Opera buildings. A rehearsal seemed to be going on, with women and men in peasant or farmer clothes from bygone days clustered around the mansion looking upward, while a couple on the wide porch sang a duet. I imagined this might have been one of the places where Enzo had acted. I could stop and ask a few questions, except I didn't have unlimited time. What I did have was no desire to interrupt their dress rehearsal or whatever it was. I would try to find another time to stop by.

Pedaling on, I slowed at the condo development where Enzo had lived. Flo had supplied me with the unit number. It was a seniors-only development and, with any luck, the neighbor who discovered the skeleton corpse on the deck next door would be home. I scanned for a security camera near the entrance but didn't spot one, which didn't mean it wasn't there. Places were getting crafty at disguising those little lenses in signage or landscaping.

I braked at the sight of a former tennis court transformed into a pickleball venue a short ways past the entrance to the development and set one foot on the pavement to watch for a moment. No wonder neighbors complained about the noise factor. The constant thwack of a mostly hard ball against a hard paddle was relentless. As I remembered it, the sound of a semi-squishy tennis ball against the netting of a tennis racket was much easier on the ears.

At one of the farther courts, two men ceased play and glowered at each other across the net. I couldn't hear the substance of their argument, but as I took a second look, who they were didn't surprise me. Scott threw a hand in the air. Herbert turned away and stomped to the serve line.

All righty, then. Guys who didn't know the meaning of play and fun despite having lunch together only yesterday? I'd leave them to it.

Before I could resume my ride, my phone dinged with a text, then another and another. I dismounted and walked the bike a few yards farther. I wanted to be out of sight of the courts. Tangling with either Scott or Herbert was not on my lunch break agenda.

Flo followed up on my query to her yesterday about Shelly's real estate.

Shelly owes BIG back taxes. Bought the building two years ago, hasn't paid a dime.

I knew she'd invested way before she started bringing in money from the costume shop. Maybe she'd sold property in New York and had used that to buy the shop.

Norland's reply was next.

Haven't seen any police action against her.

I'd been too busy to share what Delia had overheard last evening. I tapped out the gist of it.

Delia H now working for me and at Rusty Anchor. Heard Shelly and Harini argue at bar last night about cleaning up oil, possibly peanut, and camera and police.

Gin chimed in with what she'd told me Saturday evening.

Shelly said E deathly allergic to peanuts. Murder weapon?

I texted my response. **Starting to seem like it.**

Norland wrote next. **We should meet again tonight.**

Flo agreed, but what she added gave me pause.

Harini has been asking when we're meeting.

If Harini was in the room, she'd expect us to talk

about the book, not the homicide. I texted the group that thought.

Norland responded. **We tell her we're meeting at eight but the rest of us start at seven. Yes? My house is fine.**

That could work. I told them I'd have to clear it with Tim and might be a few minutes late. After the thread petered out, I rode on, hoping to reach my original destination before my lunch break ended and I had to hightail it back to the shop.

CHAPTER 51

I rode on, searching the signs for condo 38-D on Lark-spur Lane.

Once again I slowed. Units 38 and 40 in the D section were joined in the middle, with their garages abutting. In the side yard of 40, I spotted a woman on her knees in a garden patch. I walked my bike off the street onto the grass. Next to the front door, the mailbox was labeled with a metal plaque reading, "Kimuri."

"Good afternoon," I called.

She glanced up and sat back, laying her gloved hands on her knees. Her beige cloth hat with a flat top and a brim all the way around could have belonged to Vera, the fictional British detective of book and television fame. The gardener frowned at me from under it.

"If you're a reporter, I have nothing to say to you." She set fists on hips.

"I am not. But my aunt is looking to downsize, and

I'm interested in these condos. I wondered if you'd be willing to chat for a minute about your experience of living here." I'd been about to say it was my mom who was interested, but then I'd have to pull off the lie and pray this woman wasn't a present or future bike rider. If she came into my shop and figured out who my real mother was, I would be in big trouble. Much safer to go with a fictional aunt.

The woman studied me for a moment, but her posture relaxed and she dropped her fists. "In that case, sure. Come over here, if you don't mind. We can talk while I plant."

I flipped down the kickstand and joined her. Her last name was Japanese, and I'd only met one person in Westham also named that. With this person's blue eyes and pale skin, I suspected Kimuri was a married name. She picked something out of a small basket and pressed it into the dirt of the garden bed. I wasn't a gardener, but I'd seen my mom plant daffodil and tulip bulbs in the fall.

"I've met a police officer in town named Nikki Kumuri," I began. "Is she a relation?"

Ms. Kimuri softened and beamed. "She's my older daughter. I'm Ilsa, by the way."

"My name's MacKenzie. It's nice to meet you." I purposely told her my name was MacKenzie and left off my last name. She might find out who I really was from her daughter, but I didn't want to start off with my reputation as a sometimes bumbling amateur sleuth.

I pointed at her basket. "Are those flower bulbs?"

"No, it's garlic." She held up a clove.

"And you plant them now?"

"Indeed, I do. Other than hardy greens, garlic is the only food crop you can plant in the fall. It comes up in the spring and is ready to harvest and cure in July." She glanced up at me. "You asked how I like living here. It's been good, but the one thing I miss is my big garden in my old house." She selected another clove from the basket and pressed it pointy side up into the dirt about four inches from the first one.

"So the people are friendly and the management is good?"

"For the most part, yes, on both counts."

"I saw a couple of men arguing on the pickleball courts on my way in," I said. "Do you play?"

"Good heavens no." She laughed and shook her head. "What a ridiculous sport, and so loud. Plus, that Scott fellow plays. He'd argue with a lamppost."

"I gather he lives here."

"Yes. Blessedly over in the E section, not next door." She sat back on her heels again. Judging from the snowy white hair peeking out from under the hat, she might be twice my age, but her knees were twice as good as mine. "Most folks who live here are decent. Friendly without being intrusive."

I tilted my head. "May I ask, why did you think I might be a reporter?"

"I guess you don't follow the news. My adjoining neighbor died recently, and I was the unfortunate person who found his body."

"My goodness, that must have been shocking."

"It was. I stepped out onto my deck with my coffee, as I do every morning, regardless of the weather. I spotted something out of place on the deck next door, so I went around to have a closer look." She shuddered and wrapped her arms around herself. "It was poor Enzo, my neighbor next door. I called to him, but he didn't rouse, and when I touched his cheek, it was far too cold for human skin."

"How very sad. What time was that? I mean, you said you went out with your coffee, so . . ."

"Yes. The sky was beginning to lighten, so it was maybe a quarter to seven."

"Do you think he went out onto his deck the night before and had a heart attack or a stroke or something?" I tried to keep my tone casual, innocent. The last thing I needed was one more person getting their back up at my asking too many questions.

"I have no idea. But the oddest thing was, he still wore a Halloween costume. Enzo was clothed in a full-body skeleton getup, and it wasn't some chintzy nylon thing from the party store, either. This was a well-made garment with an attached hood. A skull mask had been tossed on the deck like he'd ripped it off, perhaps. I found him on November first, mind you, the day after Halloween."

"Wow," I said. "You didn't hear him fall in the night or anything?"

"I didn't. I'm a sound sleeper, partly because I use silicon earplugs, which block out most noise."

"I suppose you called the police."

"I certainly did. I must say, they asked me questions six ways to Sunday over the next couple of days and didn't let Nikki be involved. Not a soul has reported back to me about what happened, either."

"Nikki can't tell you?" I asked.

"My daughter said she's not allowed to discuss departmental business with civilians. She's a sweetheart but operates strictly by the book." Ilsa gave herself a little shake. "Anyway, Enzo's death was truly an aberration for this development. Your aunt has nothing to worry about. Why, she could move in next to me. That unit will be available soon enough, may Enzo rest in peace." She crossed herself, garden glove and all.

"Thank you for sharing with me. I'll tell my aunt, and right now I'll leave you to your planting."

After we said goodbye, I flipped up the kickstand on the bike.

Ilsa called to me. "Miss, you seem interested in the death, and there's one more thing I found strange. Enzo was lying on the deck in an odd position. It was as if he was sitting in a chair, except he lay on his side with no chairs in sight. It's not what one would expect if he'd had a heart attack and fallen."

"That's really strange."

She smiled. "I was a nurse. I notice these things."

I thanked her again and rode away. Curious indeed. Why would Enzo have been lying in a sitting posture?

CHAPTER 52

Unfortunately, tangling with Herbert appeared to be on my agenda, after all. I'd ridden only one condo toward the exit when I glanced up to see him riding toward me on a cycle matching mine. He didn't look happy. I plastered a smile on my face and prepared to keep riding.

Instead, he swerved and braked in front of me, putting a foot down. I had no choice but to do the same, especially as two cars were passing and we bikers were confined to the edge of the road.

"What are you doing here?" Herbert demanded before I could greet him.

"Hello, Herbert." His was not a question I cared—or needed—to answer. "I suppose I could ask you the same. Is the Airbnb where you're staying in this development?"

"What?" He shook his head. "Not at all. I'm, ah, here to check out a property I have an interest in."

"Your friend Scott must have recommended buying in the same development as him." I cocked my head. "You don't look old enough for a senior living community, though."

He made a tsking sound. "Of course I'm not old enough. If I retire to the Cape, I'll go gated, all the way. Besides, look at this place. It's so vanilla, so plain wrap. It was fine for my un—" He clapped his mouth shut.

"For your uncle Enzo?" I smiled and kept my tone casual.

He squinted at me. "I get it. That's why you're here. To do more snooping, more asking questions, more *investigating*." He surrounded the word with air quotes. "Scott told me all about you."

Another statement I was happy to ignore. "Do you inherit Enzo's condo?" I half-turned and gestured behind me.

"You have a nice day, Ms. Almeida." He put his foot on the pedal and rode past, nearly clipping my elbow.

I took a deep breath and let it out, then cycled on. At the corner, I glanced back. Herbert had also stopped to talk with Ilsa. I might look up Ilsa Kimuri later and see if we could have another little chat. I hadn't seen Nikki recently, but I hoped she was on the team to find out what happened to Ilsa's late condo neighbor.

Turning away, I continued my ride before Herbert spotted me looking at him. Maybe he was staying in Enzo's place. Otherwise, why was he playing pickleball here and riding down the dead man's street? These condos weren't exactly affordable for many seniors. The so-called interest Herbert said he had must be in the property sense of interest rather than being interested in living here. If he was Enzo's heir and wanted to sell the condo, I expected Herbert would come out ahead financially, if not way ahead.

Darn. I wished I'd remembered to bring up the topic of the peanut allergy. Did that kind of thing run in families? Genetic predisposition to allergies was a simple research question. Anyway, it was probably best I hadn't asked Herbert, who was already too suspicious of me and my poking around.

I added looking up allergies to my growing to-do list, which included checking in with Tim about tonight. I also wanted to call my mom about how the kiddo drop-off at new schools went. Right now? I was way overdue back at my shop. I pedaled as fast as I could go while still being a careful driver.

Biking was nearly as good as walking for doing some thinking, though, and cycling was by its nature a more solitary activity, even when one rode with others. I wondered if Flo could dig into whether Herbert was Enzo's heir, sole or otherwise, or maybe Norland had heard.

And then there was what Flo reported about Shelly's financial woes. Being in arrears wasn't something I ever wanted to experience. I hadn't bought my shop's building and invested in a business without being positive I had the funds to get it off the ground. Thanks to some excellent prior investments, I'd been able to. What had Shelly been thinking? Maybe she'd been expecting Harini to chip in more than she had. Tonight we could all try to finagle an answer out of our new member.

Last night Reba almost told me something about Peter, but we hadn't had a moment alone after dinner to talk. I'd promised to get back to her today. That needed to happen too. My mental list was getting too long to hold in my head. I crossed virtual fingers that I'd remember all of it once I was off this bike.

CHAPTER 53

It was two o'clock by the time I checked in the bike and helmet at Mac's Bikes and greeted Orlean and Delia. Both were looking frazzled as well as a bit peeved at me.

"You know I have to leave now, right?" Delia asked after she rang up a helmet and our best bike lock.

"Of course," I said. "Clear out of here. I'm sorry if I've kept you."

Delia left without delay, after which, in the shop owner's permutation of Murphy's Law, we were swamped with customers looking for all three of our Rs: rental, retail, and repair. I either had renters waiting while I rang up a sale or purchasers cooling their heels as I fitted visitors with the right size bike and explained the agreement they needed to sign. Orlean grew ever more exasperated with the interruptions to her work, so I had to mediate those interactions, as well. I didn't understand why so many people wanted to rent bikes at this time of year, but it sure made the shop's bottom line happy.

At three thirty, a tiny angel in a rainbow-striped Rasta beret bustled in.

I greeted my grandma, then added, "Sorry, I'm swamped right now."

"Sounds like I came at the right time. Why don't I handle retail?"

"Seriously?"

"You bet," she said.

I blew her a kiss and headed to the rental area with the group of five I'd kept waiting. Reba had helped out here over the years. She knew the drill. Plus, she'd been on my list of people to contact, none of which I'd gotten to.

By a quarter to five, I was as frazzled as my employees had looked when I'd rolled in three hours earlier, but it was finally closing time. Orlean had left at four thirty. Reba sat on a stool, feet dangling, reading something on her oversized phone. I brought in the Open flag and locked the door an entire fifteen minutes early.

"Man, what a day," I said. "You saved my bacon, Abo Ree."

"Always glad to help out, honey. I stopped by because I had something to tell you, but now for the life of me I can't remember what it was." She rapped on her head. "Hello? Thought? Are you in there?"

"While you're thinking, do you want a nip of my special secret sherry?"

She laughed. "You mean the bottle and glasses I

gave you that you keep in the bottom drawer of your desk?"

"The same."

"Yes, please."

I grabbed the cash drawer. Money locked in the safe, I returned with the bottle and two delicate little glasses. With flowers etched in the glass, they were flat bottomed but flared slightly at the top. I poured a couple of fingers for each of us.

"Cheers, my dear." Reba raised her glass. "Sherry should rightly be sipped from a stemmed glass, but stemless is so much more practical, don't you think?"

"I'm all about practical." I took a most welcome sip.

"Eight of these glasses were a wedding gift to Alcindo and me, except our marriage took place so long ago I can't remember who gave them to us, and the matching decanter broke and was discarded."

Reba had given me the half-dozen matching glasses when she delivered the bottle, but I'd never had them all out at the same time. We didn't tend to throw sherry parties for six in the shop.

My phone buzzed with a text. "Hang on a minute, okay?" The message was from Tim. I'd carved out a minute to text him earlier. He'd replied that all was well with the kiddos, and that my leaving for book group was fine. Now he added a piece of news.

My mom wants to come Thursday. Okay?

I texted back that she was always welcome, and she could stay in the tiny house out back. Before I married Tim, the little abode was my residence when it was parked behind my shop. We rented it out in the summer but not during the offseason. Of course Greta would be worried. Jamie was her only daughter, and the kids were two of her four grandchildren.

Tim replied immediately.

Thx. When will you be home? Ella's asking.

I tapped out an answer. Ella might be having anxiety at anyone in her life not showing up when they should.

By 5:30. XXOO to her and to you.

I took another sip.

"About Peter Z," Reba said.

Ooh. "I'm all ears, but I don't have a super long time. Tim says Ella wants to see me, so I need to get home."

"And why wouldn't she want to be with her auntie? I won't keep you long. I don't actually have much on Peter."

I sipped and waited and sipped some more. My grandmother gazed out the window.

"Abo Ree? What's up?"

"What? Oh, I was woolgathering. I'm sorry, *querida*. It's one of the perils of being old."

"No worries, but please do go on."

"You see, Peter manages my money. I do have a state teacher's pension, but the other reason I have any funds is that my Alcindo had the wisdom to prepare his estate with great care and well ahead of his death. Just now I was reminiscing about my husband, and that's a fact." She dusted off her hands. "In any event, I'm not sure Peter has his own affairs in good order. Why, his late wife was the moneymaker in that family. Now that she's gone, I rather wonder if he's having trouble making ends meet."

"What did she do for work?"

"She was an engineer and an inventor. Brilliant mind.

Peter was never a match for her, except in love. So, when Enzo threatened to withdraw his own considerable funds from Peter's care, our Mr. Zelensky was not pleased in the least."

"Do you know how he made his money? You said, 'considerable funds,' and when he came in to get a three-wheeler before he died, he readily laid out the cash."

"I'm not entirely sure, although some of it might be family money. I think he did quite well in his profession, and he must have made smart investments over the years," She brightened. "Like you did."

I had, it was true, when I was earning big bucks in the financial sector in Boston.

"You heard Enzo and Peter arguing in public?" I asked.

"I most certainly did."

"When was that? And where?"

"Let me think a minute, now." Reba pushed her lips together. "Enzo was found dead, what, Tuesday morning?"

I nodded.

"This has to have been at least a week earlier, perhaps two," Reba said. "But certainly in October. I know because it was one of those warm and sunny fall days. I was about to go into Peter's office to tell him the names of a few stocks I wanted him to invest in for me. The front door was wide open, and I couldn't help overhearing his disagreement with Enzo."

"Naturally, you lingered outside to listen." I smiled at her.

"As one does. What I heard made me quite wonder about Peter."

"Did he threaten Enzo?"

"How did you know?" Reba asked. "Never mind. I know how your brain works. Kind of like mine." She winked at me. "Yes, Peter said if Enzo withdrew his business, Peter would be ruined. He was furious about it and finally told Enzo to get out."

"I thought you told me Peter handled investments for most Westhamites, I mean, those with money to invest."

"That was what I thought. He did, previously. Ever since his wife's death, his business has suffered."

"You still keep your money with him," I said.

"Well, not all of it by any means, my dear. You know what they say. Diversify, diversify, diversify."

CHAPTER 54

I locked the shop door at five fifteen and hugged my grandma goodbye before we headed for home in opposite directions.

Peter had lost his touch in the stock market and yet threatened Enzo if he moved his money elsewhere. That sounded like a recipe for disaster—or murder. I thought back to when I'd first met Peter in the cemetery. He'd said his daughter had recently finished college and moved home, and his son had graduated from a private high school. He might be in additional debt from paying for their education.

In front of the library, I halted my brisk walk abruptly, my breath rushing in as I remembered something from that encounter on the Day of the Dead. Peter's breath had smelled like peanuts. He obviously wasn't allergic to them, but maybe he'd figured out a way to get enough of them in some form into Enzo the day before.

"Did sudden paralysis strike?" Flo asked from behind me. "Alternatively, maybe you're pretending to be a living statue." She moved up to stand beside me.

"Neither. Flo, I just remembered something."

"All right, dish. Or save it for our meeting in an hour and a half?"

I swore. "I need to get home. Can you walk with me?"

"Better, I can give you a ride." She pointed at the Reserved for Library Director sign in the small parking area next to where we stood. Next to her little red Honda Fit were two handicapped spaces and three ten-minute parking spots for library patrons who needed to run in to pick up a reserved item or drop off a book or movie. One of the posters displaying Jamie's face was stapled to the telephone pole in the grassy verge.

"You're on." Once we were underway, I relayed what Reba said about Enzo and Peter, as well as the peanut aroma I'd detected on Peter.

"Dude's my action item," Flo began. "I know he has several unhappy clients."

"Why do you think his performance has slipped, and his reputation along with it?"

"Grief, maybe? I agree with Reba that he wasn't the brains in that marriage. He could be taking something to dull the emotional pain, which would also dull the mind."

"It's been five years, though," I said. "Would his grief still be that acute?"

"Mac, you yourself do not have a dull mind. Have you not heard of addiction?"

"Ugh. Of course. My thoughts have been way more scattered with this case. It seems like we have one person who is a strong suspect, and then somebody else pops up. It's like a dog with a squirrel."

"Might you be pregnant?" Flo asked.

"What?" I whipped my head over to look at her. "No, I know I'm not."

"It's only a thought, Mac. Hormones can do a number on your thought processes."

"I suppose," I said. "I think it's more likely the combo of a homicide, Jamie missing, and being half responsible for her babies, all in one week."

"You have had the triple whammy, I agree." She turned onto my street.

"Have you learned anything else about Peter?"

"No, but now I plan to dig a lot more deeply into his finances."

"I had a couple of interesting encounters today," I began. "I didn't have time to text the group about them, but there's my house. I'll save my news for our gathering."

"Sounds like a plan." Flo pulled into the driveway. "See you soon. Do you want me to come back and give you a ride over to Norland's?"

"That'd be great, thanks." I climbed out.

I waved at Ella, who gazed intently out the front window, her face lit by the lamp next to her. A big smile took over her expression as she waved back. Was there ever a better homecoming sight?

CHAPTER 55

We got a late start at Norland's. When Flo came to pick me up at six forty-five, Ella clung to my legs, tearfully begging me not to leave. It was almost her bedtime, but I was on the verge of canceling my plans when Tim cajoled her into a laugh. He popped his head around the corner of the living room wearing her pajama bottoms on his head and promised two extra books before bed. I hugged and kissed her and said I'd make a special breakfast for the two of us in the morning.

Now the group was gathered in Norland's comfortable family room at the back of the house with drinks and Flo's yellow legal pad at the ready.

"So, what do we have?" Flo tapped her pen on the pad.

"I had a few encounters today and learned something from my grandmother," I offered. I began with seeing the argument on the pickleball court and pointed to Gin. "Your buddy Scott was one of them. Tulia, remember on Saturday when he came in with Herbert and they left before ordering food?"

"Sure."

"They were getting along fine then, but this afternoon? Not so much. And yesterday Scott brought his bike into my shop for the simplest of repairs. It would have been so easy for him to tighten his own pedal, it made me wonder if he loosened it on purpose. I didn't get a warm and cozy vibe from him at all."

"The poor man seems deeply unhappy," Tulia murmured. "It's no good to take it out on others, though."

"I agree." I told them about finding Enzo's condo and my talk with Ilsa. "She's Nikki Kumuri's mother."

"Nikki's a good officer," Norland said. "I hired her, I should know, and I met Ilsa at a department family picnic. Nice lady." When his cheeks pinkened, he avoided my gaze.

Ooh. Maybe Ilsa was his date the other day. "I liked her." I added how Ilsa described the way Enzo's corpse was positioned. "Isn't that odd?"

"She found him early in the morning, you said," Norland said.

"Yes."

"It sounds like he spent some time sitting after he was killed and was moved later," Norland said.

That was the livor mortis thing he'd explained to me. I told the group about running into a suspicious Herbert shortly after I left Ilsa, both of us on bicycles.

"Then my grandma came into the shop this afternoon," I went on." She says she overheard Peter and

Enzo having a heated discussion, with Enzo saying he was going to withdraw his investments from Peter's management. Reba thinks Peter doesn't even manage his own finances that well."

"That comports with what I learned," Flo said.

"You picked up a lot, Mac," Gin said. "All I have is what Shelly said about Enzo's peanut allergy. I dug into that a bit more. For those with allergies, peanut oil is more deadly than the peanuts themselves, I guess because it's concentrated."

"Or gets into the bloodstream faster," Tulia said.

"The first time I met Peter, I thought I smelled peanuts on his breath," I said. "Delia overheard Shelly and Harini arguing about cleaning up oil. I'd say it's not looking good for any of them."

"Right," Flo said. "Shelly is deeply in debt. She might have hoped Enzo would leave her some money."

"Do you think Delia told Lincoln?" Norland frowned a little. "Seems like important information."

"I hope so," I said." I should probably update him on all kinds of things."

"He's pretty quiet this time around, isn't he?" Gin asked.

"I guess," I said. "Maybe because he's no longer a bachelor, exactly," I said.

"Is that all we have?" Flo asked.

"I signed up to look into Enzo's past." Norland raised his hand. "He did have quite a successful career on- and off-Broadway. But get this: Lawrence wasn't his surname at birth." He gazed around at us, the hint of a smile playing around his lips.

"And?" Gin made a rolling gesture with her hand.

He leaned forward and spoke in a rasping, dramatic voice. "It was Corleone."

"You mean . . ." Tulia gaped.

"Yes." Norland reverted to his usual register. "Like in the movie, but it's also an actual Sicilian Mafia family."

Flo whistled. "And that's where Enzo got his money? He was related to the real-life Godfather?"

"Apparently," Norland said. "Ill-gotten gains of the worst kind, although I found no evidence that Enzo himself was part of any criminal activities."

"If the mob was my people, I'd also want to get out and change my name," Tulia said. "No question."

"Do you think Herbert knows?" I asked.

"Seems like it might not matter to him, from what I've heard from you all and elsewhere." Norland checked his phone. "Listen, it's almost eight. Has anyone actually read the Conte book? Harini should be here any minute."

"I read about half," I said.

"Not me," Gin said. Tulia and Flo both shook their heads.

"I finished the book." Norland shrugged. "Hey, I'm retired. You all have day jobs."

"We can talk with her about what she likes to read," I said. "And try to find out in the subtlest of ways what she knows about Enzo's death."

"Are you going to tell Harini you saw her with him and Shelly at the bank?" Gin asked.

"Maybe."

"And maybe we can also ask where they went on Halloween night after the bank," Tulia said. "That seems important."

I murmured my agreement. The doorbell rang. Norland jumped up. Gin and I both quickly pulled out our copies of the Halloween cozy. Our host returned a moment later with a hesitant Harini, book in hand.

"Sit down, please." Norland gestured to a comfortable chair. "What can I get you to drink?" He listed what he had, ending with herbal or black tea.

"An herbal tea, please, any flavor, but no sweetening. Thank you." She sat with her spine straight, as always.

"Welcome to the Cozy Capers," Flo said. "I don't believe you and I have met until now." She introduced herself and Tulia. "I think you know Mac and Gin."

"Yes. It's good to meet you all." Harini thanked Norland when he came back with her mug of tea.

I smiled at the newcomer. "As often happens, Harini, many of us haven't had time to get to this week's book."

"Because of all the commotion in town," Gin added in a casual tone, as if the five of us weren't intimately involved in trying to put the so-called commotion to rest.

"You should have let me know." Harini's voice shook a little. "I can come back another time."

Were her nerves from more than joining a new group, meeting new people? She was a ballet instructor and met the public every day in the costume shop. She couldn't be too much of an introvert.

"No, no," Norland said. "It's fine. Please stay. I actually did finish *Nine Lives and Alibis*, but we thought it would be nice to get to know you better."

"How long have you been reading mysteries?" Tulia asked.

"I can hardly remember not reading them." Harini crossed her legs at the ankles and tucked them neatly to the side.

"Same here." Tulia laughed. "My gateway drug was Encyclopedia Brown and I went on from there."

"Sherlock Holmes for me," Gin chimed in.

"As many men do, I began by reading noir," Norland said. "You know, the hard-boiled, smoking, drinking PIs written by men like Raymond Chandler and others. But after my wife died, I plucked one of her cozy mysteries off our living room shelves. I found that a story where justice is restored to the community at the end suited my mood much better. I'd rather spend my time with a book that, after you finish reading it, you feel better about the world, not worse."

"Well-put, Norland," I said. "I think that's how we all feel about the genre."

"Harini, do you have a few favorite authors?" Gin asked.

Our friendly book chat seemed to be relaxing her. *Good.*

"Living in New York, I was thrilled to find Cleo Coyle's coffee shop series," Harini began. "New York is hardly a village, but she created one with the coffee shop regulars and that little neighborhood."

"I love those books," Tulia said.

"And although they aren't cozies," Harini went on, "I've also been loving Sujata Massey's mysteries about the woman lawyer in India over a hundred years ago. India is my heritage, in case you haven't guessed."

"Those are excellent stories," I said. "The author has won lots of awards for them. Speaking of things historical, though, weren't you dressed as a jester for Halloween? It was a great costume."

"What?" Harini seemed to shrink into her chair, and the tea in her mug nearly sloshed over.

"I saw you and Shelly in costume driving through the bank that evening," I said. "I think it must have been Enzo dressed as a skeleton in the front seat, yes?"

She swallowed, her eyes darting left and right, finally settling on a spot past my right ear. "Yes, that's right."

"You must have been so upset to hear of his death," Gin said softly.

"I was." Her voice shook as much as her hand. She set down the mug and stood. "If you'll excuse me, I thought we were going to discuss a book, not a real-life homicide. Could you show me the door, please, Norland?"

Flo opened her mouth as if to object, but she closed it again.

"Of course," Norland said. He jumped up and escorted Harini out. The rest of us exchanged glances.

After he came back, he said, "We shouldn't be surprised that didn't go as planned."

"No," I said. "She was nervous even before I mentioned seeing her in the car. Sorry if I bungled getting information out of her."

"I didn't have high expectations," Gin said. "Don't worry about it."

"Do you think she was more on edge than merely meeting us merited?" Tulia asked.

"For sure," Flo said. "Listen, I should get going. Action items are to keep digging into your previous assignment, okay?"

I nodded as we agreed to disband. If we all dug in, we'd get some action soon. We'd better.

CHAPTER 56

Breakfast with the kiddos the next morning didn't go a bit smoothly. The baby was cranky, smelling vaguely of poop, and Ella was demanding.

"When is Mommy going to be home? Why can't I play all day with you, Auntie Mac?" Ella stared at her bowl of raisin bran with banana slices and oat milk. "I don't like bananas," said the girl who'd adored them yesterday. "I thought we were going to make pancakes, and my orange juice has little bits of icky stuff in it."

Somehow I soothed her. I showed her how sweet her cereal actually was and strained the pulp out of her OJ. I cleaned Luca's spit-up off of him and me and got him into a clean diaper, and I managed to get the three of us presentable and out of the house on time.

Now, at nearly nine o'clock, I was in the orderly world of my shop, where the shelves of helmets and shoes stayed tidy, where Orlean left her tools clean and in their proper places, where the rental and retail bikes remained in the neat lines I'd left them in yesterday. Where, in other words, I could control almost everything.

Maybe this was one reason parents of young children paid the high cost of day care and kept their jobs rather than staying home with their little ones. Sure, there was a career to consider, but having a world of adults to hang out with every day could be important to mental health, even if it was hanging out in online meetings and working remotely.

More power to those with infinite patience, like the stay-at-home dads and moms and the day care and preschool teachers. Some people were well-suited to spending all their time with babies and toddlers. So far, I didn't feel like I was one of them, even though I was hoping to have one and in the short term had one of each in the house.

As I hung out the Open flag, I thought about Harini and how abruptly she'd left our meeting last night. Did she have children? Was she a grandmother? I had no idea. I didn't know those kinds of things about Shelly, either. She was Gin's action item. I doubted if one's status as a parent had anything to do with Enzo's death, but anything was possible. Knowing if Enzo himself had children as well as a nephew might be important.

I shot off a message to the group.

Anybody know if Harini or Shelly has kids? Grandkids? Herbert? Enzo himself?

When no one immediately replied, I put away my phone and focused on my business, ordering in more retail items. I also checked the rentals book. We didn't have any reservations for bikes going out today, nor were any due in, which was normal for early November. We'd get another flurry of visitors wanting to ride on our trails around Thanksgiving and also at Christmas, if the weather wasn't horrible. Today's weather was chilly and super breezy, but at least it wasn't raining.

Orlean trudged in on time at nine thirty. I got a gruff greeting as she headed to the repair room, and that was it.

"Good morning," I called after her.

Delia wasn't far behind, and she wasn't alone. Lincoln paused inside the door, looking as windswept as Delia. He didn't smile.

Uh-oh. "Hello, you two." I regarded the detective. "How's it going, Lincoln?"

Delia hung up her coat and headed to the back to greet Orlean—and to leave us alone, apparently.

"Is there anything you've learned recently that you haven't told me?" he asked in a terse voice.

"Um, let me think." I hated being put on the spot. "Okay, here's something. Last night, Norland said Enzo Lawrence's actual name before he changed it was Corleone, as in the Mafia."

"Gifford shared that with us, yes."

"So, if Herbert is Enzo's nephew, why is his name also Lawrence?" I asked.

"We dug into that. Apparently Enzo's younger brother liked Enzo's name change so much, he officially changed his to match. Herbert is his son."

"Is the brother still living?"

"No."

"Did Enzo have children?" I asked.

"Not that we know of. What else?"

"Reba told me Peter Zelensky's finances are in bad shape, and she overheard him arguing with Enzo. Enzo was going to put his investments elsewhere."

"So noted, thank you."

Delia came back in but went straight to the retail shelves and began straightening stacks of shorts and shirts.

He lowered his voice. "Listen, I heard down at the station that there's been a report. Someone might have seen your sister-in-law down by the breakwater the night she went missing. As soon as we know anything, I personally will come to tell your husband and you."

"The breakwater not far from the pier?" I could barely speak around the lump in my throat.

"That's the one. I don't know anything else, I'm sorry."

"Thanks for telling me, Lincoln."

"I wouldn't get my hopes up about it, but I wanted to share what I heard." He checked his watch and made a noise in his throat. "I had to be somewhere else ten minutes ago." Lincoln went over to Delia and exchanged a few words with her, followed by a light kiss.

The breakwater. At night. I hated the sound of that. But giving way to worry right now wasn't in the cards.

"Talk to you soon, Mac." Lincoln held the door for a group of six customers who filed in speaking French, then he slipped out.

I gazed at the chattering women and men. Should I try to resurrect my French? Nah. When in Rome, and all that. I was sure they were eager to try out their English.

Hopefully they hadn't heard about our town's latest homicide.

My breath rushed in, and I ran to the door. I glanced both ways, then spotted the detective nearly to the police station. "Lincoln!" I called after him.

He half-turned, saw me, tapped his watch, and hurried on. My shoulders sank. I grabbed the nearest display bike to steady myself. He hadn't said if he'd told Tim about the report. I couldn't run down Main Street to catch him, passing the bakery on my way.

I swore to myself before heading inside. I'd have to text him. I needed to know if Tim was in worse anguish than I was right now. I could only hope that Lincoln was kind enough to spare Tim the pain until it was absolutely necessary. That is, when he brought definitive news of Jamie's death.

CHAPTER 57

The next few hours were torture. All I wanted to do was to go and hug Tim, and then visit the break-water. I wasn't sure what I would see. Lincoln had mentioned only that the station got a report of a person being seen near the breakwater the night of November first.

Those long arms of huge, sharp rocks sticking out into deep water had terrified me my entire life. They still did. Some people liked to risk walking out as far as they could go. Brave kids liked to fish off the rocks. But waves broke on breakwaters. Sharp sea urchins and slippery seaweed covered much of the barrier. I was not a candidate for venturing out farther than the dry sand where the first giant chunks of breakwater sat, and even then my body went into shivers thinking about it.

If anyone called me chicken about my refusal, I

wore it like a badge of honor. I had to assume the WPD, and maybe the Coast Guard, were now searching both sides of the breakwater for Jamie. More accurately, for her remains.

Right now, I couldn't go anywhere. I had bikes to sell, walk-in rentals to arrange, and employees who deserved to be treated well, including taking their lunch breaks before I did.

A petite woman walked in. She wore a puffy jacket and had an infant in a front carrier. When she pulled off her cap to reveal white-blond hair, I did a double take.

"Victoria?" I asked, astonished.

She laughed. "I have today off, and you were asking about Miko. I was out walking around and thought I'd bring him in to introduce you."

If I'd had whiplash when Orlean told me she played pickleball, I was really having it now. Victoria, laughing and talking to me as if we were any two women, two former classmates? The universe had stood on its end, but I wasn't putting up a fight.

"I'd love to meet the little guy. Thanks for stopping in." The store was quiet right now, and I came out from behind the counter.

The baby was facing her chest, but she slid off his warm bear-ears hat and pulled down the front of the carrier enough for me to see his face. His eyelids floated open to reveal the same pale blue eyes as his mom's.

"Aww, what a cutie." I smiled. "Hi, Miko."

"He's so easy right now. We've figured out breast-feeding. He's not too heavy to carry around. And he sleeps a lot."

"My little nephew Luca is like that, too, except we have to fix bottles."

"I wanted to ask you how those children are doing with their mom's absence," she said.

"The baby seems to be taking it in stride, but Ella's having a much harder time with her mom not coming home. Jamie, for all her troubles, has been a good mother with those two."

Victoria gazed at me as if making up her mind. "Lincoln said he told you of the possible sighting." She spoke softly.

"He did, a couple of hours ago. But he didn't say if he had told or planned to tell Tim about it. Do you know?"

"I don't believe he did. He told you as a courtesy and possibly a heads-up. We all know how upset your husband is, and rightly so."

"I'm glad he doesn't know yet," I said. "It's going to be hard enough when we hear something definitive, other than her walking in the door."

"Forgive me for asking, but if it comes to finding her remains, will you and Tim take in the children going forward?"

"I don't know. He's already in place as their legal guardian if something were to happen to Jamie, so I'd say the answer is yes. They're going to need a home, although I suppose we'd have to contact their fathers."

Victoria winced. "Fathers, plural?"

"Yes." I left it there. This wasn't the time to discuss Jamie's choices.

Miko squeaked. Orlean returned from lunch and

stopped to murmur a greeting to Victoria and the baby. Customers pushed through the door.

"I'm going to get going," Victoria said. "Little guy here is going to want lunch soon, and there's something going down at the station I might get called in for. Listen, Mac, I hope the news about your sister-in-law, when it comes, is tolerable."

"Thanks."

She cleared her throat. "And if you end up with the baby on a permanent basis, maybe we can do playdates and share information and such. Miko's a little older than Luca, so I could probably pass along clothes, too. They outgrow things so fast."

I gave a slow nod. "I'd like that. All of it."

"Great. I wasn't sure." She snugged the baby's hat back on and then her own. "Talk soon."

I stared at her back for a moment before I turned my attention to the customers. I didn't have time to dwell on this new, softer-edged, friendly version of Victoria, but I did half-wonder if I'd slipped into an alternate reality. Would the real Victoria return in a few years after breastfeeding hormones no longer circulated in her body, or had motherhood fundamentally changed her outlook on life?

She hadn't been certain I would accept her reaching out with friendship. I wasn't surprised, given our rocky past, but who was I to turn down a peace offering? If I was to become an overnight mom, I could use all the help and friends I could get, especially another baby mama.

CHAPTER 58

Lincoln returned that afternoon, shortly after Delia left for the day.

I regarded the detective. "Are you here with news about Jamie?"

"News, yes, but not about her." He folded his arms.

I glanced around, but the only customers were browsing the shirts and jackets across the store from us.

"Did you make an arrest?" I whispered.

"Yes, two."

I frowned. "Two people killed Enzo? What, was one an accomplice?"

"The co-owners of the costume shop were spotted late Halloween night carrying a stiff skeleton out of their car and around the back of his condo. The witness, who doesn't sleep well, thought it was a prank. Victoria and I have engineered some selective leaking to the press, and that made the witness rethink what he saw. The man called, and I went over to interview him. He also happens to have night vision cameras outside his condo, which is next to Enzo's. Seems to be a person fond of electronic gadgets."

"Wow. So, he lives in the condo with the driveways between his and Enzo's." Not Ilsa's adjoining condo, but the one before Enzo's. "D-36?"

He pressed his lips together and shook his head. "I am not going to ask how you knew that number."

"Never mind." These impending arrests must have been what Victoria meant when she mentioned something going down at the station. "So, you have your murderers. Why don't you look happier, Lincoln?"

"Each woman insists she didn't kill him. We spoke with them separately, of course. Ms. Hitchcock clammed up and asked for a lawyer, but Ms. Whitt had no qualms about speaking with us. She said they found Enzo dead in their shop after they closed. They'd gone into their apartment to change into costumes for the evening. When they returned, he lay dead on the floor."

"They could have colluded ahead of time to get their stories to match up."

"Maybe, but we have ways of getting to the truth, and it appears that at least Harini is telling us what actually happened."

"And, then, what, they packed him into the front seat of Shelly's car and drove to the bank?" I asked.

"It seems so. At long last we have succeeded in gaining permission to speak with several tellers at that institution. Apparently the ladies often drove through with Lawrence to withdraw funds from his account. He doesn't have a car. The difference is that on previous occasions, he would smile and greet the teller. The one on duty Halloween night thought it was strange Lawrence didn't remove his mask or wave, but she chalked it up to the driver being in a hurry."

"When instead he was sitting there dead as a post." I thought for a moment. "Those two have a lot of nerve."

"You could say that, yes."

"The women must be pretty strong to lift his dead body into the car and later out of the car," I said. "Come to think of it, I noticed Shelly's strong arms, and Harini seems to still be in good shape too."

"Yes to both. Also, the victim was a relatively slight man.

"Yesterday I spoke with the neighbor who adjoins Enzo's condo, the one who found him on his deck. Wait, did I already tell you this?"

"Ilsa Kimuri, and no, you didn't." Lincoln's heavy brows met in the middle.

"I've been busy." I hurried on so he couldn't express his displeasure. "You must already know his body was on its side but as if he was sitting in a chair. Shelly and Harini must have left him in their car all night, right? And he stiffened up in that position."

"We noticed that but had not been able to understand where the chair was. Now we might. Also, lividity indicated he'd been moved."

"Is it also known as livor mortis?"

"Yes," Lincoln said. "How do you know that?"

"Norland explained it to me."

"Then you know it's where and how the blood pools after death."

The shoppers began to approach the counter, arms full of merchandise.

"We plan to continue our questioning of the owners, but I thought you deserved to know. That said, you will keep this under your hat until further notice, Mac," Lincoln murmured. "That's an order."

"Yes, sir. And thank you, but now you still have to find the real killer."

"Yes, we do." He headed out, leaving me with a shop to run and a head full of questions. Were Shelly and Harini telling the truth? No wonder the latter had seemed nervous and Shelly had been on edge about my questions.

There were so many things wrong with what they did, even if it wasn't murder. For one, not reporting the body immediately. Two, withdrawing money from a deceased person's account. Three, transporting a corpse, not to mention leaving it outside exposed to the elements and possibly critters all night. The phrase *boggles the mind* didn't begin to cover this.

Despite their arrests, that meant the actual murderer was at large. The person who attacked Enzo with the thing he was fatally allergic to and left him dead on the floor had committed a far worse crime but was still out there walking around free. Who would be killed next?

Someone cleared their throat. I blinked. Two women and a man stood on the other side of the counter, which now held an array of shirts and biking pants.

"Forgive me, folks. Shall I ring those up for you?"

CHAPTER 59

Mac's Bikes stayed busy all the way to five o'clock, and for the last hour I was alone and wishing I could clone myself. At five fifteen, I grabbed the Open flag from its holder, the last item on my list before switching off the lights and heading home.

A couple about my age hurried up. "Are you closing?" the woman asked.

"Yes, but we'll be open tomorrow at nine."

"Can we possibly persuade you to stay open a few more minutes, please, ma'am?" Her cadence sounded southern, or at least southern Midwestern.

"Her parents were here last year and love the branded shirts they bought," the man said. "We wanted to surprise them with matching jackets, but we have to leave for the airport at six tomorrow morning."

"I'm so sorry," the woman said. "We truly meant to get here earlier in our stay. My folks absolutely adored your cute shop and the bikes they rented. You were super helpful and nice to them, explaining all about the trail and whatnot."

I gazed at their hopeful, sincere faces. "Come on in." I opened the door and ushered them inside, but I brought the flag with me and made sure the door lock clicked so no one could enter from the outside.

All of that meant I didn't leave the shop until five thirty, and it was already fully dark out there. I texted Tim that I was running late.

I grabbed one of the super bright headlamps we stocked and made sure I removed the little tab so the battery would make contact, then tucked the light into my coat pocket. Yes, streetlights illuminated Main Street, but the shops were all closed up tight and only the Japanese restaurant and the Rusty Anchor showed any signs of life. After I turned onto Blacksmith Shop Road, there would be fewer streetlights, and they grew sparser halfway to our house.

All the thoughts about all the things kept my brain too busy to really notice my surroundings as I trudged down the main drag against a cold wind that hadn't let up all day. What would the police and rescue personnel find at the breakwater, and how would Tim cope if the results were the worst?

Why were both Herbert and Peter so antagonistic toward me, not to mention Shelly? What dealings did Herbert and Shelly have to argue so bitterly about? And speaking of Shelly, did she or Harini have any inkling who left Enzo for dead in their shop? How did that person get inside, and what allergen did they force Enzo to ingest?

I came to the block that included the costume shop and halted abruptly. The wind rattled the chains the sign hung from. It blew a plastic container here and there, making it bump against bench legs and lampposts. My phone rang from my jacket pocket. I tore off my gloves and pulled out the device.

"Abo Reba? Are you okay?"

"Yes, but I heard a rumor." She sounded breathless. I waited.

"Somebody said something about a peanut allergy. Well, the item I helped that Herbert fellow find at the grocery store was a spray peanut oil. An aerosol."

OMG. "Thanks. I have to run." I ended the call and jabbed at Lincoln's number. I glanced around, but I was alone on the sidewalk except for a man who emerged from a storefront down the block, jammed his hat farther down on his head, and sauntered in the other direction.

Lincoln didn't pick up, and it was faster to speak a message than to text one.

"Lincoln, my grandmother helped Herbert Lawrence find peanut oil spray at the market about two weeks ago. Maybe that's your murder weapon. I'm at Cape Costumers and am going to walk behind it to look around." I disconnected and headed down the side street that led to the back.

Enzo and Shelly had been dating. He might have had a key to the shop. He could have let Herbert inside while Shelly and Harini were donning their costumes. Earlier in the week, I'd meant to look for a security camera back there but never got around to it.

Unlike on the other side of Main Street, the back doors of these shops connected with a municipal parking lot, not a dark, narrow alley. Still, I didn't want to linger here, since the lot was mostly empty and the lighting was inadequate. In fact, to add to my insurance of having told Lincoln where I would be, I called his number again and left the call open.

I hurried down to the rear of the costume shop. I put my fists on my knees and peered at the pavement. Surely the killer wouldn't have stupidly tossed a can of oil spray on the ground, but maybe he'd left another clue.

I pulled out the headlamp and switched on its super bright light, but I didn't slide it onto my head. Nope, no clue that I could see. Where was Nancy Drew when I needed her, or Sherlock Holmes, for that matter? I aimed the light up at the eaves and over the door, hoping I could spot a security camera lens. No luck there, either.

"Lose something?" a man's voice said from behind me.

CHAPTER 60

I whirled, thumbing off the light switch. Herbert Lawrence stepped forward, backing me up against the wall, his expression cold. He planted his right hand on the wall next to my head and leaned on it with a straight arm but kept his left hand in his jacket pocket.

I cursed mightily—but silently—at getting myself into this dangerous situation. I tried to swallow down my racing heart, which had leapt into my throat.

"Herbert, hi there. Yes, I dropped my prescription eyedrops out here a couple of days ago. I can't find them, though, so I'll be going." I tried to duck around him. Before I could, he lowered his arm to rest on my shoulder.

"You're not going anywhere, Mac." His reedy voice was grating and raspy. "Ever."

"What are you talking about?" I tried to keep my own voice from revealing the panic I felt.

"I heard you call your detective buddy."

He'd been following me. I swore again but under my breath.

"Not very competent is Haskins?" Herbert's tone was mocking, singsong. "He arrests two ladies, but they're as clueless as he is."

All I could do was listen as I thought hard and fast about my escape.

"So you think I murdered my uncle with peanut oil?" Herbert continued. "You lead a rich fantasy life for a bike shop owner."

What were my options? I didn't know what was in his pocketed left hand, but it couldn't be good, especially since I'd seen he was a lefty when he filled out the bike rental form. The dude was ruthless if he could kill his own blood relative. He wouldn't hesitate to remove me, and he was both taller and stronger than I was. My getaway would have to rely on brains and surprise. I had a life and a family to get back to.

"You bet I do." My gut turned to ice with a new thought. What if he'd learned about my own allergies and had bee venom in a syringe? I would die in short order. "Why did you kill Enzo?"

"You don't know anything about him. My uncle was a greedy old man. He was trying to keep me from my inheritance. He looked down on my late father and lorded it over me." Herbert's sneer turned to a glare. "But I'm all done with people manipulating me and telling me I can't have what's mine. Including you." His left arm started to move.

Go! Down at my right side, I switched on the light

and swung it up to shine the strong beam straight into his eyes.

He cried out. He dropped his arm and brought one hand to his eyes, scrabbling for the light with his other. I swung my left elbow up into his throat. He made a gurgling sound as the light went flying.

And I ran.

CHAPTER 61

I hadn't made it to the side street when lights and sirens roared into the parking lot from three directions. I halted and pointed toward where I'd left him, then kept moving. Now out of breath, I slowed to a walk until I was fully lit by a streetlight near the corner with Main Street but still in view of the action.

Victoria, now in uniform, came at a jog from across the street. Her eyes widened when she saw me. "Mac, are you all right?" Her hand rested on the weapon in her duty belt.

"I think so."

She listened to a crackling radio. I leaned against the lamppost. How had Herbert been able to come up behind me with no warning? He'd clearly heard me leave the message for Lincoln. The wind must have masked any noises of his footsteps tailing me, or maybe he was the man I'd seen go in the opposite direction.

Either way, I'd once again demonstrated that I was not a trained officer who knew better than to let someone sneak up on them. I set my hands on my knees, leaning halfway over.

"They have him," Victoria told me. "Hey, you need to sit down?"

"Just trying to catch my breath." I took a few deep inhales and exhales, then straightened.

"Come over to this bench," she insisted.

I let her guide me to one of the many sidewalk benches Westham featured. It was a welcome offering that let tourists and residents alike sit and appreciate the scenery or give their feet a break from walking and shopping. At the moment it was a place to rest after sprinting away from a murderer.

"Thank you." I sank onto the seat, my heart rate finally slowing to normal.

She pulled out a sturdy cell phone and texted something, then looked up. "Nikki's coming to sit with you until Lincoln's free. In the meantime, want to tell me what happened?"

Not really, but I knew I had to. "I think Herbert was following me. He must have overheard me call Lincoln, saying Reba had helped Herbert find peanut oil spray in the market. You know about Enzo's severe peanut allergy?"

Victoria nodded. "In combination with several other health conditions, being sprayed in the face with oil wasn't a recipe for survival. How did you escape the younger Lawrence's attack back there?"

"I blasted his eyes with a super bright light, then I

elbowed him in the throat. All I needed to do was get myself out of his grip and run, and that's what I did."

The chief smiled at me. "That's the best self-defense method, Mac, for anyone, but especially women. Get free and run. Good job." Her phone vibrated. "I'm needed elsewhere. You okay?"

"Yes. Thank you."

Nikki drove up in a cruiser and parked. "Nice job back there, Mac," she said after sliding out.

Victoria waved and bustled off toward the parking lot.

"Thanks," I said. "Is Herbert okay? He made an awful sound when I elbowed his throat. I mean, it was self-defense, but I wouldn't want to kill someone."

"He's fine enough to gripe in a raspy voice about his handcuffs being too tight." She gave a low laugh. "I'd say you didn't do any permanent damage."

"Is Lincoln there?" I asked her.

"Yes. I'm to give you a ride home and he'll be by as soon as he can. Okay?"

"I can't think of anywhere I'd rather be than home. I'd appreciate a ride."

Before I got out in front of the house, I turned to her. "Would you please ask Lincoln not to come by before eight o'clock? We have little ones to put to bed."

"Will do."

"Thanks for the ride, Nikki."

"We aim to serve." She smiled and drove away.

Me, I headed into a houseful of loved ones, small and large.

CHAPTER 62

I was greeted by a house fragrant with the aroma of spaghetti and meatballs and the sounds of a little girl laughing with her uncle. After I walked in, I said to Tim in a quiet aside that I'd had a little adventure on my way home but that I was fine and would tell him about it after the little ones were asleep.

When he opened his mouth to ask for more, I shook my head, laying an index finger on my lips. "Later."

The next two hours held only the best of home life: food and fun, baths and books and bottles, plus a few hugs and kisses for good measure. Tim read Ella to sleep while I cleaned up in the kitchen. He and I settled in on the couch with small glasses of port and spoke quietly. I'd barely finished relating the short version of what had happened in the parking lot when the doorbell rang at exactly eight o'clock.

"That's Lincoln at the door," I told Tim as I stood. "Don't be alarmed. I knew he might stop by."

"I hate that you were in danger, my love." He kept hold of my hand. "I'm not sure how much more worry I can take."

I faced him again. "I'm sorry. I know this is a horrible, stressful time. Listen, I'll tell Lincoln to go away. I can talk with him tomorrow." I squeezed my sad, beautiful husband's hand and leaned in to kiss him.

Gazing into my eyes, he took a deep breath in and let it out. "No. Let him in. I want to hear what happened. Then he'll leave, and we'll be alone. It's okay."

"You sure?"

"I'm sure."

"Let's talk with him in the kitchen."

A moment later Lincoln sat at the kitchen table with us.

"Will you have a little port, now that the case is solved?" I waved the bottle at him.

"That sounds heavenly. I can't do it, but thanks. I'd accept a tonic, though, particularly if you have something with caffeine."

I smiled at his use of the traditional Massachusetts term for a soft drink. "Coke?"

"Perfect, thank you."

I poured, delivered, and took my seat again next to Tim.

Lincoln took a sip from the glass and set it down. "I appreciate that you let me know where you were headed, Mac, and I know I'm not alone in this room in being relieved you once again rescued yourself from a dangerous situation."

"Amen," Tim murmured.

"To date you have been quite resourceful in that regard," Lincoln added.

I held up my palm. "Guys, please don't scold me. I do enough self-flagellation for all three of us. Lincoln, were you pretty sure it was Herbert who killed Enzo?"

"I wasn't sure of a thing, unfortunately," the detective said. "The tip you relayed from Reba about him buying the aerosol peanut oil was crucial."

I took a tiny sip from my glass. "Victoria said something about Enzo having other health issues that combined with his allergy to kill him."

"Yes. He had congestive heart failure and possibly an issue with his kidneys."

I thought back to when I met Herbert. "I first met Enzo's nephew when he came into my shop the day Enzo's body was discovered. In fact, you were leaving as he entered, remember? It was early afternoon. Herbert referred to the death as murder. I knew the news about the body had been released, but I'm pretty sure you hadn't declared it a homicide yet, at least not publicly."

"We had not," Lincoln said.

"I wish I'd taken note of that at the time. Of course, he knew it was murder. He had committed it."

"Indeed."

"How are Shelly and Harini holding up?" I asked.

Tim gave me a quizzical look. He hadn't been involved in this case at all. What with his worries and the kids being here, I hadn't shared much of what I'd been learning along the way. I gave him a thumbnail about

Enzo's corpse and the costume shop owners' role in how it came to be lying on his deck in a strange position.

"That's heavy," Tim said. "Those poor ladies, to do something as stupid as that."

"Indeed," Lincoln said. "To answer your question, Mac, Harini has opened up and told us all she knows, which is considerable, about Shelly and her shenanigans in New York and here. It isn't pretty."

"There's a man named Xavier Casbohm in the Barnstable correctional facility who knows Shelly," I said. "You might want to have a chat with him."

"We can do that."

"So Dayton Scott wasn't involved at all?" I asked.

"No. He appears to be merely a cranky old man."

Tim's attention had been going back and forth, as if he was watching a tennis game.

"I had no idea all this was going on," he said.

"I didn't want to bother you, honey."

The doorbell rang again. Who in the world could this be? "I'll get it." I stood.

I opened the front door to Nikki Kimuri. She didn't smile, and her expression looked stricken. My heart sank.

"I need to speak with Haskins, Mac."

I wasn't going to ask. "Follow me." When we got to the kitchen, I said, "She's here for you, Lincoln.

"A word in private with you, sir, please." She gestured toward the living room.

He rose.

"Please keep your voices down," I said. "Two little children are asleep in the adjoining bedroom and the door is open."

"We'll step outside to the back instead." Lincoln ushered Nikki to the back door and closed it behind them.

Tim yawned. "Sorry, sweetheart."

"Don't apologize. It's been a day for both of us."

Lincoln gave a little knock at the door before coming back in. Nikki followed behind but stayed near the door, her uniform hat in her hands.

"Tim," Lincoln began, "I'm very sorry to inform you that we believe we have recovered your sister's remains."

CHAPTER 63

Tim went quiet. He sat so still I wondered if he'd stopped breathing. All the color drained from his face. I reached for his hand and held on tight. He gazed at Lincoln with the saddest look I'd ever seen on him or anyone else.

"You believe you've found her," Tim whispered. "Is there some doubt?"

"Not much, I'm afraid, but we need to officially identify your sister," the detective said. "From what you told us about her height, weight, hair color, and what she was wearing, we're pretty sure it's her."

"Where . . ." Tim's question trailed off.

"We received a report of a woman fitting Jamie Brunelle's description who was seen venturing onto the breakwater on the evening you said she went missing," Lincoln said. "I'm not sure why this witness didn't come forward earlier. We'll have to wait for the medical examiner's official autopsy results, but they've released a preliminary report. If it's any comfort, the death so far appears to be accidental, not self-inflicted nor at the hands of someone else."

"You mean she might have slipped on the rocks," I murmured.

"Exactly." Lincoln clasped his hands behind his back.

Not suicide. Not murder. Small comfort indeed, and it didn't take away from the sad, immutable fact that she was gone. I was at least glad she hadn't felt she needed to end her life.

"Thank you, Lincoln." Tim's voice was low, gravelly.

The detective cleared his throat. "I'm afraid we'll need someone to make the official identification."

I raised my hand. "I'll do it."

"No, I should," Tim said. "She's my sister."

Lincoln stepped to Tim's side and laid his big hand gently on Tim's shoulder. "Let Mac go."

"Pa will come and sit with you." I took Tim's other hand as well and kept my eyes on his as I spoke to the detective. "It won't take long, right, Lincoln?"

"No, and I'll drive you there and back," Lincoln said.

Tim gave me a nod, then folded his hands on the table. I was more than surprised he hadn't broken down sobbing, but of course he'd been expecting this announcement sooner or later. Still, he was a tenderhearted man given to tears. I knew they would come later, and even now his shoulders sagged as his chin dropped.

"Let me call my father. I'll be right back." I kissed Tim's forehead and hurried into the other room.

"Pa," I began when he picked up the call. "Please come over as soon as you can. The police found Jamie's body. I need you to sit with Tim while I go with Lincoln to identify her. Can you do that, please?"

"The poor man. Of course I'll come, darling. Be there in five minutes. I'm honored you asked me."

"Can't think of anyone more comforting than you. Thanks."

I quickly hit the restroom and grabbed my coat and bag. Back in the kitchen, Tim had his face buried in his forearms on the table.

"Officer Kimuri will stay until we return," Lincoln said.

I rubbed Tim's shoulders and kissed his head. "Pa will be here in a few minutes, my sweet." To Nikki, I added, "Do you know Joseph Almeida?"

"I do. You're lucky to have him as your father."

I smiled, albeit wanly. "I am."

CHAPTER 64

As Lincoln drove me to our destination a couple of towns away, he shook his head. "That's the worst part of my job."

"Telling someone their loved one is dead?"

"Yes. It never gets easier, never less painful."

I thought of Belle speaking in Jamie's voice. "You know how good Belle is at imitating voices," I began.

"I do."

"Last week, a couple of days after Jamie didn't come home, Belle spoke in her voice. She said, 'I can't do it anymore. I just can't,' or something like that. At the time, I didn't know if she meant staying sober or staying alive. It's an odd kind of comfort to know her death was an accident, not by suicide."

"I understand, Mac."

We rode in silence for a minute. "Lincoln, my grand-

mother told me you and Delia lost a child. I'm so sorry.
I never knew."

"We did, our little Sylvie, the sweetest child you'd
ever meet. Her death drove the worst wedge between
Delia and me. We grieved so differently and couldn't
figure out how to talk about it. We both took a long
time to heal, and I can't tell you how glad I am she has
agreed to love me again."

"I'm glad you're both happy." We rode in silence for
a minute. "Getting back to Jamie, was she found in the
ocean?"

"Actually, no. Well, not completely. A woman out
fishing in a boat spotted something between the rocks
halfway out the breakwater. It was Jamie's corpse. Waves
had broken over her, but she hadn't been completely
submerged. The Westham harbormaster and her team
did the recovery."

"I was out on the pier looking at that breakwater a
couple of days ago." I shivered. "Why didn't anybody
see her until now?"

"She was on the side away from the pier. For anyone
looking from the shore, she was shielded by an extra
large block of granite. It took a boat to spot her. Victoria's team was monitoring the coastline for any re-
ports of a body washing up, but they hadn't inspected
both sides of the breakwater, and there's no security
cam pointed at it."

"Too bad. She's been gone a week," I said. "Her
body must have taken a beating."

"It has, plus there are marine scavengers and the natural decomposition process. Apparently the ME thinks

there's enough of her intact to be recognizable, but I must caution you, it won't be pretty."

"Another reason for Tim not to have gone."

"You are absolutely correct," Lincoln said. "He shouldn't have to remember her that way. So you know, they'll show you only her face, and we'll be behind glass."

"I appreciate that."

"Tim will have enough to deal with telling little Ella her mother won't ever be coming home," he said softly. "You will, too, I expect."

"I think Cokey will be a help. Her mother handed her off to Derrick when Cokey was two and she's never seen her Maman again."

Lincoln gaped. "You're kidding."

"I'm not. After they conceived Cokey, the mother refused to marry my brother. She went back to France, where she was from, and gave birth there. Two years later, she apparently was all done being Cokey's mom and told Derr to come get his daughter. I don't know if she met someone else or what, but she hasn't been in touch."

"Derrick's a good man," Lincoln said.

"Totally. He never hesitated to be a single dad. Anyway, Cokey can help Ella see that she'll be okay. They're already besties, according to Ella."

We reached the medical examiner's facility, a satellite of the main office in Boston according to Lincoln, and I carried out my solemn obligation. He was right, it wasn't a pretty sight. But I had no doubt that the pale, still, somewhat disfigured face I viewed through the glass was Tim's sister's.

We drove slowly back to my house. I stayed quiet most of the way, and Lincoln let me be.

I finally spoke. "What makes them think Jamie died accidentally?"

"She doesn't have a wound or contusion to indicate she'd been struck. And if she'd wanted to jump into the water, she could have cleared the rocks. Her abrasions are consistent with slipping and scraping on the rocks, which are rough and jagged. Being as inebriated as she was, she would have had difficulty extracting herself, or she might have passed out."

"Thank you. Poor Jamie."

"She seems to have struggled a great deal in her life. Unfortunately, some people's body chemistry makes them prone to substance abuse."

I let out a noisy breath as my thoughts strayed to the murder case. "You know, usually I feel better about the resolution of a homicide case. This one leaves me uneasy, and it's not the emotional overlay of Jamie being missing—and now found. Do you know what I mean?"

"I do. Perhaps it's the idea of a nephew murdering his uncle for money. I find that unsettling in the extreme."

"Maybe." Or maybe I'd never know.

He pulled up in front of the house. I stayed seated for a moment.

"Thank you, Lincoln."

"It's not too late for you to attend the academy and join us for real, Mac. You have a gift for this investigation business."

"Yeah, no, but thanks for the compliment." I smiled.

"I'm going to be pretty busy for the foreseeable future."

"Take care of your man. It'll be rough going for a
while."

"I promise." I opened my door and slid out.

"Please ask Nikki to come out now. She's free to go,
unless you both want her around."

"I'll tell her. We'll be fine."

He gave me a mock salute. "You take care now."

That was definitely the plan.

CHAPTER 65

The next Sunday at one o'clock, I sat over brunch at Jimmy's Harborside with the Cozy Capers. Our table for five was next to one of the big windows at the back, but I'd taken a seat with my back to the water view. I didn't need to look at the breakwater where poor Jamie lost her life.

The bar area was packed with men and women in dark blue New England Patriots jerseys and T-shirts. I didn't follow football, but the local team was apparently doing pretty well this season. I knew Derrick and Mom were watching at the parsonage while they cooked something together for family dinner. She'd long ago imparted her love of the sport to him, and it had become a special bond between them. They were probably both wearing jerseys right now.

Gin and I had walked over here together and had each ordered a Bloody Mary. Flo and Norland followed suit, and we now had a platter of fried calamari in front of us to share. Tulia, also clad in a Pats jersey, lifted her glass of ginger ale.

"Here's to Jamie's memory, and also to a successful resolution of the case." She clinked glasses with all of us.

"Amen." Norland sipped his drink. "Mac, how are Tim and the children doing?"

"Tim's taking her death hard, but he's trying to hold it together for the kids," I said. "It helps that Greta came Thursday, and his dad arrives with the two oldest children tomorrow. With the help of her two grandmas, I think Ella is starting to realize her mom won't be coming home."

"Good. Of course the older two will be sad about her too," Gin said. "When is the service?"

"Her memorial service will be Friday morning in my father's church, with a wake on Thursday from four to six." I hadn't thought we needed a wake, but my mom had pointed out how well-loved Tim was in the community, and that lots of folks would want to stop by and pay their respects, even if they hadn't known Jamie. "You're all invited to both."

"Is the wake at the Chapman Funeral Home?" Gin asked.

"No," I said. "We decided the church hall would feel like a more friendly place, since there won't be a casket involved."

"We'll be there." Flo raised her eyebrows. "But I don't think the town should allow anyone to walk out on the breakwater. Why don't they put up a fence across it at the low tide mark?"

"Then people would gripe about their personal freedoms," Tulia said. "At least the warning sign at the beginning is large and clearly worded about the dangers of walking on sharp, wet rocks."

A cheer went up from the bar. Tulia whipped her head around to check the big television screens in that area a few yards away.

"Touchdown for the Pats." She turned back to us, grinning, then popped a crispy morsel of calamari into her mouth.

"Mac," Norland began in a gentle voice, "are you and Tim now de facto parents to Jamie's children?"

"We are." I traced a line in the condensation on my glass. "We've been granted temporary custody. He and I are still discussing things, but it looks like we're going to begin the process of legally adopting Ella and Luca. I guess you can call me Mom now."

"You'll be the only mother Luca knows." Gin also spoke tenderly.

"And Ella will be fine, eventually," Tulia added. "Look at the family support she already has."

"She will be," I said. "I, however, have quite the challenge in front of me, even after Tim heals from the acute stage of grieving. I hope I'm as resilient as Ella already seems to be. You know? I mean, I adore those little guys and I've only known them a week. But I also don't know anything about being a mother."

"You were raised by a good one, though." Gin reached over and squeezed my hand. "Nobody really knows how to be a parent before they give birth or adopt, and we have no doubt you're going to be awesome."

I wasn't so sure, but I had no path other than forward. Tim and I had hoped for our own biological child, and that might still happen. For now and for the future, we had children in our family, and together we would figure it out.

"I know what we can do," Tulia said. "We'll throw you guys a shower for both kids!"

"Good idea," Flo said. "You're going to need a lot of stuff."

Norland gave a thumbs-up and Gin nodded.

My eyes filled. "How did I get such good friends?"

Gin reached over and squeezed my hand. "It's what friends do."

"If I can change the subject, Mac," Norland began. "Are there any details about the case you haven't already shared?"

"Weirdly, I'm relieved to be talking about homicide instead of parenting, and I'm sure there are lots of things that slipped through the cracks." I stirred my drink with the celery stalk that served as a swizzle stick and took a sip.

"I mean, we know about the horrible stunt Shelly engineered, with Harini's help," Norland continued.

"There goes our newest book group member," Flo said.

"What I don't know is what Shelly had over Harini to force her to cooperate," I said.

"You didn't hear?" Norland asked. "I learned from my sources that Harini apparently had a weakness for nice jewelry with a big price tag. She stole a few pieces from a ballet school parent and never got caught. Shelly caught word of it and has used the knowledge as leverage ever since."

"No, I hadn't heard." I shook my head.

"Besides herself, Harini also supports her younger sister, Alisha, who has Down syndrome," Gin said.

"I met them both out walking last week." I frowned. "Who's going to look after Alisha now?"

Tulia shook her head. "I hope she has another relative."

"Care can be so expensive," Gin said. "Harini might have been desperate not to be exposed for her thefts, or maybe that was why she stole jewelry. To sell the pieces, not because she wanted to own and wear them."

"Possibly." I frowned. "Lincoln did say Harini was happy to tell them every detail of what happened, while Shelly clammed up and demanded a lawyer."

"Harini might get some sentencing leniency for that," Norland said.

"I hope so," I said. "There was also the conversation I overheard where Herbert said Shelly owed him something and she said she didn't. I have no idea what that was about."

Flo raised a finger. "You missed our jail visit on Thursday. I went without you."

"Yeah." I blew out a breath. I munched a perfectly battered and fried calamari and one of the accompanying deep-fried slices of jalapeño pepper, which they had blessedly seeded before battering, so it wasn't too spicy. "I had way too much going on at home."

"Of course," Flo said. "I didn't mean to blame you. Anyway, I was able to speak with Xavier, and I got him to open up a little. He told me he'd done a bit of work for Shelly. It was under the table and outside the law. He'd also assisted Herbert in forging a few documents. Don't ask me how he and Herbert connected, unless it was somehow via Enzo being associated with both Herbert and Shelly. Poor Xavier is always the one who gets caught, but he was happy to dish about what he knew."

"Interesting," Tulia said, except her attention was again on the game.

"That doesn't explain how Herbert and Shelly were connected," I observed. "But maybe we don't need to know."

Our server returned, a young guy with full lips, blond gelled curls atop his head, and a tight, V-necked red T-shirt featuring the Patriots' mascot in its tricorn hat. He asked if we were ready to order meals. I went for the lobster quiche and a refill on my drink.

This was the first time I'd relaxed away from home since everything went down on Tuesday, and I was going to take advantage of it. Tim and Greta had taken the children, plus Cokey, to an indoor playground for the afternoon, making me temporarily a free woman.

"Did anybody else wonder if Dayton Scott was involved?" I asked. "He and Herbert were friendly, and I thought maybe they worked together, but it doesn't appear so."

"Scott's nothing more than a cranky old man," Flo said.

"That's what Lincoln said." I surveyed the group. "Do we have any other loose ends?"

"It doesn't seem like it," Gin said. "Although I now wonder who will inherit Enzo's estate, if Herbert was his only next of kin.

"He must have named a secondary beneficiary," I said. "Maybe a nonprofit like the Bay State Light Opera organization or some cause he cherished."

"That would make sense," Tulia chimed in. "Anything else we haven't tidied up?"

"Not about the case." Norland cleared his throat. "But Ilsa wondered if she could join the book group."

"Who's Ilsa?" Tulia asked.

I gazed at Norland, but he just blushed.

"She's Westham PD Officer Nikki Kumuri's mom," I said. "Ilsa was also the person who reported finding Enzo's body. She lives next door to his condo. I met her when I was poking around Enzo's place."

"Sure, invite her to the next meeting," Gin said. "Hey, why are you blushing, Norland?"

He rolled his eyes. "She and I happen to be seeing each other. There, the secret's out. Satisfied?"

Tulia grinned again, but this time at Norland. "Way to go, man. We're all for happiness around here."

"Have any of you read the Maisie Dobbs historical mysteries?" Flo asked.

Gin nodded. Tulia shook her head.

"Only the first two," Norland said. "I liked them, but then I got busy with something else.

"I have," I said. "It's a long series. I loved watching how Maisie's life changes."

"I was thinking this is like our final reckoning. You know how at the end she always revisits places and people who were part of a case?"

"And we do that by meeting like this." I smiled at Flo. "You're right. This is our final reckoning."

Another roar went up from the game watchers. Tulia jumped up and moved over to watch the big screen.

I twisted to gaze, finally, at the breakwater. I didn't think a fence would have kept my troubled sister-in-

law from making a bad choice there or elsewhere, but I
hoped she hadn't suffered too badly as she left our
earthly plane.

Enzo either. I sent out an intention into the universe
that his be the last homicide in Westham for a long,
long time. Our book group could get back to discussing fictional murders, and I wouldn't have to be pursuing real-life killers when I should be focused on being
happy with my new children, their uncle-father, and all
the good things about life.

Recipes

West African Peanut Stew

Neli makes this stew for the family on the day before Halloween. Versions of this stew are eaten all over West Africa.

Ingredients

4–5 pounds skinless chicken parts, legs and thighs are best, bone in

Salt and pepper to taste

4 tablespoons cooking oil such as olive oil or canola, divided

2 medium yellow onions, roughly chopped

1 green pepper, diced

4 large garlic cloves, chopped

3 tablespoons minced fresh ginger (from a 2–3-inch piece)

6 cups sweet potato (about 3 large) cut into 1-inch cubes

2 cups (16 ounces) canned crushed tomatoes or chopped fresh

¾ teaspoon cayenne pepper

6 cups chicken broth, divided

1 teaspoon fish sauce (can be Thai or any other fish sauce)

1 whole habanero pepper

1 cup creamy or crunchy natural peanut butter at room temperature

1 bunch cilantro or parsley, thick stems removed, washed and chopped for garnish

Directions

Rinse chicken parts, pat dry, season with salt and pepper, to taste. Heat 2 tablespoons oil in a large stew pot or Dutch oven till hot but not smoking. Brown the chicken over medium-high heat in batches (4–5 pieces at a time), about 3 minutes per side. Once chicken is browned, set it aside.

Pour 2 additional tablespoons of oil into the pot and add the onions, pepper, and ginger. Cook, stirring, until fragrant and somewhat softened, about 3 minutes. Add garlic and sauté for 1 minute. Add the cubed sweet potatoes, tomatoes, cayenne pepper, and 4 cups of chicken broth. Return chicken to pot. Enclose habanero in a tea ball and add to the broth with the fish sauce.

In a bowl, whisk the peanut butter with the other two cups of broth. When fully combined, pour the mixture into the stewpot. Bring the stew to a boil, reduce heat to a steady low simmer and cook, uncovered, for 1 hour, or until chicken is tender and falling off the bone.

Remove stew from heat. Using tongs, lift chicken pieces out of stew, remove meat from bones, and shred. You won't need the bones for this recipe. Return shredded chicken to stewpot. Season stew with salt and fresh pepper, to taste.

Ladle stew over hot cooked rice into shallow bowls. Garnish generously with fresh herbs and serve with a bottle of hot sauce. Enjoy!

Halloween Muffins

Tim makes these pumpkin-based muffins with Ella on Halloween morning. Not too sweet, they're a great breakfast or snack choice to counter the influx of candy later in the day.

Ingredients

2 teaspoons pumpkin spice blend (or 1 teaspoon ground cinnamon, ½ teaspoon ground ginger, ¼ teaspoon ground nutmeg, and ¼ teaspoon ground allspice or cloves)
1 teaspoon baking powder
½ teaspoon salt
1¾ cups whole wheat flour
⅓ cup old-fashioned oats, plus more for sprinkling on top
2 eggs
1 teaspoon vanilla extract
⅓ cup oil
½ cup maple syrup or honey
1 cup pumpkin purée
¼ cup milk

Directions

Preheat oven to 375 degrees F. Grease a standard muffin tin.

Mix flour, spices, baking soda, salt, and oats in a mixing bowl. Break eggs into the dry mix and stir briefly with a fork. Add other wet ingredients and stir with a fork until just mixed.

Spoon into muffin tin. Sprinkle oats on top if desired. Bake 20–25 minutes until tops are golden brown.

Enjoy with coffee or tea, next to your eggs or as an afternoon snack.

Crabbies

Astra makes these yummy appetizer bites for Sunday dinner. According to Lyndsie Reynolds, the author's friend, who gladly shared the recipe, it's easy to double the amounts. That way you can keep a bag of tasty bites in the freezer for a quick appetizer for gatherings or with a glass of wine while you wait for dinner to cook.

Ingredients

Package six English muffins
5-ounce jar Kraft Old English Cheese Spread
8-ounce can lump crab meat, well drained
1 stick butter, room-temperature softened
    (doesn't matter if it's salted or unsalted)
1 tablespoon mayonnaise
1 tablespoon finely diced onion or shallot
½ teaspoon garlic powder (if your butter is unsalted, you can use garlic salt)
½ teaspoon Lawry's Seasoning or Old Bay powder
Pinch of regular or sweet paprika
Pinch of pepper
Pinch of salt if there's none otherwise, as in the butter or garlic powder

Directions

Split English muffins in half (forking method is best to split as it leaves you with the nooks and crannies in the muffins).

Mix all the ingredients with a fork, except the crab meat. When combined well, fold in the crab. Spread over the 12 halves of muffins. Place on a cookie sheet(s) and put in freezer for about 2 hours or until hard and easy to cut.

Cut each muffin into quarters and put in plastic container using parchment paper to separate layers of appetizer bites. Keep frozen until needed.

When needed, broil frozen bites for 5–7 minutes, depending on distance from broiler. Keep an eye on them. Serve immediately.

Cinnamon Scones

Being a baker, Tim whips up scones for breakfast at home one Saturday morning. Ella loves them. Recipe adapted from Smitten Kitchen.

Ingredients
1¾ cups unbleached white flour, plus more for
    counter
6 tablespoons granulated sugar, divided
1 tablespoon baking powder
½ teaspoon fine sea salt
8 tablespoons unsalted butter, cold, diced
¼ cup half-and-half or 2 tablespoons each milk
    and heavy cream, cold
1 large egg
2 teaspoons ground cinnamon, divided

Directions
Heat your oven to 375 degrees F. Line a baking sheet with parchment paper.

In a large bowl, combine the flour, 3 tablespoons of the sugar, baking powder, and salt. Pinch the butter into the dry mixture with your fingers or cut it in with a pastry cutter until it resembles coarse cornmeal. Make a well in the center and pour in the half-and-half, then the egg. Use a fork to gently combine the egg and cream in the center, then use it to combine everything into a rough mass. Knead the mixture a few times into an even mass.

On a lightly floured counter, roll the dough to roughly a 10-by-6-inch rectangle, a little smaller than a piece of paper. Sprinkle 1 tablespoon of the remaining sugar and 1 teaspoon of the cinnamon over half of the rectangle, then fold it in half. Roll the dough out again into an 8-by-6-inch rectangle; sprinkle another of the remaining tablespoons of sugar and the last teaspoon of cinnamon over half, then fold in half again. Pat the dough into roughly a 6-inch circle and cut with a sharp knife into 6 wedges. Evenly space the wedges on the pan, sprinkle with final tablespoon of sugar, and bake until slightly golden at the edges, 15–17 minutes.

Visit our website at
KensingtonBooks.com
to sign up for our newsletters, read
more from your favorite authors, see
books by series, view reading group
guides, and more!

Become a Part of Our
Between the Chapters Book Club
Community and Join the Conversation

Submit your book review for a chance to win exclusive
Between the Chapters swag you can't get anywhere else!
https://www.kensingtonbooks.com/pages/review/

01 14

J J